KNIFE EDGE

A KYLE PAYNE THRILLER

JT SAWYER

INKUBATOR
BOOKS

Published by Inkubator Books
www.inkubatorbooks.com

Copyright © 2024 by JT Sawyer

JT Sawyer has asserted his right to be identified as the author
of this work.

ISBN (eBook): 978-1-83756-466-8
ISBN (Paperback): 978-1-83756-467-5
ISBN (Hardback): 978-1-83756-468-2

PROLOGUE

Tucson, Arizona
Three Months Earlier

MANNY TORRES THREW DOWN HIS LAST ONE-HUNDRED-DOLLAR bill on the table in the VIP room of the strip club and headed to the private exit at the back.

Torres knew he shouldn't have ventured out this late from his safehouse on the east side, but old habits die hard. Some just dug their tentacles deeper into a man's soul with each passing year.

Stepping out into the dimly lit parking lot, he motioned for his driver in the black Audi in the distance to pull up.

The fresh air coupled with the recent hit of cocaine made his nose tingle, and he felt a sudden rush of exhilaration. The latter came as much from the drugs coursing through his veins as it did from knowing Vincent Delgado was finally in custody with the Americans, having been taken down by a

DEA Task Force working in conjunction with the Mexican Federales.

With Delgado in a federal prison in Phoenix, there would be some breathing room for Torres to expand his services amongst the rival cartels dotting the border from Tijuana to Ciudad Juarez.

While Torres was known by the slang term El Camello – the camel, which translated to drug dealer – he considered himself more of a scientist than a simple drug peddler, for Torres was the creator of a new type of fentanyl, one that he called TNT, that was about to flood the North American market.

When Torres was sixteen, he'd watched a TV interview with the owner of the Rolex watch brand, which forever changed the trajectory of his life. The wealthy executive told his listeners that the key to being a successful businessman was to find something they excel at and make themselves indispensable to a company.

While Torres seared that advice into his psyche, it wasn't until he graduated with a degree in chemistry that he realized his potential in formulating designer drugs and making himself truly indispensable to the Culebra Cartel in Mexico City.

When the Culebras were obliterated in a cartel turf war a few years later, Torres relocated to Ciudad Juarez, offering his services to the current cartel leadership that controlled the lucrative drug market across the Southwest.

A year later, he saw the same pattern repeat itself with a small but well-armed cartel taking down the Ciudad Juarez crew in a brilliantly orchestrated hit.

Over and over, the shift of power occurred, but Torres was always spared and subsequently recruited by the new kingpin to create a signature brand of designer drugs unique to that cartel.

Then nine months ago, Vincent Delgado swept into power, eliminating his competitors along the border and consolidating his grip on all drug distribution into the Southwest.

That should have meant a good payday for Torres, but Delgado believed prosperity resided in relying on cheap fentanyl from China, which was responsible for flooding the US market.

So for the past few months, Torres had lain low at an old friend's townhouse in Tucson, trying to determine his next move.

But with Delgado now in custody, it seemed like the tide was about to change considerably, and the former kingpin's son, Emilio, was interested in returning to an emphasis on designer fentanyl, which had a much higher addiction rate without the fatalities associated with the Chinese pharmaceuticals.

As Torres had often told his cartel overlords, you can't have future addicts if your end users are killed by the product.

Now, Torres saw an avenue back and knew he would be able to use his unique skills to create a more refined version of fentanyl that would saturate the Southwest and beyond.

Torres waved at his driver again. The man had his head back and appeared asleep. Torres muttered a curse in Spanish as he strode across the nearly empty parking lot.

He stopped at the driver's side, rapping his bony hand on the tinted window. "Cabron, wake up. Take me home."

Torres pressed his face in closer, letting his eyes adjust. His ribs compressed. He shuffled back, feeling bile rushing up into his throat at the sight of the gaping wound where the man's throat should be.

"*Madre de Dios.*"

He turned to run but felt something prick his back

through his silk shirt. A second later, a nerve-racking jolt shot through his body. He collapsed to the ground, his body jerking in spasms.

Two men in black masks moved into his peripheral vision. The larger of them stood over him, depressing the Taser again and sending another flood of searing electricity through Torres' quivering body. All Torres saw was the excitement in the man's eyes along with the faint tattoo of a coiled red viper on his neck.

The shorter man squatted down, glancing at his phone, then at Torres' face. "Yeah, it's him."

The bigger man grunted in approval. "Let's wrap him up and get the hell out of here. We've got a long drive."

Torres wanted to scream, but his jaw was frozen, his mind trying to fight back the urge to vomit. Another jolt from the Taser racked his body into uncontrollable spasms. He felt himself being lifted and saw the stars in the night sky as he was carried a few feet towards a white utility van.

They tossed him inside like luggage; then the shorter man climbed in and zip-tied Torres' wrists to a horizontal brace in the van's side panel.

Torres forced himself to think back to the men's voices. *Americans. Not cartel. Who, then? Feds. Maybe DEA?*

In all his years working as a chemist for various cartels, there had always been an understanding of his importance, and he was treated with respect, given his specialized skill set.

But these thugs struck him as gang members unaffiliated with any cartel.

The shorter man slid a dark pillowcase over Torres' head, then removed the two Taser leads from his back. "Relax, Manny. In about four hours, we'll cut you loose, that is, if you cooperate and tell us what we want to know."

He felt some sensation returning to his face. "I don't know

anything. I'm just a businessman out of Mexico visiting family here."

"Well, in a few hours, I'm going to ask you very nicely, just once, about the ingredients for that new fentanyl brand of yours, and I expect a little more honesty." He felt the man pat him on the cheek. "Because the padded shed I've got made special for you out in the woods... ain't no one gonna ever hear your screams, amigo."

Torres felt his heart punching through his ribs as he slid his knees up into his chest as the van sped away.

And with each passing mile, he felt his hope flutter away like grains of sand in the wind.

CHAPTER 1

Upper Peninsula, Michigan
Present Day

KYLE PAYNE GLANCED AHEAD AS THE BRONCO BOBBED ALONG the dirt road, the sight of another law-enforcement vehicle making him wonder what he had gotten himself into, especially since this was supposed to be time off from pursuing killers and thugs.

"You sure picked the right week to visit," Darryl Payne said to his son. "This poacher I've been after has been an elusive SOB, and I can sure use the extra set of eyes on the ground." Payne Sr slowed the old Bronco, making a right turn onto a narrow jeep trail.

Payne had left out the part about his vacation time actually being disciplinary leave from the CIA. While his father knew who his son's employer was, Payne was not at liberty to discuss current geopolitical events.

And even if he did, he had no desire to rehash the bitter

memory of a recent mission in Romania that had gone south due to the death of a fourteen-year-old trafficking victim who was attached to a civilian he had been sent to extract. A civilian drug peddler with connections to the Romanian mob who was deemed a high-value asset by some suits back at Langley, who merely planned to employ Payne's considerable personnel-recovery skills and then toss him to the wolves once the op had ended.

It was only upon arriving at the extraction site that he learned the drug dealer had been informed by Payne's superior that the girl was part of the deal and would accompany him in his new life. When Payne tried to free the victim, the man drove a switchblade into her ribs.

If I can't have her, no one will. The thug's words still echoed in Payne's brain.

After the girl died in Payne's arms, he reluctantly completed his mission, but delivered a battered asset to the senior CIA case officer running the operation, who painted a picture of Payne being out of control and violating mission parameters. After nearly fifteen years with the agency, Payne could live with his actions abroad though he was still haunted by the terror on the dying girl's face.

But now, Payne felt like he was standing in front of multiple forks on a murky trail, unsure of what came next or if he'd even return to the CIA.

His father glanced over at him with a grin. "You're making your old man's day being here. Just hope you don't get bored traipsing through these woods again."

"Happy to help. Just point me towards the fight, *old man*," said Payne with a slight chuckle.

Darryl Payne slowed down further as the road grew rutted. "Just remember, you're back in the States and not with your agency pals in Africa or the Middle East."

"Meaning?"

"You know what the hell I mean. I shouldn't have to remind you that I'm a game warden who still has to follow the rule of law."

"So no shallow graves in the backwoods, I get it. But given the dirtbag you're after, I bet you wish things were different." Kyle flared an eyebrow. "You know, when I was a kid, you used to regale me with stories of your own dad and his buddies dispensing some Old West justice to poachers and anyone else who dared to cross their families."

"Another era, son. And back before the jury of the internet, which likes to pass judgement without caring to know the reality on the ground."

"You're worried about what people will say online? Never thought I'd see the day."

"I couldn't give a muskrat's ass what outsiders think, but what I do care about is an inordinate amount of attention being drawn to our wilderness areas up here and them becoming overrun with city folks from downstate."

That was something that made sense to Kyle given his father had spent the past thirty-one years busting dope growers, illegal woodcutters and bear poachers in a region where the few law-enforcement rangers juggled a multitude of duties that were spread around a large law-enforcement district.

It was his father's sense of justice that had led him into his own version of policing the world's ills when he joined the CIA after college.

Only the rules of engagement overseas were far different and sometimes nonexistent.

At the end of the trail the Bronco came to a halt by two game wardens standing next to a Ford F-250. The men walked over to Kyle's door, all of them exchanging handshakes as he stepped out.

"Damn, boy, what they feedin' you back East?" asked Grady Pope, a tall man with a thick black beard.

"Probably married a good cook while he was gone, is more like it, and didn't think about invitin' us country folk to the celebration," said Bud Brown, who was casually resting a meaty hand on the AR-15 rifle hanging in front of his barrel chest.

"Too many dinners in fancy restaurants schmoozing clients, to answer your first question," Kyle said in the direction of Grady. "And to answer yours about being hitched, I'm still off-leash," he replied, looking at Bud.

Kyle grinned at his father's colleagues from the Department of Natural Resources, who were more like uncles to him than family friends. Collectively, the three men possessed over a hundred and fifty years of fieldcraft, tracking and manhunting skills. They had been Kyle's first mentors, and the skills he'd honed in these very woods had saved his life countless times during numerous covert operations abroad.

But it was his time with the CIA's elite Ground Branch, and later as an asset recovery specialist, that took those skills to another level. His father was the only one privy to the nature of his real job. To anyone else, he used his cover alias as a risk-management consultant for private corporations with employees working overseas.

Kyle patted Bud on the arm. "So, when you guys gonna step down and make room for some new blood out here? You fellas got more miles on your engines than my old man's Bronco."

Bud faked a slow punch to Payne's ribs. "Sounds like you're gunnin' for my job, but I still got a few trails left in me. Darryl's Bronco is gonna give up the ghost before me."

Grady smirked. "Besides, the rookies we keep getting up here are all from below the bridge and don't know a bobcat from a bear since they spend so much time behind their desks."

The age-old rivalry between those born below the Mackinac Bridge and those who were from the Upper Peninsula was still, and always would be, a point of contention.

"Speaking of bears. What you got for me on that poacher?" asked Darryl, who was outfitted with a small camouflage daypack and an AR-10 slung on his right shoulder.

Bud leaned back, removing a ruggedized tablet from the tailgate. He tapped on the screen while giving an irritated glare at having to put on his reading glasses. "Our drone still has him a half mile west of here, skirting along Tamarack Swamp. He's probably heading to a rendezvous site to get picked up on one of the old logging roads."

"You think it's the same guy I nearly got zinged by last month?" said Payne Sr, glancing at the live video feed on the screen.

"Yeah, it's him alright," said Grady. "Same MO for dropping bears that we've been seeing for quite a while. Uses bait piles of fresh meat mixed with tuna near the den sites to lure the sows out, then takes down her and the cubs." He thrust his thumb over his shoulder. "Bastard killed a mom and two cubs on the other side of the hill late last night where we set up those trail cams."

"After the gallbladders?" said Kyle, figuring the lucrative international black market in Asia hadn't eased up since his last visit home two years ago.

Bud licked his lower lip, his eyes narrowing. "That and the latest thing is to use the paws for ashtrays. Must somehow make cigar-smoking more enjoyable for the rich pricks who can afford five K a pop for a trophy."

Kyle had to hold back his fury at the thought of such a magnificent animal facing such an inglorious fate at the hands of a poacher.

During his time involved in ops in Africa, he'd encountered numerous poachers, but they were desperate men trying to prevent their impoverished families from starving. Here, in the US, the poachers were mainly only interested in the bears' gallbladders, which they then sold to a middleman, usually out of China or South Korea, who would turn around and auction off the organs for top dollar to apothecaries around Asia.

Darryl Payne removed the rifle from his shoulder, doing a partial chamber check. "Alright, you guys head on foot towards the north end of Tamarack Swamp while Kyle and I make a beeline due west from here. We should be able to box him in before he gets to his ride."

"Roger that," said Bud, who tucked the small tablet into a pocket in his BDU pants. "I'll give you an update on his location in thirty minutes once we reach Knob Creek."

Kyle watched the two seasoned manhunters venture down a deer trail before disappearing in the thick foliage. He returned to the Bronco, grabbing his tattered daypack from the rear seat along with a spare rifle.

"Thought you might like that Mk12 better than an AR," said his father.

"I'll never turn down a rifle with a long reach."

"I imagine you're not accustomed to using your shootin' skills on poachers, though."

"No, but in my experience, evil is still evil regardless of what side of the globe you're on."

The two men walked alongside each other as they moved down the old dirt road, their eyes habitually scanning for people tracks amidst the plethora of white-tailed deer, squirrels and the occasional porcupine. Somewhere high up in the white pine trees, a blue jay sounded the alarm call, as they always did when a two-legged intruder or another predator was in the region.

Darryl glanced over at his son's tan face. "I know we haven't had much time to talk since you got in last night, but I get the feeling that something's on your plate. Everything alright?"

Kyle didn't even know where to begin. He needed a break from the politics plaguing his job at the agency.

"Just taking some time to sort through what I want to do with my life. Been slogging around the planet on government-sponsored trips for way too long, and things feel just as chaotic now as they were when I first started with the agency. Not sure I'm even making a difference anymore."

"Because of the tangled bureaucracy you've told me about or because of our enemies outmatching us?"

"Well, a problem with the former leads to problems with the latter, and the past few years the agency has spent more time bowing to public perception than bolstering assets towards our asymmetrical warfare efforts abroad and at home. The enemy is at our gate, and instead of charging at them with spears, the policy makers signing off on our budget want to replace our spears with white flags."

"So what now? It's not like you to take time off. Not that I mind it one bit."

They paused at a small stream that intersected the road, each of them taking turns hopping on rocks to get across.

Kyle inhaled deeply, enjoying the aroma of cedars. "Honestly, I'm not sure I'm gonna go back to that line of work. I put in for all the vacation time I've accrued and took off the next three weeks. I'm planning to go to Arizona after this to visit my friend John, who retired a few months ago."

"The guy with the vintage motorcycles you've told me about?" Darryl fought back a partial scowl. "The one who recruited you out of college, right?"

"That's him. We're gonna take a long road trip. See some of Old Route 66 from Flagstaff to Santa Monica. We've always joked around about how we've spent so many years fighting overseas that we've never really enjoyed our own country or seen its sights."

The overgrown road narrowed and came to a dead end where a fallen log blocked the path. Kyle had gone deer hunting here in high school and remembered when the forest service blocked off vehicle access to the swamp to protect the watershed.

The weathered tree trunk was large enough that they had to straddle it. Once on the other side, both men focused their senses on the terrain ahead. Darryl veered off to the right, slowly proceeding through second-growth poplar saplings.

While Kyle would have preferred a GPS unit to help reacquaint himself with the terrain, he knew his father was following the topographic map burned into his brain from a lifetime afoot in this region.

Darryl raised a finger to his lips, indicating their conversation would have to continue later.

Strangely, despite the remoteness, Kyle felt his iPhone vibrate in his cargo pocket. Whatever was going on outside of this reality would have to wait.

Coming to a small clearing of grass, Kyle pointed to the cluster of ravens circling overhead. His father gave him a knowing nod, both men knowing that a raven sign like that indicated a recently killed animal.

Sixty yards later, they came across a gutted black bear beside a bait pile of sardine cans. Steam was still rising off the animal's innards.

Kyle was no stranger to blood and guts, but seeing the horrific fate of this huge creature made his own stomach churn like a cement mixer.

His father paused to take a photo of the carnage with his iPhone, then pushed on, following the boot prints in the mud.

After twenty minutes of trekking, the walkie-talkie on

Darryl's tactical vest emitted a single squelch. He paused beside the trunk of an immense silver maple tree, placing the radio up to his lips. "Go."

"Drone's nearly out of juice and was recalled to my location," said Grady. "Last fix on the subject was at that crook in the swamp where it veers due east for a few hundred yards not far from a rock escarpment."

"I know the one. We're only five minutes out. Hold up by that series of knolls beyond the swamp in case he slips by us."

"Copy that."

The game warden looked at his son. "Stay behind me. Remember, you're just along for the ride."

Kyle grinned. "Take your kid to work week with a semi-auto rifle, it seems."

The two continued on, descending a gentle slope cloaked in young oak saplings. The damp ground muffled the sound of leaves, and they covered the distance quickly, arriving at the snaky section of the swamp that Grady had mentioned.

Darryl squatted in the brush beside a fallen log while Kyle did the same but, out of habit, provided rear cover protection, briefly focusing on the route they'd just taken before shifting around and studying the swamp's contours.

A few seconds later, some raucous blue jays sounded their alarm.

Kyle's eyes darted a hundred yards to the right. A sleek figure in camouflage was winding through some raspberry bushes, the small thorns causing his garments to get hung up. The man's bulbous backpack was clearly bloodstained at the bottom.

"Cover me," said Darryl as he walked through the brush to the clearing fifteen feet ahead. He fixed his rifle on the young man working his way through the thicket.

"This is a DNR game warden behind you. Drop your weapon."

The poacher froze, tossing his scoped Marlin rifle on the ground. He turned his head slightly, revealing an unexpectedly youthful face. He couldn't have been more than sixteen.

"Now lower that backpack slowly and turn around."

The young man complied, his lips trembling and his face growing ashen.

Kyle kept his rifle trained on the poacher. *This kid couldn't have dropped a bunch of black bears alone. He must have...*

The air erupted with gunfire; two rounds penetrated the young poacher's chest. Another barrage peppered the maple trees near Darryl, clipping him in the shoulder.

Kyle saw a man in mottled green clothes with a scoped rifle spring up from a clump of saplings on the opposite hilltop and bound away.

Emerging from the brush, Kyle jogged towards his father, who was lying on his side. "You good?"

The older man rolled to his right, grimacing as he gave a scornful look at his bleeding shoulder, which had suffered a grazing wound. "Ah, shit."

Kyle removed his bandana and wrapped it under his father's armpit, then over the injured rear deltoid before tying it off.

Both men glanced at the dead poacher a few feet away. "Musta been the gopher. Thought something was off," said Kyle, who refocused his eyes upon the hilltop for a second.

Darryl leaned against the log, bracing his arm against his torso.

Kyle rested a hand on his father's knee. "You gonna be alright?"

Payne Sr nodded, removing his own first-aid kit and popping a few ibuprofen.

"I'm gonna stay on his trail and push him towards Grady

and Bud," said Kyle. "This guy intentionally shot at you. If he gets away again, it's going to mean more game wardens in his crosshairs out in these parts or somewhere else."

"I'll radio the guys and give 'em an update."

Kyle took off, sprinting along the base of the hill to the other side.

Tracking a man bolting through the forest wasn't difficult. Displaced leaves and splayed mud were evident for several hundred feet. The nagging question on Kyle's mind right now was whether the poacher was button-hooking to either side to set up an ambush, or if he was truly fleeing the area in an effort to make it to his vehicle.

There were more game wardens killed in North America by ambush than any other on-the-job hazard. It was the one thing that had caused a lot of sleepless nights when he was younger, wondering if his father would return home safely.

He thought back to the dead teenager. It was more than just the poacher trying to eliminate a loose end by killing his errand boy. He was also targeting a game warden, and Kyle knew that poachers like that often accrued a decent body count before they were brought down.

Kyle gritted his teeth. *That bastard tried to kill my father.*

He followed the tracks through the pines, finally catching a glimpse of the man in the distance as he scampered up a vertical escarpment. It was a ridgeline of basalt that extended for a half mile to the east of the swamp. Kyle figured his primary escape route must have been cut off to risk climbing a fifty-foot rock face.

But Kyle knew a quicker way to the top. He veered to the right, sprinting towards a slope. His daily regime of jogging six miles each morning enabled him to keep up a frantic pace without getting winded.

Arriving at the top, he turned and trotted through the knee-high vegetation and young saplings. A minute later, he neared the end of the escarpment where it abutted the swamp below.

A grunting sound emanated from his left. He crouch-walked to the edge of the rock formation and saw the poacher grasping for a final handhold near the top.

Kyle towered over the man, the poacher's hands clinging to the thick rootlets that snaked along the basalt.

"Game's over," said Kyle. "You lose."

The man leaned back slightly and peered up. His face was red, and sweat streamed down his cheeks. "Shit, you ain't no game warden."

"You're sure right about that. That also means I'm not bound by any of their laws."

The man chuckled as he pulled himself up. "Screw you. This isn't the 1800s."

Kyle stepped back, pointing his rifle at the man's chest as he crested the top and sat down like he was going to enjoy the sunset.

"Take your rifle off and toss it on the ground by my boots."

The man came to a kneel, then stood, slowly removing the weapon and casually dropping it on the ground. "Anything else, Davy Crockett?"

Kyle heard some blue jays squawking behind him and turned slightly to see Bud and Grady in the distance as they made their way along the edge of the swamp below the rock formation.

He'd only turned a second, but the poacher rushed at him with a blade he must have had concealed in his sleeve. For a man his size, he moved with surprising speed.

Payne sidestepped, swinging the rifle buttstock at the man's face. The glancing blow connected with the right cheek, spinning the man slightly. The poacher came back around with a wild swing of his knife hand, close enough to slice Kyle's jacket.

Kyle had backed so much into the thick saplings that he couldn't angle the rifle muzzle at his opponent. He tossed it aside and removed his folding blade.

"Not a good idea, man," he said. "I'd just sit your ass down and surrender. I'll only give you this one chance."

"And spend the rest of my life in prison for whacking that kid. No way. I ain't ever going back to jail. I can live off the land out here just fine."

The man lunged again, this time with a straight thrust. Kyle parried it with his empty hand, blocking the attacking forearm while sending a downward slash along the inner arm, slicing the brachial artery.

"Thirty seconds and it's all over. You sit down now and apply pressure to that wound and you might just live."

"Fuck you." The man was staggering from blood loss as his blade hand turned crimson, but Kyle was running out of room to retreat. At the next half-assed attack, Kyle darted on an angle to the left and shoved the man aside. The poacher's left boot struck a jagged rock, sending him tumbling over the escarpment.

For a brief second, Kyle saw the man's eyes widen in terror as his mouth hung open in a scream. The stocky body careened against some rocky protrusions before impacting on a car-sized boulder below.

Kyle wiped his blade off on some leaves and folded it up before returning it to his pocket. He glanced over the edge. "Your days of slaughtering animals are over," he told the glassy-eyed figure below, then for a moment he scanned the forest in the distance, figuring Bud and Grady must have already walked around the other side by now.

There was no emotion or ethical dilemma stewing in Kyle over what had happened. As far as he was concerned, there was one less parasite plaguing these woods, his father and friends were out of harm's way on future outings, and the bear population would no longer suffer, at least for a while.

Gazing at the dead man made Kyle wonder. Could he follow in his father's footsteps and become a game warden?

But then, he'd had his fill of hunting down men and killing them.

———

Kyle made a makeshift sling for his father's arm while Grady and Bud took photos of the dead men.

The trek back to the vehicles went without incident, and the wardens discussed how they would have to return in their ATVs to retrieve the bodies.

Kyle sat in the Bronco with the door open, swigging down the cold coffee still left in his cup. He felt his iPhone buzz again for the third time since they'd arrived. He pulled it out, seeing it was from John Heller, along with several messages. Kyle heard a gravelly voice on the other end.

"Hello, who is this?" said the stranger.

"Who the hell is this?" snapped Kyle.

"Sheriff Bill Rudensky, out of Pineland, Arizona. John Heller has been in an accident, and I was hoping this number might lead to his family."

The Bronco suddenly felt claustrophobic, and Kyle stepped out. "I'm about as close as you'll get. John doesn't have any remaining family alive. What happened? How is he?"

"I'm, um, I'm afraid he's dead. It was a rollover accident on the highway east of Pineland."

Payne's ribs constricted.

The overhead birdsong faded away, the world becoming a shade paler than he could last recall.

CHAPTER 2

Twenty-Four Hours Later

THE GRUELING DAY OF TRAVEL, HOPPING FLIGHTS FROM THE TINY airport in Marquette, Michigan, to Chicago and on to Phoenix Sky Harbor, happened in a blur. All Payne could remember was getting into his hotel in Phoenix at midnight and collapsing on the bed.

The next morning, he did the monotonous drive in his rental car out of the city and onto Highway 87 heading northeast. The weak engine of the Honda Accord had barely handled the elevation gain after departing Phoenix, but it was the only vehicle available on short notice.

As the highway climbed to the north, the columnar saguaro cacti disappeared and transitioned to the scrubby forests of junipers near the city of Payson and finally majestic ponderosa pines once he crested seven thousand feet in Pineland.

The town wasn't on the way to anything of significance.

On an Arizona map, it barely registered as a minuscule speck. Four hours from the Grand Canyon and less than two hours northeast of Phoenix, Pineland was mostly frequented by seasonal hunters and summer visitors wanting to escape the triple-digit heat of the Sonoran Desert. It had a population of three thousand people, whose lives mainly centered on tourism, hospitality and the Tanner Steak Company.

Surrounded by thousands of acres of federal wilderness, the topography where Pineland was situated was a belt of coniferous trees that was only fifty miles wide but extended on an angle across the state for three hundred miles from western New Mexico at one end to just past Flagstaff on the other. On either side of that high-elevation belt of trees was desert.

For Payne, he had originally hoped it would be the kind of place to relax with John Heller before setting off on an epic motorcycle trip across the West. Now, his visit to Pineland was to say goodbye to an old friend.

And those he could count on one hand.

How can John be dead? Is this really happening?

Payne remembered his agency colleagues joking with Heller that he was too ugly to die, after which Heller simply shot them one of his venomous glares, which shut down any further comment, followed by Heller cracking a joke.

Payne drove through the six blocks of downtown, pausing repeatedly to let tourists cross the street. Finally, he pulled the red Honda up in front of the sheriff's department.

The one-story building before him, with its floor-to-ceiling windows, gave the impression it had once been a grocery store. The parking lot was empty except for two 4x4 Ford trucks with Pineland law enforcement emblems on the sides and a grey minivan. There was a phone booth with a muddy exterior in the corner near the sidewalk, and Payne tried to recall the last time he'd seen one that was operational.

But then the whole town had a vintage vibe to it, and he wasn't sure if the city council had opted for that look or if it was just trapped in another era due to budget constraints.

Payne took a swig of the tepid coffee he'd picked up near the airport, dreading the coming conversation. He knew speaking with the sheriff was the first step in learning more about Heller's death, but it also meant further confirmation that his friend was gone.

Gone for good.

And despite his father's earlier comments about how "God's plans are shrouded in mystery," those well-intentioned words didn't ease the pain of knowing a door had been forever closed.

The sheriff's words from yesterday's shocking phone call were still ricocheting through Payne's psyche. He tried to suck in a deep breath, feeling like he was freefalling through an abyss.

How can John be dead?

Payne thought back to the numerous battles abroad that Heller had been in during his three decades with the CIA, some of which Payne had experienced alongside his mentor over the last ten years.

He survives all that and ends up dying in a fucking accident on the highway?

Payne shook his head, trying to wrap his brain around the new reality.

He stepped out of the vehicle, the aroma of pines wafting over him. From the parking lot, he had a full glimpse of the town's main street, which was little more than trinket stores interspersed with snack joints. If he blinked, he could be transported back to his hometown in the Upper Peninsula. The only difference was that there weren't mosquitos and black flies assaulting him.

He headed to the front entrance, stepping into the lobby. A

gold bell clanked against the glass door as it shut behind him. The air inside was cool and slightly musty like he'd entered through the basement.

The interior of the police department was a patchwork of marble flooring coupled with faded wallpaper with images of cowboys chasing down cattle. In the center of the lobby was a curved reception desk whose right end was covered with acrylic racks containing maps and tourist brochures.

Payne noticed a sign on the nearest door to his immediate left, indicating it belonged to the director of the visitor bureau. He thought back to the sign on the edge of the parking lot, which revealed this building also housed the offices for the city council and the fire chief.

With the lack of bustle inside, he figured everyone was out to lunch or occupied by business elsewhere. The fifty-something woman behind the desk glanced at Payne before returning to her computer monitor. Her bronze nameplate read *Barbara*.

"Be with you in a minute," she said, frantically clicking on her mouse as she moved it around.

In the reflection of the framed photo on the wall behind her, he could see she was playing online poker. A second later, the woman blew a strand of red hair off her nose and mumbled a curse as she leaned back.

Her formerly excited expression turned sour. She gave Payne a plastic smile. "What can I do for you?"

"My name is Kyle Payne. I spoke with Sheriff Rudensky yesterday about my friend John Heller."

Barbara glanced down the hallway, then stood up, moving around the desk towards Payne. "I, um, I was so sorry to hear about John." She bit her lower lip and stepped closer, resting a hand on Payne's forearm. "Such a tragedy. John seemed like such a nice man."

"You knew him?"

"Mostly in passing. He came in here asking about fire-wood-cutting permits when he first moved to town, but I told him he'd have to go up to the Forest Service office in Payson. After that, I'd run into him at the diner once in a while. He was very pleasant, unlike a lot of the Phoenix folks who just want to be left alone in their mansions in the woods."

Payne noticed how, the entire time she was speaking, her tone shrank into whispers dependent on the noise coming from the back room.

She flicked her head to the right. "Sheriff Rudensky is in his office. Just follow me. He can fill you in on the details."

Her yellow floral-print dress and coiffed hair were in stark contrast to her immaculate white sneakers, which squeaked with each step on the tiled floor.

Walking past two closed offices and an empty employee lounge, Barbara paused at the half-open door of the rear office and cleared her throat while pecking out a sheepish knock. "Sir, there's someone here to see you."

The sheriff was standing along the back wall behind his desk, rummaging through some files in a steel cabinet, apparently unaware that there were software programs for such things.

In the opposite corner was a tattered Arizona flag on a wooden pole propped against the wall, the threadbare cloth looking like it had served many generations of law enforcement officers prior to Rudensky.

The lanky figure slowly closed the drawer, holding a manila folder in his left hand. He walked past his desk towards the door, extending a hand towards his guest. "Kyle Payne. Sheriff Bill Rudensky." He thrust his chin towards the hallway. "Barb seems to forget that I can hear everything that goes on up front."

The two men shook, and Rudensky motioned for Payne to

sit in one of the faux-leather chairs in front of his desk. The secretary excused herself and closed the door.

Payne opted to stand, folding his arms and waiting to hear the sheriff's full breakdown of events surrounding the rollover.

The sheriff cradled the folder and leaned back on the edge of the desk. "So, you said on the phone that Mr. Heller was a good friend of yours?"

The words barely percolated through Payne's rattled brain. He pushed back the wave of grief.

The sheriff repeated the question, looking intently enough at Payne to make him think his reaction was being scrutinized.

Payne nodded, glancing around the walls at the variety of commendations and training certificates nestled between numerous mounted deer heads. In the right corner was an antiquated security camera, angled out towards the windows at the front of the office.

"John and I used to work together on the East Coast. We had a motorcycle trip along Route 66 planned. We were supposed to leave next week."

"My condolences on your loss. I recall seeing Mr. Heller coming into town on his bike once in a while… a vintage Indian motorcycle."

"Yeah, he was pretty fond of that old-timer."

"Just curious but what line of work were you guys in?"

"International consulting. We did risk management for corporations who had their employees overseas." He always kept it brief and found that most people rarely ventured beyond the elevator pitch. If they did, he had a lengthy cover story with a detailed background that the intel wizards at Langley had created, complete with an online history, resumé and the requisite social media profiles.

Oddly, Rudensky handed the folder to Payne. Inside were four photos and an accident report.

Why's he showing me this?

The images showed a mangled vehicle on its side, and Payne had a hard time imagining that the crumpled heap had once been Heller's Toyota 4Runner.

"I reckon he was humming along that remote stretch of Highway 260 at about fifty-five miles per hour and didn't slow down before the hairpin turn that comes up out of nowhere."

Payne scrutinized each image, but there wasn't much to decipher. It looked like Heller had plummeted off the side of a cliff. He glanced up at the sheriff. "Are there any more photos of the site?"

Rudensky shook his head. "Nope, afraid not."

He must have more photos than this. No way only four were taken of the entire scene. And the way he keeps studying my reactions, he must be searching for some information.

"You said your deputy found John unresponsive?"

"He died shortly after my officer arrived. EMS showed up a few minutes later, but Mr. Heller had suffered too much internal damage."

The sheriff walked around to the other side of his desk, pulling out a clear evidence bag and holding it up. Inside was a gold watch, cell phone and a Spyderco folding knife. He handed it to Payne. "Just don't open it up or touch anything inside."

Payne gazed at the watch, jostling it so he could see the underside where the word *Kalimera* was inscribed. He thought it was strange that a law enforcement officer was readily handing over an evidence bag to a man he'd only met minutes earlier.

What's he fishing around for? Does he want more info on Heller? But why would he need that for an accident report?

"I noticed that too. Is that a person's name?" said the sheriff, who leaned in closer for a quick glance at the inscription. The odor of cigarette smoke on the man's breath caused Payne to lean to the side, which must have given the man a hint, as he walked back to his seat.

Payne thought about the small retirement party for Heller back at Langley four months ago when he'd presented him with the watch.

"It's Greek. Means good day." The saying was a Heller classic and one he'd often spouted when the chips were down on an op. Rather than being a fatalist, Heller always said: *each day is a good day as long as your friends are on either side of you when the sky rains daggers down upon your world.*

Rudensky glanced at the evidence bag. "That phone only had two numbers on it. The last one he dialed a few times in the hour leading up to his death appears to be your number, but probably didn't get a signal. My data forensics guy said the text just read *HVT 3106.*"

Again, he felt like Rudensky was studying his response. He returned the man's gaze, looking through him until the sheriff broke contact.

How is it a one-horse town like Pineland has a data forensics guy who can hack into someone's phone and retrieve their texts? That's bullshit. He must have really wanted to know what was on John's phone, but why?

"Kinda cryptic, don't you think? That message mean anything to you, Mr. Payne? It could be of help in my investigation."

Payne glanced at the phone, wishing he could climb through it and ask Heller what the hell the message was about.

HVT always meant high-value target during missions, but is that what John was referring to?

He glanced up at the sheriff again. "You made it sound

like it was a pretty cut-and-dried fatal accident caused by a rollover on a winding road. My only question is, why was John driving so far from his cabin late at night? What's out that way?"

The sheriff shrugged. "Keep going east another thirty miles and you hit the Apache rez. He mighta been headin' to the casino for a drink or to play the slots. Not much else out in those parts."

Except John was neither a drinker nor a gambler. He'd been sober for the past twelve years, and Payne found it unlikely the man would spend his retirement playing games of chance in some rural casino.

Payne placed the evidence bag on the desk. "Where's John's body? I'd like to see it."

"You said you were a friend not family."

"I'm about all the family he had."

"I'll have to look into it. It's outside the usual protocol. Plus, the coroner in Payson is a bit finicky about who steps into his place."

This guy is seriously going to deny me seeing John's body? He casually drops an evidence bag in my lap but now suddenly has some protocols about visiting the dead?

The sheriff rubbed the back of his neck, gazing at the old clock on the wall. "I guess I can bend the rules a bit. But you won't like what you see. Car wrecks of this nature are pretty gruesome."

Rudensky stood, heading to the door and opening it. "Tell me when you're going, and I'll make a call over to the county morgue so they expect you."

Payne walked past him, not bothering to extend a handshake.

Something was off.

Way off.

Payne's headache was getting worse, and he knew it was

more than jet lag and elevation changes. When he first arrived in town, he thought he'd be getting a glimpse into Heller's last few moments on Earth and making final arrangements for his friend.

Now he had more questions than answers and a nagging suspicion that Pineland was about to become a staging area for an investigation of his own.

CHAPTER 3

IN A TOWN WITH A POPULATION OF ONLY A FEW THOUSAND people, your restaurant choices were limited to Jake's Truck Stop at the west end or Monique's Diner near the center of downtown. Short of that, the city of Payson, thirty minutes to the west, was the only other option.

Given the two rats he'd seen fighting over garbage by the overflowing trash bins outside the truck stop, Payne decided to drive the three blocks to Monique's. While he wanted to get to the morgue, he was low on fuel.

Twenty minutes later, he polished off a plate of grilled chicken and potatoes. On any other day, the meal would have tasted fine, and he might have even considered ordering a slice of homemade apple pie, but everything he'd eaten had the texture of cardboard since receiving the grim news yesterday.

"Passin' through?" asked Connie, the waitress.

Her soothing voice didn't match her weathered face, and she looked like someone who had grown up under Arizona skies. Given she appeared to be in her fifties, he figured she was a part-timer. Maybe semi-retired.

"Just here for a few days." He leaned back, figuring this was the hub of town where all the drama and gossip between locals unfolded. "Was supposed to be meeting my friend John Heller but got word that he died in a car wreck the other night."

She clutched her order pad close to her chest. "Lord. I just heard about that this morning when I got in. I am so sorry." She thrust her chin towards the corner booth. "John was a regular ever since he moved here. Such a sweet man, always quick to crack a joke if the opportunity presented itself, and he was always spending time at the VFW in Payson, helping out other veterans."

Payne recalled Heller speaking fondly of barbecues at the VFW. Given his extroverted nature, it seemed like a good fit and a way to meet other locals.

"Who was he helping out exactly?" asked Payne.

Connie shrugged her shoulders. "Don't recall any names. He just mentioned a young fella who seemed kinda lost, and John was trying to get him back on his feet."

Sounds like the Heller I knew. Always looking out for others.

She slid into the seat across from Payne, her painted red nails tapping on the edge of the table.

Payne looked at the waitress, whose expression had softened. "The sheriff indicated that John had a rollover after taking a turn too hard."

She bit her lower lip. "Mmm, don't know how that could've happened. There's only one major switchback, and you'd have to be blind, drunk or stupid to not see it coming."

Payne appreciated her forthright response even if it was gruff. Connie struck him as the kind of woman who would let you know exactly what she thought of you, which could be why there was the lack of a wedding band on her finger.

He glanced out the window at the cloudless cobalt sky.

"Don't suppose it was raining that night? Maybe that obscured visibility on the road?"

Connie slid her hands beneath the table, fidgeting for a while. "Nope. July through September is when our monsoons come in. It's been drier than a rattlesnake's noggin."

She glanced at the line cook on the other side of the counter where completed orders were stacking up, then patted Payne on the hand. "Sorry again to hear about John." She slid out of the booth.

He gazed up at her, wanting to get her take on one angle of the story Rudensky had discussed. "I appreciate you taking time to talk with me, Connie. One last thing, what would be of interest to someone heading east on that road at night?"

"Apache rez. They've got a good dinner buffet and pretty decent slots. Other than that, it's a mind-numbing drive to the New Mexico border and then a few hours northeast to Gallup. And all of the tiny towns like this are surrounded by national forest, so it's no-man's-land in most areas."

"They serve alcohol at the casino?"

She shook her head. "They're dry like the rest of the rez. Anyone who wants to get liquored up usually does it here in Pineland at the Red Bandit Bar." Connie gave a nervous glance at the cook, who was trying to shimmy another plate in between the others. "Gotta run."

Payne swiveled in his seat, staring out beyond the greasy children's handprints on the window towards the rest of downtown. He remembered when he helped move John out here four months earlier, wondering what kind of trouble his old mentor would drum up. Only he figured that would be along the lines of practical jokes with neighbors or carousing with fellow vets.

After finishing his coffee, Payne stood up and tossed down a twenty-dollar bill. He noticed a sheet of Connie's notepad resting on the seat where she'd just been. The top corner had been hastily torn off where she must have plucked it from the pad. He picked it up, focusing on the scribbled words.

Garrett Wheeler. Infinity.

He tucked the paper into his jacket pocket. *Is that someone in town or on the rez? And what the hell's Infinity? The guy's car?*

Connie was juggling multiple plates on her arms in the far corner, and he felt unsure about questioning her since she'd clearly left the message in such a fashion for a reason.

Payne headed outside, inhaling air that wasn't bacon-laced.

He walked to the corner of the building near the dumpsters and leaned against the brick wall, removing his phone and entering the name Infinity in Pineland, Arizona. The only thing that showed up was the web listing for Infinity EMS. He tapped on the staff listing, but it only showed a group of first responders huddled in front of a building beside two ambulance bays.

He glanced down the street, recalling seeing such a place. It was on the west edge of town across the street from a mechanic's garage.

Payne wondered why Connie had been so secretive about how she provided the message.

He thought back to the other patrons and the staff. *Was someone inside watching her?*

Payne got into the Honda and pulled out, slowly heading through downtown past a shuttered pizza joint, an outdoor retailer and a pioneer museum.

He stopped at one of the town's two stoplights, watching the tourists trickle across the street. A group of four thirty-something friends were taking their sweet time walking as they laughed about something on their phones. The women wore bright-colored blouses and designer sunglasses, while the men were clad in chinos and loafers.

Must be Phoenicians enjoying their getaway to the high country.

He watched them pass, envious of their jovial disposition.

When the light turned green, he continued west for two miles, passing some vacant lots, a cemetery and a barn offering pony rides.

He drove by the mechanic's garage and continued a hundred yards farther into the parking lot for Infinity, pulling up beside a grey Subaru Outback.

Payne exited his own car and walked into the small lobby. The odor of bleach filled the air.

The front desk was lacking a receptionist, but a stout man with a beard wheeled his chair out from the office on the right. "Howdy. Can I help you?"

"Hello. My name's Kyle Payne. I'm looking for Garrett Wheeler."

"I'm Marcus, Wheeler's better half here," he said with a grin. The man glanced over Payne from head to toe. He crept his chair out farther, then shouted down the hall towards the ambulance bays, "Garrett, get your ass up here. Some guy from the city wants to talk to ya."

Before Payne could respond to the presumptuous comment, a lean man in his early thirties emerged from the bay, walking like he was striding across the ring towards an opponent.

"Name's Kyle Payne." He shook each of their hands before turning his attention back to Wheeler. "I'm in town visiting a friend." He cleared his throat. "Actually, it's about a friend who was killed in a car crash east of here. John Heller."

Marcus and Wheeler shot each other knowing glances.

"Geez, you're the second person to show up here asking about that poor fella," said Marcus. "He sure has a lot of interest for a guy who's only lived here a few months."

"Who else was enquiring?" asked Payne.

"Lady out of Phoenix," said Wheeler, his jaw tightening as he spoke. "Said she was with the insurance company. Asked about the crash, the weather and the road where it happened. Usually, those agents just have the photos from the sheriff sent over to them, but she said she's up here for a few days to check things out along with some other unrelated accidents in towns farther north."

At the ringing of the phone on his desk, Marcus slid back into his office.

Wheeler's eyes darted towards the front door. "Why don't we step outside for a minute so we're not interfering with Marcus' work?"

Out in the parking lot, Wheeler walked to the edge of the building, standing under the shade of a lone pine tree beside the twin ambulance bays. "I'm sorry to hear about your friend. Didn't know him, but seemed like an interesting guy from what I've heard." He waved a hand in the air. "Word gets around in a small town."

"Interesting in what way?"

"He'd only been here a few months and had already helped an old couple stranded on the highway, brought a load of firewood to the VFW cookout, and always helped out his neighbor, Heather, and her little girl, Zoe." Wheeler dug the toe of his black boot into the pine needles. "Most of us up here are used to rich folks from Tucson or Phoenix snatching up acres of land to build their McMansions and then turning their noses up at the locals when they're strollin' through town. But not Heller. Seemed like a real good dude."

"That he was." He glanced down at the sliver of tattoo

showing under the short-sleeve work shirt on Wheeler's right arm. "Rangers, eh?"

"Yes, sir. Did six years and just got out last fall." Wheeler gestured towards his hip. "Medical discharge. Fucked up my joints from too many jumps and all the other fun stuff they had us doing." He looked over Payne's face. "You an army guy?"

"No, I never had the distinction of serving. Just been slogging away at a government job longer than I should have been." He stepped closer. "I got the accident report from the sheriff. I didn't see much about the EMS response other than that John was DOA upon the ambulance getting to him. So I thought I'd drop by here to see what else I could find out."

He didn't want to mention the note Connie left, figuring Wheeler would have surmised that Payne learned of the medic on duty from the accident report.

"It was the kind of carnage we typically see at high-speed rollovers. You arrive on scene, and it's like something out of a movie. I've seen people survive such things, but, man, that 4Runner looked like it had tumbled round and round about twenty times. I figured it would be a tag-and-bag as soon as I stepped out of the ambo."

"You think he swerved to avoid a deer or something?"

Wheeler shrugged. "Could be. Or maybe he was just not paying attention as he approached the switchback. But, still, I've only seen vehicles get that mangled when they're going ninety miles an hour, which you can't really do on that stretch of road at night with all its ups and downs."

"Can you tell me more about what you guys saw?"

"It was actually just me. I was finishing my night shift and coming back from a call to someone's house in the boonies, so I got to the crash site a few minutes after the deputy got there."

"You guys always work alone?"

"Not usually but we're pretty understaffed right now. The other medic called in sick that day, so it was just me and Deputy Lenny Firth, who was on scene when I arrived."

"And John had already died by the time you got to him?"

Wheeler folded his arms, pivoting slightly to the side like he was about to run for cover.

Something has this guy spooked. That's not like any Ranger I've ever crossed paths with.

Wheeler licked his lips. "Heller had been pulled out of the vehicle and was lying flat on the ground. It seemed like he was convulsing slightly as I approached, but he expired just as I walked up."

"Is it standard procedure for law enforcement to remove an accident victim like that? My understanding is you wait until medical help arrives so they can provide neck support so no further spinal damage occurs."

Wheeler flared an eyebrow. There was a pregnant pause as the man gazed up at the trees to the right. "Technically, you're right. That's not SOP, but those guys with the sheriff's department, they, well, they kinda play by their own rules most of the time, to be honest. And Firth said he saw Heller was barely breathing, so he thought it best to get him out in case I was running late."

"Rudensky said the crash occurred along a remote stretch of Highway 260. That kind of thing happen in that area a lot?"

"First time since I've been on the job. I grew up in Payson, and most rollover accidents I used to hear about occurred on the switchbacks up north by the town of Strawberry."

Payne rubbed the back of his neck, noticing that each time he mentioned Rudensky's name, Wheeler looked away. Payne also wondered if the medic had reported his concerns up the chain of command, or if he was trying to avoid conflict with the sheriff's department. "Any thoughts on why someone would be driving that road at night?"

"Not at that time. Most of the folks who frequent the Apache casino don't start rolling back home until a few hours before sunrise. The only other people on that road are the workers finishing the midnight shift at Tanner Steak Company."

Connie and the sheriff had both failed to mention that. "Is that a slaughterhouse?"

"Not exactly. They're a distributor of grass-fed beef obtained from ranchers in northern Arizona. They ship stuff all over the country. And if you ask anyone here, Levi Tanner and his company are the economic lifeblood of this town."

The walkie-talkie on Wheeler's belt notified him of an alert. "I gotta run. I hope this was of some help. And, again, I'm sorry for your loss." He brushed past Payne, trotting back to the front entrance like he was about to break into a sweat if any more questions were asked.

First the cryptic numbers on John's phone, then the waitress at the diner dropping a breadcrumb to come here. Now this medic who's acting like he's standing on hot coals.

What the hell is happening in this town?

CHAPTER 4

PAYNE WALKED BACK TO HIS CAR. HE LEANED ON THE HOOD FOR a moment, staring across the road towards the mechanic's lot, where dozens of vehicles were parked behind an eight-foot-high fence topped with rusty barbed wire.

It was the navy blue SUV near the side that caught his eye. Caved-in passenger compartment, shattered windows and mangled sides. It looked like it had been hit with a wrecking ball.

He walked across Infinity's lot and crossed the narrow two-lane street. Stopping at the fence, he scrutinized the rear of the Toyota 4Runner.

Has to be his.

On the right was a Prius with a crumpled rear end. To the left was a Chevy Colorado pickup, the front end missing a bumper, which led Payne to think this was a salvage yard in addition to the impoundment lot used by the sheriff's department.

He glanced around the property, then along the shoulder of dirt where he was standing, noticing a set of smaller tracks in the soil beside him. Given his background in tracking animals and people over the years, he could tell from the crisp details in the diamond tread patterns that they were recent prints. And the length looked three inches smaller than his size eleven boots, so he surmised it was a woman or an adolescent, with the former being more likely.

That insurance agent was following a similar set of clues. But why wouldn't she just inspect the vehicle with the mechanic?

Payne walked a few feet to the right towards a waist-high gash in the fence. He crouched and passed through, moving around the pickup truck and stopping at the 4Runner.

He rested a hand on the driver's side.

So this was where it all ended for you, my friend. Wish I coulda been there for you.

Payne skirted around the front, pausing to gaze through the passenger's shattered window. He saw something metallic just under the seat, standing out from the micro-shards of glass. Payne leaned inside, removing the object. He turned over a tarnished carabiner in his hand.

He knew Heller was a skilled climber and had mentioned something a few months ago about getting involved with local search and rescue, but why was this piece of gear randomly lying under the seat?

Payne glanced around the interior flooring in the front and back but didn't see anything else. Nothing else at all, and Heller was the kind of guy who always had emergency equipment in case of a vehicle breakdown or to help someone stranded along the road.

Payne rubbed the side of the carabiner as if it would give up its mystery. He tucked it in his pocket and glanced around the rest of the interior.

Both airbags had been deflated, but the appearance of the right one caused his eyes to narrow. There was blood spatter on the white fabric. The head impact matched the one on the driver's side, where Heller's face had clearly slammed forward. And there were visible teeth marks present.

Shit. John wasn't alone.

His mind raced back to conversations with Wheeler and Rudensky.

They knew all along. At least Rudensky did since one of his deputies was first on scene.

Payne's eyes shifted along the interior for any other clues. When he had finished, he continued walking around the front again, finally squatting down to examine the flattened tires.

And what he found next made his chest constrict.

CHAPTER 5

IT WAS SUBTLE, SOMETHING ONLY A PERSON WITH A TRAINED EYE would recognize... someone who had ambushed vehicle convoys like Payne.

A series of uniform slits were evident in the front tires of the 4Runner. They were characteristic of the multiple puncture marks created by a spike strip. Payne had used Stinger tire deflation devices more than a few times in western Pakistan and central Africa to disable trucks. The 4Runner's tires bore identical marks.

But this wasn't a vehicle in the middle of a war zone.

This was a targeted attack on Heller. Or maybe on who was with him?

Despite the warming rays of the sun on his face, he felt an icy chill run down his back.

He removed his iPhone and took some photos of the Toyota, then stepped back through the opening in the fence, staring at his old friend's vehicle.

A second later, Payne heard the sound of crunching gravel. A man with a grey beard and dressed in dirty coveralls emerged around the side of a white van a few rows down from the 4Runner. Behind him were two younger men in greasy shirts who came up alongside their boss. By the looks of their oaken arms, the latter two must have lifted engine blocks for fun. One had red hair and a lengthy chin beard, while the other had a shaved head and a dangling earring of what resembled a fang.

"Need somethin', mister?" said the older man, whose embroidered name tag indicated *Earl*.

"Just curious. This the 4Runner from that crash along 260 the other night?" He was plumbing for the man's reaction.

"Hell if I know where they're all from. My tow-truck driver just hauls in the wrecks, and I hold 'em for the sheriff until he's done with them."

"This is private property, and we seen you takin' photos," said the man with red hair. "Hand over your phone; then you can be on your way."

Payne pointed a finger straight down. "You're right. Where you're all standing is private property, but the shoulder of this road is state land."

All three men stepped through the opening in the fence.

"Get his phone, then tenderize him a little bit so he don't bother us again," said Earl, who folded his arms and stood behind the other two like he was about to coach a wrestling match.

Things suddenly seemed beyond verbal de-escalation.

They sure don't want me walking away with photos.

"You know, for a tourist town, you guys are very unfriendly. How about this… I get in my car and drive off, and you two get to keep eating solid food?"

The redhead grinned. "Shit, old man. After we're done, we oughta toss your body in the arroyo out back and let the coyotes finish you off."

"Ain't much meat on this string bean," said the other man, who was now cracking his knuckles.

It was something he'd heard since he was a kid. And his average size and build was something he'd turned to his advantage during many fights, using his speed, skill and experience to turn the tide on much larger opponents who'd underestimated him. While Payne had been trained in a variety of combatives, he relied on only a handful of moves derived from the Filipino martial arts, Krav Maga and Brazilian jujitsu.

The redhead stepped forward with a slow confident stride.

And he never had time to react.

Payne shot in and sent the tip of his hiking boot into the side of the man's left shin. It was a practiced strike, designed to hit the tibial nerve. The debilitating blow was quickly followed up with an elbow slamming into the man's jaw as Payne threw his full weight into the vicious strike.

Something cracked and shifted, the stunned figure careening into the fence and slumping to the ground.

Payne saw the blur of a fist coming at his head from the other guy. He parried the punch with a double-arm block, then drove his right forearm into the man's neck repeatedly. Then he stomped his heel down on his opponent's instep, the delicate bones of which readily snapped.

The figure groaned, trying to fight through the pain and sending a limp swing at Payne's ribs.

Payne issued several right hooks into the man's face, then a roundhouse kick into the left knee, toppling the figure beside his redheaded co-worker. He turned to face Earl, but the mechanic was nowhere in sight.

Several loud whistling sounds emanated from the direction of the garage, followed by the sound of barking as dogs moved towards the fence.

Payne trotted across the road towards his rental car.

Heading out of the lot, he watched two Rottweilers inspecting the fallen men along the dirt shoulder.

His headache from jet lag and the changes in elevation was returning, compounded by the adrenaline surge from the fight. He decided to drive west for a while, recalling the coroner's office in Payson was only thirty minutes away.

His mind was swirling, and he had gathered far more questions than answers since arriving in Pineland only hours ago.

One thing was certain. Someone had laid a trap for his old mentor.

And whoever it was had the training and resources to catch such a wolf.

He took a deep breath. *What the hell did you get yourself into, John?*

CHAPTER 6

AIDEN CAVELL WAS ON THE BACK PORCH OF HIS FORTY-ACRE retreat in the forest, mounting a new Leupold scope on a hunting rifle he would soon be handing off to an accomplice for a forthcoming job. The Beretta BRX1 was a bolt-action rifle whose serial number had been recently ground off and was capable of punching through a vehicle windshield at high speed, which was why Cavell had selected this tool.

Unlike Cavell's other weapons, this rifle was designed for a onetime use. It would have served as a fine big-game rifle, but Cavell had little experience hunting animals in the wilds. His prey lived in the urban jungle, and he'd amassed more than a dozen kills during the past ten years as the head enforcer for a Serbian crime syndicate out of Riverside, California. It was there that he honed his shooting and tactical skills under the watchful eyes of battle-hardened men who'd seen action in the wars that raged through Eastern Europe.

He would have preferred the warm weather of California over the snowy winters of northern Arizona, but Cavell had been approached a few months ago with a lucrative opportunity in Pineland that he couldn't resist.

Levi and his younger brother, Davey, had both been in the same group home in Phoenix with Cavell during their adolescence, so when Levi contacted Cavell about assisting him with a business venture, wintering over in the Southwest suddenly became more appealing.

During their youth bouncing around those group homes, Cavell had been a brawler with a penchant for violence and a checkered history in the juvenile system. But he also protected the Tanner brothers like they were his own family.

After Levi and Davey had been adopted by the wealthy Tanner family in Pineland, the two boys took on the father's last name, trying to erase the memory of their brutal past. Except for cutting ties with Aiden, whom they looked after from afar, sending him funds for bail, paying his lawyer fees, covering medical bills, and most recently buying a parcel of remote forest near Pineland for Cavell to use as a base for the new division of the Tanner brothers' empire.

He gazed towards a clearing in the forest where a dozen of his men were training in live-fire drills with their AKs as they trotted towards mannequins clad in state trooper uniforms. These were simple bounding drills that focused on shooting and moving while providing cover fire to your teammates.

While the majority of Cavell's crew were toughened criminals, they were loners, and he needed them to gel into a unit. The drug-running operation that Cavell and the Tanners were getting underway was going to require disciplined men with tactical skills and not just brawlers, especially since the forthcoming business would venture across state lines.

Cavell's buzzing iPhone disrupted his thoughts. He tossed down the tiny hex tool for the scope and snatched the device off the table. "This about my Jeep upgrades, I told you before to just get it done."

"It's not that. Something's come up down here at the

yard," replied Earl's gruff voice. "Some guy was poking around and taking photos on his phone of that 4Runner that was in the crash the other night."

Cavell arched up. "What guy?"

"Never seen him before. Looked like someone out of the Valley. He dropped Billy and Tate like they were ten-year-old girls. Never seen anyone move that fast before."

"So you don't have his phone?" Cavell kicked an empty gas can off the porch, sending it clattering onto the driveway.

"No, sir."

"Then get rid of the vehicle."

"The sheriff hasn't signed off on it yet. I can't just bury something connected to a fatality like that."

"Do it. I'll deal with Rudensky." He glanced up at a raven drifting over. "This guy, what did he look like?"

"About your height and size. Except he was dressed in boots and cargo pants like some of the hikers we get up here, but he sure didn't move like 'em."

"What was he driving?"

"Red Honda Accord. Headed east after pulling out of Infinity's lot."

"He musta been talking to the medic who handled Heller." Cavell sighed, rubbing an old knife scar on his forearm. "Alright, you take care of your end, and we're good. Just make sure that Toyota is buried so deep even archaeologists a thousand years from now won't find it."

Cavell hung up and palmed his phone, pacing on the wraparound porch as a burly man with a braided ponytail walked up. Randy Barr was his second-in-command and helped oversee daily operations and tactical training for the other sixteen members of his cadre, men who lived in trailers and cabins spread around the property.

Given they needed to stay low profile, the encampment was set up like an army basecamp with a kitchen, chow hall, and communal center for training. The only individuals who left the site were those accompanying Cavell or Barr during infrequent resupply trips to Pineland or Payson.

"Trouble?" said Barr.

"Could be, but it's just one guy. Apparently, he was checking out that 4Runner we toppled. It's not him who worries me as much as that medic who showed up at Heller's crash."

"You want me to pay Wheeler a visit?"

Cavell nodded. "Send some of the boys. Tell 'em to find out who Wheeler talked to about the crash. Do it discreetly even if it means waiting until he's off-duty."

"And this other guy you mentioned?"

"I need to find out who he is first and whether Heller told him anything."

"I'm on it." Barr stepped off the porch, heading to a large Quonset hut that served as the garage for their numerous vehicles.

Cavell clutched his iPhone, thumbing the side as he decided whether or not to make a call. His business associate would want to know about the aftermath of Heller's death.

He pressed the number. A second later, he heard the anxious voice of Levi Tanner.

"I'm about to give a presentation. What's up?" said Tanner.

"That problem we discussed the other day, it may still be lingering."

"I thought you took care of it. You told me it was a done deal."

"It was. Except there's another party who seems to be interested in the details."

"Is this a local issue?" Levi asked, and Cavell could hear a rare trepidation in his boss' voice.

"No. Outsider. Don't have anything on him yet, but I will."

"Do whatever it takes to keep our timeline with the initial production run on track. Make it look like this guy suffered a hunting or hiking accident or just completely erase him. People go missing all the time in the backcountry."

"Alright, but we need to meet again. I need to hand off this rifle to your brother so he can handle his end of things north of the border."

"As soon as Davey gets word on the target's location, I'll get in touch. Right now, I gotta run. Take care, my friend."

Cavell tucked his phone in his back pocket.

He grabbed the Beretta off the porch table and walked back inside his house. After returning it to the gun safe in the back room, he removed a tarnished Glock 17 from the shelf and tucked it into his beltline. This was a weapon that required no familiarization.

He needed more information on the newcomer in town, and the sheriff would be his best source for that.

CHAPTER 7

THE TRIP TO THE CORONER'S OFFICE IN PAYSON DIDN'T YIELD anything of help. The chief medical officer indicated Heller had died from massive internal bleeding and multiple organ failure resulting from the crash. At Payne's request, Heller would be cremated once Rudensky's investigation was over.

He didn't suffer for long. Those were the coroner's words ricocheting around Payne's brain as he walked back to his car.

He leaned against the hood for a moment, clenching his fist.

I can't guarantee the same for those behind John's death.

The thirty-minute drive back to Pineland went by in a blur, and it wasn't until he was near the diner that he even realized where he was.

He pushed on east for another twenty-five minutes, eventually turning right along a seldom-used dirt road and heading up towards Heller's place.

The cabin looked like more of a modest guest house than a full-size dwelling. There was only one other residence on the narrow dirt lane that led a mile down from the main road, and Payne remembered the privacy offered by the pines was the main attraction for Heller when he'd purchased the place last fall.

The twenty-by-thirty dwelling was situated on three acres of heavily treed land surrounded by miles of Apache-Sitgreaves National Forest. The structure was just above a slope of open ground that provided a vista of a grassy meadow below. To the rear were some game trails that led into the densely populated forest of pinyon pines and junipers.

Because the older structure had required a new septic system and water cistern, Heller had purchased the property at a fraction of its true value.

On the side of the building was a large propane tank and the pump for the cistern along with two large solar panels, which provided backup electricity. To the left of the back door was a one-car detached garage.

Payne killed the engine and exited his car, half expecting his old friend to stroll onto the porch and bark out a joke about Payne's choice of vehicle.

Instead, the ravens and the wind were his only company.

Payne removed a bronze key from his wallet, then headed to the back door, walking up the steps. He unlocked the deadbolt on the windowless steel door and stepped inside, disarming the alarm keypad on the wall, which he'd installed for Heller.

The air smelled of cigar smoke mingled with juniper, and Payne figured Heller must have recently enjoyed one final sit-down by the stone fireplace, staring into the glowing embers, unaware that the sand in his hourglass would soon be down to its last few grains.

Payne walked through the twelve-foot hallway, passing a bedroom on either side and a bathroom on the left. He paused in the entrance of the room on the right, which Heller had converted into a reading room and small office. Payne glanced over the dog-eared books on the shelf to the right. Most of the titles were vintage volumes of Zane Grey Westerns, whose Arizona settings had left a lasting impression on Heller in his younger days and had, ultimately, drawn him to this region.

The bedroom across the hall was pretty sparse with a wooden floor and a neatly made bed with a twin mattress pressed against the wall by the window. Heller used to joke about having spent so many years sleeping on a narrow pad on the ground during field ops that he would never need anything more than a cot when he was retired.

When Payne asked him about female companionship, Heller simply replied, "That's what her place is for." Based upon conversations since his retirement, Payne hadn't heard any mention of a woman in his friend's life.

He strode through the hallway past the bathroom and storage closet and into the living room on the left. The kitchen was on the right with a round antique table made of walnut and two wooden chairs opposite a breakfast bar by the sink.

Payne opened the fridge, seeing a carton of carryout from a Chinese restaurant. Other than a bottle of orange juice, a block of Cheddar cheese and some butter, the place was as sparse as the rest of the dwelling.

But then Connie said he was a regular at the diner. Maybe he was in town a lot.

Although Payne couldn't recall any Chinese establishments other than the one he drove past in the town of Payson on his way to Pineland.

The sound of a dog barking shot his attention to the dining room window. He stood to the side, peeling back the curtains. An Aussie shepherd was chasing a tennis ball that had landed near the rental car. The dog retrieved its prize, then raced back to a young girl standing near the house Payne had passed on the way in. It was a run-down structure with a gutter hanging partly off the front, a torn screen door and several missing slats from the porch steps.

The girl looked no more than ten and had pigtails down past her shoulders. A few more throws, then the two disappeared around the other side of their house.

Payne walked to the living room and sat on a recliner beside the lifeless fireplace.

He took in the photos on the walls, which contained images that only a handful of people in the world could identify. There was Heller standing on a rocky ridgeline south of Abalessa, Algeria, after he and Payne's team had completed a month-long mission to take down an arms dealer.

Another photo showed Heller sitting cross-legged on a beach, staring at the waves rolling in after completing a JSOC jungle training exercise in Surinam. What the photo didn't reveal, and what Payne recalled all too painfully from that time, were the hundreds of insect bites on Heller's back and arms, making it look like he had been peppered with buckshot.

With each glance at the photographs, Payne ran through the locations and memories, often feeling like leaning over towards the empty couch and provoking his mentor into recounting an old, shared story.

A few moments later, there was a knock on the door. Payne reached for the iron poker beside the fireplace. Standing up, he moved to the door, then heard the voices of two women whispering.

He peeked through the peephole and saw it was the girl from the adjacent property along with an older woman he presumed was the mother.

Payne sighed, leaning the poker beside the wall, and opened the door.

Immediately, the Aussie shepherd darted inside and trotted towards the recliner.

"Oh, my gosh, I'm so sorry," said the woman, who called at the dog to return. "We just got Mochi recently, so we're still working on the whole listening thing. He's used to getting treats from John." She held a hand up to her mouth, then let it slide down her chin. "Or was."

He could see her eyes growing misty while the girl just buried her head in her mother's side.

"I'm Kyle Payne, a friend of John's."

She thrust her hand out, vigorously clutching Payne's as they shook.

He noted her firm grip and calloused hand.

"Lordy, forgive me, I'm Heather Ryland, and this is my daughter, Zoe. We live just down the road, as you mighta guessed."

The dog had made its rounds of the house and now returned to the girl's side.

"John spoke often of you. At first, I wondered if you were his son." Heather tucked her hands in her jeans pockets.

Kyle smiled, the first time a genuine emotion other than grief had trailed across his face. "Do you want to come in?"

He stepped back and returned to the recliner as the two visitors sat on the couch across from him. The entire time, Zoe had only once made eye contact, and her mother seemed fine with not prodding her to socialize. The girl's gaze was fixed on Mochi, her arm wrapped around the dog's neck.

"I'd offer to get you both something, but I'm afraid there's only OJ in the fridge."

Heather gave a nervous smile, glancing around the room, then clutched a belt loop on her pants as if it were a lifeline. "It's OK. We can't stay long. I heard the car drive up and figured it was someone from John's family."

"I'm afraid John's family is all gone. He had an older brother, but he died a few years back."

It was just now, with Heather leaning back, that he could

make out the imprint of a revolver on her right side under her untucked shirt.

He glanced at her trim figure and athletic arms, figuring she probably knew how to wield such a weapon. And being alone out here with her daughter meant she was probably always armed, which wasn't unusual for such a rural area.

Zoe leaned into her mother. "Can Mochi and I go play out by John's garage?"

The mom shook her head. When Zoe asked a second time, Heather swiveled in her seat, giving the girl a firm stare. "I said no. You can wander around in here, but that's as far as you go. Got it?"

Zoe nodded. She got up and walked into the reading room with Mochi in tow.

Payne glanced at Heather's hands, which were vigorously squeezed together like she was trying to contain something in her palms.

She lowered her voice to a murmur. "Did John say anything to you in the past few weeks about any recent events in these parts?"

The way she said "events" made him think she wasn't talking about the county fair or an incidence of stormy weather.

"Nothing out of the ordinary. The last we spoke was three days ago, mostly about our upcoming motorcycle trip."

Heather slid closer, her nails biting into her hands as her grip intensified. "There's been a lot of creepy guys hanging around town. They're part of some militia-type group, I think. I've caught them eyeing my little girl more than once when we're in town. Makes me nervous as hell. I'm not too worried out here, but now that John's gone, well, this neck of the woods makes me feel like we're on the far side of the moon sometimes."

Payne lifted an eyebrow. "Militia… in this town?"

"They're fringe-dwellers, living on the county line. Not sure if they're actually militia, but that's the rumor. Bunch of 'em living in the back forty, doing Lord knows what."

He could hear the little girl singing in the other room. "I'm sorry you and Zoe have to deal with people like that. She sure seems to love her new buddy, Mochi, though, which has to go a long way towards making her feel safe."

Heather nodded, a tremulous smile appearing for a brief second. The woman unclasped her hands, rubbing the palms on the sides of her jeans.

"Why doesn't the sheriff do anything about these goons in town?"

She rolled her eyes. "Not sure he's got a pair, if you know what I mean. Rudensky and I went to high school together, and he was always the kind of guy who knew what to say to convince you he was right even though you knew he was full of shit. He shoulda been a politician. Now, all that being said, his daughter Emily and my Zoe are best friends, so I'll cut 'em some slack."

She waved a hand forcefully in the air like a conductor. "But that man needs to do something about the garbage on the streets before it affects the tourists coming up here." Heather glanced at the fading rays of sunlight in the window. "Well, I'd better get back. Have to pull a pork loin out of the smoker on my patio before the bears show up for dinner."

She called for her daughter. Zoe and Mochi appeared in the hall, and the trio headed towards the front door. "You're welcome to join us, if you'd like," said Heather.

He walked them to the porch, inhaling the rich aroma of smoked meat coming downwind. "I appreciate the offer, but I need to head into town and get a few things."

Payne was actually starving, but he needed a break from people for a while, which was why he'd come out to the cabin. A lot of it had to do with the tumultuous events of the past couple of days, but he also had a narrow bandwidth for socializing. He didn't mind it. In fact, on rare occasions, he craved it in small bouts.

But anything beyond one person was a crowd, and if small talk was involved, then his eyes began to grow glassy. Maybe it was because he grew up in the woods and had sought refuge in the wilds after his mother's death when he was ten, or it centered around his years in an occupation that involved endless bouts of silence during missions. Either way, Payne abhorred lengthy conversations and mundane gossip.

"Maybe another time, then." She smiled, the tension seeming to drain away after having revealed recent events in her life. "I home-school Zoe and run a bakery from home, selling to the shops in Pineland and Payson, so I'm around most of the time except weekends, when I do the farmers' markets. Feel free to drop by if you need anything. Any friend of John's is a friend of ours."

"Thank you. I will."

After Heather and Zoe left, Payne sat down at the dinner table and cracked open a can of tuna he found in the cupboard. With the addition of some honey mustard, cheese and crackers, it would make a suitable dinner.

He'd had far worse.

Payne watched the plum-orange slivers of sunset flittering through the trees outside as he mulled over the day's events and the revelation about Heller's vehicle. If he were back at work, he'd contact his team's intel targeter and have her track down every connection, however nebulous, to the mystery surrounding Heller's death.

Only this mystery seemed to surround an entire town, and he didn't have access to drone footage, security-cam hacks and digital wiretaps. He would have to work this operation alone, which meant old-school methods, starting with visiting the site of the crash, then working back from that point to Heller's last couple of days.

John didn't seem distressed when we spoke this past weekend, so whatever happened must have unraveled quickly.

Heather and Zoe wouldn't be of help other than to know about his comings and goings.

And those two shitbags at the mechanic's yard were just hired help with a snail's IQ between them, but the owner, Earl, probably knew far more than he'd let on.

Then there's Wheeler. Maybe I can catch him off-duty away from prying eyes and see if he's more receptive.

He shoveled down the last bit of tuna, thinking back to the odd round of questioning at the sheriff's office.

Rudensky… he has to know everyone in this town and all their dirty secrets. Is he leveraging such things for his own gain, or could someone be leveraging him to keep things about John's death quiet?

That last consideration concerned him the most.

He would have to steer clear of the sheriff for now. Payne reflected on his own years of recruiting and handling assets in far-off lands. The approach was always the same: locate the individuals who are economically disadvantaged, and provide some financial incentive at the end of the tunnel.

Only Payne didn't have a duffel bag of cash from Langley to help him out here. He'd have to see what details he could gather on his own to fill in the gaps of what he'd learned since arriving.

And the best place to begin was with the woman who laid down the first breadcrumb. Connie had to be a goldmine of local information, so he would start with her in the morning.

Right now, his brain was foggy, and he needed some serious sleep.

But before he could lie down, he needed to make a run into town to get a few groceries for breakfast and a bottle of ibuprofen for his headache. Glancing at the pathetic cast-iron poker resting against the door reminded him he also needed an equalizer.

He tossed the empty tuna can in the trash, then swigged down some water. He headed into the bedroom and slid back the nightstand. To anyone but Payne or Heller, the knotty-pine walls would look like a professional paneling job.

But Payne had spent a few days after move-in installing a gun safe behind the boards. It was a small safe that he'd bolted to the concrete foundation. He pushed on the panel, releasing the spring-loaded magnetic catches. Payne swung open the door and shuffled in closer, pressing his thumb on the biometric keypad.

The four-inch-thick steel door popped open. He glanced over the familiar rifles and pistols. A Benelli shotgun, an HK pistol in 9mm, a .357 Smith & Wesson revolver, a Ruger MKIII .22 pistol, an AR-15 rifle, and a Remington 700 rifle. Just the right tools to cover a variety of bases from hunting and home defense to personal carry.

He grabbed the HK pistol and removed the magazine, then did a chamber check. Seeing it was empty, he replaced the magazine and racked a round, then slid the pistol into a Kydex holster that was on the shelf. Payne glanced around the interior again, realizing that Heller originally had two HKs.

Rudensky didn't mention a pistol found at the crash. And John never travelled anywhere without his HK.

Payne thought it unlikely that it had been in a lockbox in the vehicle. He gritted his teeth.

Which means Rudensky's deputy or the mechanic pilfered the weapon.

He glanced back inside the safe. On the lone shelf at the top, he noticed a reusable ice pack. He pulled it out and flipped it over in his hands. It was a flexible four-by-eight pack with clear fluid inside.

He wondered about its purpose, then slid it back on the shelf for a closer look at another time.

Payne stood up, tucking the HK pistol under his shirt. He exited the room, turning off the lights and heading out the back door of the cabin before activating the alarm system.

He paused, feeling a pull towards the garage, and walked over to the side door. Using the same key from the house, he unlocked it and flicked on the fluorescent lights.

To the right was a workbench with neatly organized tools arranged on the pegboard attached to the wall. Most of them were connected with Heller's interest in motorcycle repair.

Beyond that were several sleeping bags draped over the rafters along with an assortment of camping gear. On the opposite wall was a rack lined with a shovel, rake, hoe and other landscaping tools along with some backpacks and large plastic crates.

He gazed at the four empty pegs on the wall near the corner where Heller usually stored his climbing gear. The harnesses, rope, helmets and ring of carabiners were all missing.

Payne thought about the lone carabiner he'd found in the 4Runner but couldn't draw any conclusions. *So what happened to all of his climbing stuff? Did he lend it out?*

He stepped inside the garage, reviewing the contents on the walls again but seeing that everything was intact.

He had purposely avoided the prize gems parked in the middle of the floor. On the left half was an Indian Scout motorcycle and beside it a Harley-Davidson Cruiser, each of them laden with saddlebags for the upcoming trip. Heller had worked hard to restore the vintage Indian, and it was a treasured friend. The Harley had been Heller's first bike, but he'd let it gather dust once the Indian's restoration was completed.

Now, the two motorcycles sat dormant, maybe indefinitely.

Payne stepped closer, running his hand along the Indian's handlebars. After a few minutes, he pulled his eyes away and retraced his steps to the exit.

He flicked off the lights and locked up, leaving a part of himself inside.

———

The woman remained hidden in the thick cluster of manzanita shrubs fifty feet from the back of the cabin. She knuckled her right quadriceps to prevent another cramp.

Since arriving two hours ago and trekking through the woods from her vehicle, Lara Medina had only managed to visually inspect the garage through the windows before the stranger drove up. Posing as an insurance agent with the medic at Infinity hadn't provided much info about the death of Heller and his passenger. She hoped the old man's place would reveal more and that her undercover work wasn't about to go down in flames.

With the death of her confidential informant in Heller's vehicle, she was running blind now. Three months ago, she had been following Manny Torres, a key player in the Mexican cartels. Torres was more than a drug mule or crime boss; he specialized in the production of synthetic drugs like fentanyl, high-grade methamphetamines and designer PCP. Whichever cartel he was working for usually ended up dominating the drugs trade within six months.

Medina had hoped that following Torres would lead up the food chain to the next kingpin. Instead of playing catch-up in the years to come, she and her taskforce could then take down the players in their formative months.

Or so she figured.

Until Torres disappeared outside a strip club in Tucson. The van used in the abduction was tracked as far as the northern outskirts of Phoenix. And there the trail went cold. No Torres, no evidence of his remains in the desert.

But a few weeks later, her DEA colleagues along the border apprehended Pineland resident Michael Portman, who was about to deliver a shipment of stolen firearms to a cartel crew out of Nogales.

After a lengthy interrogation by Medina's boss, Portman was given the choice of spending twenty years in federal prison or becoming a confidential DEA informant in Pineland, working directly with Medina.

Unlike other hardened criminals Medina had dealt with, Portman seemed like a misguided young man who had gotten sucked into a get-rich quick scheme. When it was revealed that he worked at the Tanner Steak Company in Pineland and that it was one of Tanner's associates, Aiden Cavell, who had convinced Portman to run a shipment of stolen firearms to the border, Medina and her boss knew they had their inside man.

For Medina it felt like that initial meeting with Portman was light-years away. Now, here she was, with her leads gone and months of investigative work about to dry up... until Heller's and Portman's paths had somehow intersected earlier this week. The only thing they had in common was that both men frequented the VFW in Payson.

According to what she'd dug up on Heller, he had no next of kin, so she figured this new arrival in the Honda Accord must be a close friend.

But someone out of state, given he's driving what looks like a rental car.

She had watched with interest as the woman and her daughter from down the road came by for a visit, but she'd not dared get within earshot of a window due to the presence of the dog.

Fortunately for Medina, she was no stranger to stakeouts, having worked undercover narcotics in southern Arizona before transferring to the DEA's Phoenix branch two years ago. Though most of her time was spent in the Sonoran Desert, tackling cartel drug busts, she didn't mind the lack of skin-crisping heat here in Pineland.

Medina watched the man exit the cabin and arm the alarm system before making a brief stop in the garage.

She had already positioned her iPhone to snap a clear photo of her subject as he stepped off the porch.

He moved with a quiet confidence, gazing at his immediate surroundings and the area around his car. She wondered if his situational awareness came from being either a cop or a combat vet, or both.

Especially since Heller had a background in the military.

All she'd discovered about the old man was that he once served in the US Army Special Forces decades ago.

Afterwards, he disappeared off the radar. No tax filings. No utility bills. No house. Nothing. A few years later, he surfaced as an employee for an international consulting firm, which, in Medina's experience, meant he was probably someone deeply embedded within the State Department or even a spook.

Medina watched the Accord head down the dirt road. She waited for five minutes to be sure he was gone, then stood, shaking each leg to regain circulation.

She walked around the side of the cabin, seeing a narrow horizontal window slightly ajar that hadn't been open upon arriving. It was in the room where she'd heard the girl singing. It's location above eye level and twelve-inch width was going to require some yoga moves to enter, but it was one of the only windows at the cabin lacking a security sensor strip.

Medina stood on her toes and used her folding knife to pry off the screen and leaned it against a tree, then hoisted herself up on the window frame before shimmying inside, eager to see what other clues she could locate about Heller's involvement in the sudden hotbed of criminal activity that had descended upon Pineland.

CHAPTER 8

Tanner Steak Company HQ

"So you see, my family business started with a dream. My father, God rest his soul, wanted to sell only the finest and most humanely processed beef from local ranches that would not only provide customers with quality, grass-fed meat but also support the ranching industry and provide local jobs to support our amazing community. But dreams can only point the way. Eventually, success in any endeavor in life will always boil down to hard work, commitment and surrounding yourself with the right people."

Levi Tanner clasped his pasty hands together, smiling at the twenty junior-high students seated on folding chairs in the employee cafeteria in the company warehouse eight miles northwest of Pineland.

After fielding questions for a few minutes, he passed the mantle to his vice president, who completed the tour of the facility.

Tanner headed down a spacious hallway lined with photos of employees, company banquets and various business awards. At the first intersection, he made a right turn. He then walked down a narrow corridor in the thirty-thousand-square-foot facility that served as the hub for processing, packaging and shipping out steaks and burgers to his thirty-three distributors around the US.

Another right turn and he proceeded towards a lone door at the end of the hall.

The armed guard standing at the entrance nodded and stepped aside.

"Afternoon, Barry. How are things with you and the wife these days?"

"Very good, sir. Still getting used to being new parents."

"Ah, so you're on your ninth cup of coffee today." He swiped his keycard to the stairwell entrance. "Or is it the ninth pot?"

The burly guard chuckled. "Depends on the day, sir."

He patted the man on his thick forearm. "Enjoy your new youngster and give my best to your lovely wife."

"I will, sir. Thank you."

Tanner ducked into the stairwell, trotting down three levels to the sub-basement that ran under the facility. Years ago, it had been used as the subterranean unit for keeping meat refrigerated until packing day.

During the past two months, Levi Tanner had had the entire basement retrofitted with an industrial-grade ventilation system and employee living quarters with a separate entrance on the building's seldom-used north end.

Until his other drug-production facility was up and running at the new property in the next county, this place would serve its purpose.

Which was for creating that initial run of designer fentanyl.

The guard wasn't privy to what went on beyond the first floor except that it was Tanner's R&D department, and besides, everything was protected by NDAs.

Tanner trotted down the steps, his designer penny loafers clacking on the cement. On sub-level two, he paused before a retinal scanning device mounted on the wall and leaned into it while placing his right hand on a biometric scanner.

Then Tanner grabbed a pair of clear eye protection off the wall rack and placed them over his face, carefully readjusting his thick crop of black hair.

A second later, the vault-like door hissed open from its vacuum seal and swung outwards on automated hydraulic arms.

He stepped into a ten-by-twelve chamber lined with hazmat suits on the sides along with respirators. He didn't bother with either, knowing his visit would last less than ten minutes, well below the forty-minute health-risk window affecting the unprotected.

The door behind him closed. A stream of cool air from the overhead vents rushed along the room. A second later, the door ahead opened in a similar fashion. This time the vast room beyond was illuminated like a baseball stadium.

And in this instance, Tanner always felt like he was the celebrity about to pitch the first ball.

He strode inside the fentanyl-production wing of his new business enterprise. The eighteen employees clad in protective garb averted their eyes as he moved past, focusing even more intently on their work.

Tanner moved alongside a sixty-foot-long walkway that was nestled between conveyor belts on either side. He barely noticed the assembly workers, some of whom belonged to Cavell's crew. Reaching the end of the production line, he was greeted by a gangly figure in an oversized hazmat suit that made him look like a swollen tick.

Miles Avery had been in charge of company logistics when Tanner's father first started the company twenty-two years ago. And Avery was proud of the fact that most of the employee-of-the-month plaques on the cafeteria wall belonged to him. His life revolved around his job, and Tanner knew that the man would fall on his sword for the company, regardless of the product rolling onto the loading docks.

"Good afternoon, Mr. Tanner," said Avery as he looked up from the tablet in his hands. "You'll be happy to know that we are nine hours ahead of schedule this week so far."

Levi went to pat him on the shoulder but retracted his hand after noticing the blue-green dust on Avery's protective suit. "If this all goes well, then you can expect a similar production run next month… and a bonus to match it."

Avery's face seemed to fill the visor in his mask as he grinned. "Thank you, Mr. Tanner."

Avery had always been a sheep. An efficient employee but consigned to be little more than a drone in the hive. And once Tanner had worked out the kinks with production after a few more shipments, he would have Cavell eliminate the less efficient employees.

Then, with Cavell's mob connections, Tanner would be able to send a tidal wave of fentanyl into the streets of America and quadruple his current income. Despite being the CEO of a company that netted a quarter billion in yearly revenue, Levi Tanner had an insatiable appetite for power, and that only came through an endless supply of hard currency.

Two years ago, he'd discovered the ceiling in his industry, which was being buffeted about by cheap Argentinian beef being imported into the US for a fraction of what he was paying local ranchers. Bovine diseases had also been rampant in the American West, which had caused his beef supplies to dwindle. Then the ranching industry itself was fading into the sunset as land was being bought up by developers, and the cowboys themselves were bowing out of the brutal work required to tend cattle in the unforgiving Arizona backcountry.

Each year brought more uncertainty. And Levi Tanner had spent a childhood riddled with uncertainty, hunger and fear.

While he was always grateful for the business that his adoptive father had schooled him in, it was time for the Tanner Company to embark upon a more lucrative venture.

Now, the only thing that could interfere with his plans were the Mexican cartels. They distributed the lion's share of fentanyl, but with his brother Davey's help, Levi was confident that the cartels would soon be embroiled in a war that would decimate their ranks.

Tanner yanked the tablet out of Avery's hands, staring at the production graphs. "Nine hours. Not bad, but not where we need to be if we're pushing out the first shipment on Saturday. Ramp up everyone's schedules to fourteen-hour days."

Avery arched up, peering through his dusty goggles. "Um, that kind of duration might lead to quality-control issues, in my experience, sir."

"How many more men will solve that problem?"

Avery glanced at the assembly line. "Six."

"Take care of it."

"Very well, sir. I will further increase…"

Tanner pushed past him, making a beeline for a worker near the bathroom who had just removed his respirator and lit up a cigarette.

"You fucking idiot," he snapped. "Are you trying to get us all killed? This entire room is filled with chemicals." Tanner smacked the cigarette from the man's mouth, then stomped it out on the ground.

"I'm sorry, sir. It won't happen again." The lanky figure nervously scratched the stubble on his chin.

Tanner pivoted hard to the right, sending the back of the tablet into the man's face. The figure recoiled into the wall, holding his broken nose as blood streamed down his lips. Tanner swung again, this time sending the edge of the tablet into the man's trachea. A crunching sound followed, the figure collapsing to the ground.

Tanner straddled the thrashing worker, then used both hands to swing the tablet down upon the man's face. Bone and blood sprayed onto Tanner's slacks.

The man's body had gone limp, but Tanner kept on hammering away until the face was unrecognizable and spinal fluid and blood were oozing out of the ears.

He stood up, a furrow of sweat on his brow. Turning around, he saw the assembly line workers had stopped and had their eyes upon him.

He gazed into their masked faces. "Did everyone just get the memo about not smoking or otherwise fucking up my factory?"

Bobbing yellow heads vigorously responded, then quickly spun around and returned to their duties.

Tanner walked back to a wide-eyed Avery, shoving the bloody tablet into the man's chest. "Looks like you'll be needing seven men."

CHAPTER 9

IT WAS 9 A.M. WHEN PAYNE PULLED INTO THE BACK OF THE parking lot for Monique's Diner. He figured Connie began at 6 a.m. when the place opened. With any luck, she'd be stepping out to take a smoke break, given the nicotine-stained teeth he'd noticed the day before.

As he sat in his car, he thought about the discovery of tracks outside Heller's cabin this morning. They were the same diamond tread pattern found on common hiking boots... the same pattern he'd seen next to the salvage yard. Payne had only found a trace of dirt in the spare bedroom where the culprit had entered a narrow window that Zoe must have left ajar.

If it was the same person, the woman who had been at Infinity before him, then she sure as hell wasn't an insurance agent. The fact that nothing was taken or disturbed in Heller's cabin made him think she was there on a fact-finding mission.

But fact-finding for who?

Now, he wished he'd talked Heller into getting some surveillance cameras set up on the property.

Payne watched the other patrons coming and going from the diner for a few minutes. Ninety percent of them wore dusty jeans, cowboy boots and drove old pickups, which meant few nonresidents from downstate. Since it was a Wednesday, he wasn't surprised at the ratio, and he figured the scales probably shifted on weekends when the Airbnbs and motels filled up with city folks.

Fifteen minutes later, Connie emerged from the back door. She paused under the shade of the overhang, pulling out a cigarette and lighting it up before plopping down on a plastic lawn chair situated beside an overturned crate used as a makeshift table. She rested her phone on her leg and began scrolling.

Payne exited his vehicle, sauntering towards her so she didn't get alarmed. "With how busy you must be inside, your feet must be grateful right now," he said with a smile.

She held up one hand, blocking the sun beyond him. "Well, you come back for the apple pie?" Connie glanced nervously at the back door, then used one foot to shove it closed.

"I think you know why I'm here." He leaned against the wall so he could have a clear view of the rear parking area and either side of the building. "Why the note?"

She cleared her throat, then took a drag on the cigarette. For a moment, he saw her fingers trembling. "This may seem like a small town, but it has its share of secrets just like any other place."

"Those must be some dark secrets. You could have just told me outright to go see Wheeler. Why leave a cryptic message like that?"

She thrust her chin at the back door. "Jerry, the dipshit cook you saw in the kitchen, also owns this place. He's married to Sheriff Rudensky's kid sister. The less the sheriff knows about anyone's business, the better off you're gonna be."

Her honey-sweet waitress façade was peeling back to reveal a Connie with some thorns. Exactly what he was looking for. He needed to take a leap and see how sharp those thorns were. "And you don't trust the sheriff, is that it?"

"Hell no. That prick's only in office because of the war chest he raised last fall, with help from his pal Levi Tanner. Tanner's the one who holds the reins in this town."

"Tanner… the owner of the meat-delivery company?"

She took another drag, then gave a nod. "They sell locally raised beef from the cattle ranches in the area. Ship fancy steaks and burgers all over the country." She finished her cigarette, then tossed it on the ground and stamped it out with her tennis shoe. "They are THE business in Pineland, which is both good and bad."

"How so?"

"Good because this town's economy was drier than a lizard's ass before Levi Tanner's father opened his company twenty-some years ago. That brought in a lot of jobs and also saved a bunch of nearby ranches. Bad because Levi, that cross-eyed bastard, doesn't have his dad's scruples. He likes to throw his weight around on the town council and anywhere else he can."

Payne thought of his experiences dealing with local warlords who were ruling African villages. "There's always somebody at the top of the heap, kicking sand in the face of anyone who looks up, even in a small town like this."

"I'll tell you this much, that company brought this town up from the ashes. I remember what it was like before old Tanner arrived, and half the businesses downtown were boarded up."

He put his hands on his hips. "So, again, circling back to my original question… why point me in the direction of

Garrett Wheeler? I spoke to him, and he was pretty short on details about John's crash. In fact, he seemed downright spooked to talk about it at all."

She turned her head away, rocking one leg on her knee. "Look, I only know what I heard from the rumor mill, but that was from one of my good friends who knows Garrett. Apparently, when he arrived at the crash site, he saw Lenny Firth, the deputy, trying to treat Heller."

"He mentioned that. So?"

"If you'd let me finish and not interrupted me, I'd be explaining that to you right now."

Payne sighed. "Alright, go on."

"Anyway, as Garrett was walking up, my friend said that he swore that he saw a big streak of blood on the guardrail."

"That, he didn't mention." Payne chewed on his lip. *Wonder if Wheeler was worried about getting into trouble with Rudensky for sharing that information?* He shot a glance at Connie, who averted her eyes. "Did he say what he thought it was from?"

"Sorry, hon, you'd have to ask him that. But seems to me that since your friend John didn't go through the windshield, that musta meant he was buckled in, so where'd the blood on the damn guardrail come from?"

Her lips seemed primed to move like she wanted to continue her theory. Instead, she got up and headed to the door, pausing to rest a hand on his shoulder. That soothing look crept over her face, so she was again like the amiable waitress he'd first met earlier. "Careful how far you go digging. There are a shit ton of badgers in these parts, and they have pretty savage claws."

"Thanks for the heads-up. One last thing… know where Wheeler lives?"

She frowned. "Third house down on LaRue Drive, four

miles east of here. You probably passed the road on the way over."

"Connie, I sure appreciate you talking with me."

The woman's lips were tight as she nodded before heading inside.

As he headed back to his car, he wondered if Connie had always had a prickly nature or if life in boom-or-bust Pineland had shaped her. He figured it was a little of both, but angled more toward the latter influence.

———

LaRue Drive proved to be harder to find than expected. The sign was missing, and it wasn't listed on Google Maps. The latter was no surprise given that many rural areas in the US were marked as big blank spots. Still, Payne had to reference the four-mile mark that Connie had mentioned and do several turnarounds before he eventually located the road.

The fourth house was indeed Wheeler's, as evidenced by the same grey Subaru Outback parked in the drive that Payne had seen outside Infinity.

A former Ranger driving an Outback… that just seems wrong.

Payne got out of his rental and walked up the steps. The door was slightly ajar, and he pushed it open and poked his head inside. "Garrett, it's Kyle Payne. We met yesterday at Infinity."

Silence.

A burning odor.

He removed his HK pistol from the concealment holster under his T-shirt. Walking down the hall, he glanced into the dining room on the right and the staircase on the left before proceeding into the kitchen.

On the stove was a pot of oatmeal scorching over the

flames. He turned it off and gazed out the open back window, seeing three motorcycles near a detached two-car garage.

A second later, he heard thumping, followed by the shouts of someone in pain. He made his way to the sliding door, which was also ajar. The breeze wafting through the house was the only reason the smoke alarms hadn't gone off.

He stepped onto the sandstone patio, hearing another thump from inside the garage.

"Best drop that pistol," said a gravelly voice over Payne's right shoulder as a man stepped out from the side of the house with a shotgun. "Do it now!"

CHAPTER 10

PAYNE HAD LITTLE CHOICE. TURNING TO SHOOT WAS SURE TO GET him plugged full of holes, and he couldn't duck back inside the house. He lowered the HK and tossed it on the hammock to the left.

"And that folding knife clipped in your pocket."

Payne complied, turning slightly but seeing the man readjusting his position to stay out of reach.

"Now, head into the garage."

Payne glanced at the burly figure and saw that he had a thick grey beard that extended to his chest. He was keeping his distance, making any type of disarming move impossible.

Payne reluctantly moved towards the side door, turning the handle and stepping inside. The air smelled of sweat and blood. Wheeler's wrists were tied with rope, and he was strung up to the wooden rafters, and there was a small pool of crimson on the dirt floor below him.

Two men in leather biker vests had clearly been taking turns using Wheeler as a punching bag, and they now turned towards the fresh meat.

"Found this one coming out of the house. He was carrying

a pistol. Saw him pull into the driveway in a red Honda Accord," said the bearded man behind Payne. "That car sound familiar?"

The tallest of the three men stepped away from Wheeler and glanced over at Payne. He had slicked-back hair and a gold hoop earring on his left side. The man's breath reeked of alcohol as he barked at Payne, "Who the fuck are you?"

"Just a tourist. I thought this was the hostel, but I guess I was wrong."

The man's right eye twitched; then he gazed at his two accomplices. Finally, a faint grin crept out. "By the description of your vehicle, you must be the guy who laid out Hedley's fellas at the garage."

Payne gazed over at the medic, whose right eye was partially shut from the swelling. He was pretty sure Wheeler was as tough as they came, but everyone had their breaking point, and two-on-one odds meant his willpower would soon be dwindling.

"So what is it you fine gentlemen want to know, exactly?" asked Payne, taking a brief glance at his surroundings for weapons of opportunity. Wheeler had an assortment of tools, from pruning saws and shovels to a hammer on the workbench and a fillet knife hanging on the wall. Any of them could be sufficient equalizers, but they were too far to reach.

The tall man rushed forward, sending a blinding straight punch into Payne's solar plexus. He'd been hit hard there before, but he recognized this immediately as a superbly placed punch from someone with boxing skills.

He recoiled against a post, the surge of bile rushing into his throat as he fought to breathe. He gasped, leaning his hands on his knees.

"I ask the questions, shitbird."

"Yes, sir. You're the man in charge. You've made that

clear." He was still too far away to reach the hammer on his right.

"I'll only ask one more time: who are you?"

"Name's Kyle. Came out here to talk to Wheeler, but I can always drive by tomorrow since I can see you're busy."

The man lunged at Payne again, who backed up slightly. The incoming fist struck his abdomen but was half the force of the earlier strike. He collapsed to the ground, rolling beside the workbench.

This time, the leader removed a Bowie knife from behind his back. "I need to brush up on my filleting skills. Maybe after that, you'll be a little more cooperative."

Payne sat up on one knee, waving a hand. "No, please, I'll talk." With his other he grabbed a clump of dirt. He pivoted to the left as the man approached so the bearded thug wouldn't have a clear shot.

Then Payne sprang up. He threw the dirt at the tall man's face, then spun back to grab the hammer and slammed it down on the guy's skull. It sounded like a bundle of dry twigs had just been snapped as brain and shattered bone spewed out of the gaping hole. Payne drove a stomp kick into the man's chest, sending him back into the bearded thug.

Payne blitzed forward, now slamming the hammer into the armed guy's right cheek, then another strike down on his left collarbone, which shattered like it was plastic. With the leader's lifeless body slumping to the ground, Payne grabbed the shotgun and violently twisted it to the left, yanking it free. He squeezed off a single round into the goon's chest and pivoted around towards Wheeler's location.

The man with the stringy brown hair beside Wheeler fired off a wild round from his pistol, which struck the window next to Payne, before bolting behind some tool carts and crashing through the door on the opposite side.

Payne sprinted towards the exit, taking aim and sending a

single shotgun slug into the man's right hip. The biker crumpled to one knee before tumbling into a woodpile. He watched the incapacitated figure for a few moments to make sure he wasn't an immediate threat, then returned to Wheeler.

Payne picked up the dead guy's Bowie knife and used it to cut the medic free, easing him to the ground. "You moonlighting as a training dummy?"

Wheeler clutched his sides. "You're fucking funny." He spit out some blood and wiped his lips, glancing at the dead men. "Don't take this the wrong way, but what the hell are you doing here? And how'd you even know where I live?"

"Small town, remember." Payne removed the weapons from the dead bodies and placed them on a workbench near the window. "You know these guys?"

"Not really. Seen 'em around. Unfortunately, Pineland has been plagued with roaches like this for the past few months. They've got a spread of land northwest of here. From the rumors, it's supposed to be a militia though they all look more like a motorcycle gang to me."

"And they were beating on you, why, exactly? My guess is that it had something to do with what you saw at Heller's crash site the other night."

Wheeler dragged a shirtsleeve across his bruised face. "Not so sure that was an accident. Deputy Firth told me not to talk about what happened, saying some shit about it spooking tourists from driving that way, but I knew something was off. And he and Rudensky aren't guys to screw with." He wiped his sweaty, bloodstained brow. "There were some things that sure didn't add up, and since these goons here were asking me about what I'd told you at Infinity earlier, I'd say you're on track."

Payne thrust his chin towards the side door. "Hang on, and we'll continue this discussion."

A few minutes later, Payne returned, dragging the wounded biker by his collar. He shoved him against the legs of a table saw. The groaning figure shrieked in pain, his jeans soiled with blood from the grievous bullet wound, which had shattered the right pelvis.

Payne kneeled in front of the man and waved the shotgun towards the guy's face. "Typically, a giant slug to the hip bone will cause so much internal damage that a person bleeds out within about ten minutes. So tell me who you work for, and I'll see about easing your pain."

"You crazy, man. My boss will kill me if I talk."

Payne pressed the barrel of the shotgun on the man's mangled pelvis, causing him to recoil in agony. "Give me a name."

The thug shook his head.

Payne used the barrel to push open the unzipped leather jacket. He peered at a tattoo on the man's neck, then yanked down the sweaty collar to see the remainder of the design. "This tat… where'd you get it?"

"The Q."

"Huh?"

"San Quentin, man."

Wheeler moved in closer, gazing at the crude artwork, which showed a serpent entwined around the neck of a dragon. "That mean something to you?" he said to Payne.

He nodded. "There's a splinter group in the Serbian mafia that have those. Sadistic bunch. Didn't think they were out here, though."

"And you know that how, exactly?" inquired Wheeler.

"I used to travel a lot. You should try it."

"Pff, it sounds like I spend my vacation time in different places than you do."

Payne pressed the shotgun into the tattooed man's hip again. "I'm still waiting for the name of your boss."

The biker shuddered, clutching his sides as he lay on his back. "Aiden Cavell," he muttered. "Runs an outfit north of town and is part of the Serbian mob out of California."

"And how many of your buddies hang out at his club-house, sharpening their blades?"

"Fifteen or so, depends on whether Cavell has a run down to the border."

"A run for what?"

"Stolen firearms. He heads down there once a week."

"To do what with them?"

Tears streamed down the man's cheeks as he clutched his sides. "He got a buyer who gets them to the cartel. Cavell's arming one of the smaller outfits across the border." The biker was gasping for air, his words blurring and his face growing pale.

Payne leaned the shotgun against the post, then helped the man sit upright. "So, why'd Cavell send you and your fellow cavemen to knock Wheeler around?"

"We was told to find out what he said to anyone about that old man's car crash. Said he mighta seen some things he shouldn't have."

Payne glanced out the open door towards the motorcycles. "Tell me about the little compound Cavell has just in case I decide to pay him a visit."

The man groaned, shaking his head, greasy wisps of brown hair floating down over his face. "Cavell knows how to be a ghost." The biker's voice lowered, his eyelids flutter-ing. "You ain't never gonna get to him."

Payne thought back to hunting down warlords in Afghanistan and Africa during his years with Heller. "Good thing I know a few things about flushing out ghosts."

The biker's chest sank in as he collapsed to the side, sput-tering out his final breath.

Payne stood and offered Wheeler a hand up.

The former Ranger accepted. "Thanks for showing up when you did. I owe you one."

"I was betting on you the entire time."

"Uh-huh, right." He hobbled to the door, pausing to glance back at the bloody garage floor. "You handled those fellas like you've done that kind of thing before. You sure you weren't in the military?"

"Positive."

"You in some kind of anti-gang taskforce? Is that how you knew about that tattoo?"

"Look, the reason I came here was to ask you more about the crash site. You wanna tell me what you really saw out there after you arrived?"

Wheeler grabbed a water bottle off the workbench and swigged down the fluid. "What I noticed didn't add up one bit." He canted his head towards the dead bikers. "You sure you want to know? Seems like what happened to your buddy has really stirred up a hornet's nest."

"Since I arrived here, things haven't added up. And in my experience, when my hackles get raised, my instincts are usually pretty spot on. I want to get to the bottom of how my friend died because, based upon the little I've already uncovered, it sure as hell wasn't from an accident."

Wheeler shuddered out an exhale. "While I was walking from the ambulance to Mr. Heller's 4Runner, I saw Deputy Firth get up from Mr. Heller's side and then go to the front end of the vehicle. It looked like he tossed something over the rim of Deer Canyon."

"What was it?"

"Not sure. It looked like a small duffel bag. And it looked like there was blood on the guardrail. Hell, I don't know what Firth was doing. My attention was focused on Mr. Heller after that. But I, um, was too late."

"John was buckled in, right? There was no indication from

the photos Rudensky showed me that he went through the windshield, but he also said there were only four photos taken of the accident site. After we spoke at Infinity, I walked across the street to the tow yard and had a look at the 4Runner. The glass was cracked but still intact."

"Firth told me he pulled Heller out of the wreck, so that would definitely indicate that the driver had been wearing his seatbelt."

"Then what does your experience as a medic and a soldier tell you about the blood on the guardrail?" While Wheeler pondered the question, Payne continued, "There was another, separate bloodstain on the deployed passenger airbag. Two people were inside."

Wheeler narrowed his eyes. "That's not possible. Only Heller was there when I arrived."

"And how long were you on-site for?"

"Just a few minutes. Long enough to get some help bagging the body and getting it loaded into the ambulance."

"So you never saw inside the Toyota?"

Wheeler shook his head. "No, but I've seen blood spatter on the dashboard and driver's side before in a major collision or rollover. That's not uncommon."

"This was from someone's face being slammed forward. There were even tooth marks on the airbag directly in front of the passenger's seat. That kind of thing only happens with an extreme high impact or from an IED exploding at the rearward of the vehicle."

"Shit."

"Yeah, exactly. So think back to when you first arrived. Was there any blood visible on the pavement by the passenger's side? Or any evidence of another victim? Anything at all that seemed odd?"

"Not necessarily odd but more of a lack of protocol... Deputy Firth wasn't gloved up. That's usually the first thing first responders of any kind are trained to do, especially at a gnarly crash site like this. As soon as our vehicle stops, we're donning our gloves as we step out of the ambulance. It's second nature. I've been called to other vehicle incidents with the Pineland deputies, and they're always gloved up."

"Unless there wasn't enough time." Payne paced back and forth by the workbench.

"I don't follow. Time for what?"

He shook his head. "Just thinking aloud." His head was swirling with too many details from what Wheeler had shared and the cascade of events since he'd arrived in Pineland.

He realized that the smell of body odor and blood was assaulting his nose, making his brain foggy. He needed to step outside and get some fresh air.

He headed through the side door as Wheeler trailed behind. Payne pointed to the three bikes. "Once these guys don't report back to their boss, their buddies are gonna come looking for them."

Wheeler wiped his bloody nose again.

"Tell you what," Payne said. "I'm staying at John's place. You can lie low there for a while. No point in staying here for now."

The medic nodded, thinking. "Thanks, but I got someone I can stay with for a bit until I can decide what to do next. Just not sure what to do with these bodies and the motorcycles."

"Leave it all here. I'm going to stick around in the woods out back and see who turns up."

———

After exchanging phone numbers, Wheeler left, and Payne moved his rental car a quarter mile away to a parking lot for a wilderness trail.

Trotting back to Wheeler's house, he headed into the woods behind the back porch where he had a clear line of sight to the driveway and garage. He crouched in a thicket of oak saplings and leaned back against the trunk of a large tree.

Forty minutes later, a vehicle rolled up, and Payne was surprised to see it was one of the tan law-enforcement SUVs he'd seen yesterday at the sheriff's department.

A deputy stepped out, placing an ivory-white cowboy hat over the flossy silver hair on his head. He was older than Rudensky and had a bow-legged walk.

The deputy glanced at the three motorcycles before heading to the garage. The fact that the man didn't approach the house and hadn't removed his service pistol made Payne wonder what he already knew.

If he was responding to the shots fired earlier, he's not very worried and is also a little behind the damn clock on getting here.

The deputy walked to the side door, shoving it open and standing in the entrance. He shook his head, clearly muttering a curse at the scene before him. The man backed up and grabbed the radio attached to the shoulder of his uniform.

"This is Firth," he said, his voice loud with emphasis. "There's a bloodbath out here, and none of these dudes are Wheeler."

There was another voice barking back at him, but Payne could only make out snippets.

"What do you mean what do I mean… there are three dead guys in the garage and no signs of Wheeler. What do you want me to do?"

The deputy paced back and forth while the other man spoke. Again, Payne could barely make out the voice, which sounded modulated. "Copy that. I'll lock the place up, but someone's going to have to take care of these bodies."

A minute later, the deputy closed the side door, then

walked to the steps of the rear porch and headed inside the house. Moments later, Payne heard the front door; then he saw Firth head to his SUV before backing out.

After the deputy departed, Payne sat in place for a while, contemplating the strange turn of events.

Firth. That was the guy on scene at John's crash. He's clearly on someone's payroll, especially since he had to report back on his findings here.

Was he talking to Rudensky or someone else?

Payne glanced back towards the garage.

It sure seems like I need to zero in on this guy Cavell. If he's with the Serbian mob, then Pineland is about to be swallowed up by a black hole.

His mind kept racing back to what Wheeler had revealed about Firth's actions at the crash site.

It looks like a visit to that stretch of road is in order... to see what, or who, was thrown over into the canyon below.

CHAPTER 11

It was 2:30 p.m. when Payne pulled his rental car into Zolly's Gas Station. The retro image of a toothless clown beside the logo above the store made him wonder how many families would choose to simply drive on to the next town for fuel.

Partway through refilling the Honda, a blue Ford Explorer pulled in on the other side of the pump. An older model vehicle, its paint was chipped. A thirty-something woman with dark hair in a tight ponytail stepped out, making brief eye contact with Payne before heading to the pump.

In a short-sleeve blue shirt, her tan, athletic arms were evident, and he couldn't help noticing her tight jeans, which hugged her legs down to her hiking boots. He scanned back a few feet to the oil patch she'd just walked through and studied the tread marks, which bore a resemblance to the diamond pattern he'd seen along the shoulder near the mechanic's yard.

She rested both hands over the top of the pump and looked straight at him. "You look like someone who could use a coffee. How about I buy you one?"

"Not sure, but is that a question or a request? Sounds like a request."

The woman frowned. "A little of both, I guess," she said, and he caught a slight Mexican accent.

"This sure seems like something beyond being small-town friendly. Is this your thing... stalking strange men at the gas station to see if they take the bait?" He removed the nozzle and returned it to the pump.

"Just a cup of coffee. I'm not luring you into a cellar somewhere in the sticks. Not yet anyway." Her eyes darted towards the front windows of the minimart, then immediately towards a cat walking along the edge of the parking lot.

She's someone on high alert. Or maybe that's just her usual MO.

He glanced at her footwear again. "Let me guess, despite your hiking attire, I bet you're an insurance agent out of Phoenix who wants to pitch me a deal I can't refuse."

Her eyes widened slightly. "Now who's the stalker?"

Payne leaned back against his car, staring into her almond-colored eyes. He glanced up at the overhead security cameras, noticing that she was keeping her back to them. "Wanna tell me why you're so interested in the car fatality that happened on Highway 260 the other night? And why you interviewed Wheeler and were checking out the 4Runner involved in the accident?"

She slid on her mirror sunglasses. "I have a hunch your friend John wasn't alone on that ride. If you want to hear more, then meet me in thirty minutes at Amaretto's Café in Payson."

Now he was really curious.

She didn't seem like a private investigator, but there was definitely an edge about her. "You realize there's a coffee place just a half mile away?"

The woman gazed down the street, then back towards

Payne. "As you might have already noticed, everybody is into everybody's business here." She turned, heading back to the driver's side.

"You know, women usually give me their name before they ask me out."

"It's Lara, Mr. Payne."

He watched her slim figure slide into her car and drive off, wondering how the hell she knew his name.

Maybe she's a bounty hunter with that swagger.

But who's the bounty she's after?

Regardless, he was interested in what this woman – Lara – had to say, and it didn't hurt that she was easy on the eye.

CHAPTER 12

THE WIND HAD PICKED UP DURING THE PAST THIRTY MINUTES AS Deputy Lenny Firth stood on the rim of Badger Canyon, watching a cluster of tumbleweeds blow along the dirt road until they met with gravity on their way over the rim.

It wouldn't be the first time he'd seen such a sight. Firth knew of plenty of isolated rocky chasms in these parts that held their share of bones, most of them put there by him over the years. He retrieved the HK pistol that was tucked in his beltline beside his duty pistol and examined the weapon. Firth had lifted it from John Heller before yanking his body from the wrecked Toyota 4Runner. It would make a nice addition, he thought, to his collection of firearms that he'd obtained over the years.

His thoughts were interrupted by the noise of an approaching vehicle. Seeing it was Aiden Cavell made him draw in a tightened breath. Firth tucked the HK back in his beltline but kept his hand resting lightly on the grip.

The surly figure pulled in beside Firth's SUV. Cavell stepped out. Despite the warm weather, he donned a leather jacket, flinging his long dark hair back as he gazed towards the canyon like a tourist seeing it for the first time.

The deputy moved closer, his eyes darting along the trees to the south, then back at Cavell. "You're an hour early."

"Well, I thought I'd enjoy the scenery for a bit." He waved a hand out at the rolling terrain. "Wanna tell me why you didn't clean up the mess at Wheeler's?"

Firth balled his sweaty fist, glancing nervously down the road. "Went out there, planning to help with covering up the evidence trail on his death, like you said, but he was gone. And your boys were plugged full of holes. That ain't my job. They were your crew."

Cavell rubbed his chin. "When I last spoke to my guys, they were just finishing up with Wheeler."

"Well, someone finished things up alright, but Wheeler was nowhere in sight. Looks like he was cut loose and drove off in another vehicle by the looks of the tracks in the driveway." He stepped closer to Cavell. "That fucking medic needs to be put down. If he talks about what he witnessed at the car crash, then we got a serious problem."

"Well, maybe you should've been more careful when you dumped that body over the guardrail." Cavell narrowed his eyes, gazing along the winding road, then back towards the deputy, who was tapping his boot on the ground. "You seem a little jittery, Lenny. Is there something rattling your cage you wanna tell me about?" Cavell thrust his chin towards the road. "Or maybe you're expecting company."

"Look, you wanted Heller and his ride-along dead, and they're dead. I'm done doing your dirty work, Aiden. Your guys are supposed to be badasses, and they can't even handle a simple job like snuffing out Wheeler, even with three-on-one odds." Firth glanced to the south again.

———

Cavell shook his head, a faint grin emerging. "You know, the problem with this whole operation since we put it together is that there are too many damn fingers in the pie. It's time to streamline."

"Well, that would probably be a…" Firth gasped as Cavell shot a straight jab into the man's trachea, the cartilage crumpling. Another strike and the trachea completely collapsed. Firth staggered back, clutching his throat as all color drained from his cheeks.

Cavell grabbed Firth's collar and dragged the stumbling, helpless figure towards the canyon. "You getting here so early makes me think you and the sheriff were planning an ambush. And I thought we were just startin' to become friends. How wrong can a man be?"

Without waiting for any kind of answer, Cavell shoved the officer over the rim, watching his body careen off numerous boulders along the nine-hundred-foot drop until his inert bulk pancaked onto a sandstone slab at the bottom.

He returned to his vehicle, grabbed a can of Heineken from the back seat and swigged down the warm beer. He sat on the Jeep's rear bumper, watching a plume of dust in the distance as another vehicle sped towards him.

A few minutes later, a tan truck with the Pineland Sheriff's logo rolled up. Bill Rudensky exited, fixing his white cowboy hat and glancing around. He adjusted his tactical vest before sauntering over. "Where the hell's Lenny?"

"More like what part?"

"Huh?" Rudensky's eyes darted around the juniper trees, then over towards the cliffs.

"What part of hell do you think someone like Firth will end up in for all the dirty shit he's done for you and your predecessor over the years?"

Rudensky folded his hefty arms. "You been up here a few

months, and you think you got the lowdown on everyone in Pineland?"

"Not everyone. Just the key players." Cavell glanced towards the rim. "And now the chessboard is down another piece, which makes the outcome of the game a little more predictable."

Rudensky's lips grew flat. He swallowed hard, walking past Firth's vehicle. He cautiously approached the rim while casting the occasional glance back at Cavell, who remained at his Jeep.

"God. What did you do, Aiden? You crazy fuck." He hurried back towards Cavell, his right hand wavering near the side of the duty pistol on his belt.

"Firth knew too much and was no longer of any use. Besides, by the look on his face and yours when I showed up earlier than expected, I'd say you two boys were hoping to turn me into vulture fodder, but unfortunately that didn't work out so well for Lenny." He grinned, waving a hand towards the rocky edge where Firth had met his death. "God, I love all the canyons in this state. It's like there's a garbage disposal unit around every bend."

The sheriff reached for his Glock.

Cavell deftly closed the distance and had a seven-inch blade already at the man's throat. "You really want to join your compadre?"

Rudensky let out an audible sigh, his shoulders sagging. He waved his hands. "Easy, Aiden. Easy."

"Levi put you in power in this pathetic town so our operation would avoid any speed bumps. Unless you want those photos documenting your numerous flings down in Phoenix to be broadcast all over the news from here to the border, you'd better rethink where your loyalty lies, or your wife and kids are going to be living under a cloud of scandal for years to come."

The sheriff gulped and licked his lips. "There's no need for any of this. My loyalty is to you and the Tanners."

Cavell flicked the blade over, slicing the sheriff's chin with a small nick. Then he stepped back, waving the blade like a conductor as he spoke. "Good to hear of your newfound wisdom. Especially since you're an accessory to Firth's murder now. Dispatch records are gonna show you were headed out here at precisely the time of his death."

Rudensky patted his shirtsleeve against his chin to stem the bleeding. "You just killed an officer of the law. You're not gonna pin that shit on me."

"That badge isn't as shiny as you'd like to think it is. You and your pal Lenny are sinners, not fucking saints." He feigned a knife thrust at Rudensky's stomach, forcing the sheriff to lean back into the side of the truck.

He smiled and patted the officer on his shirt. "Not many of your kind know but most of these vests have a small jelly spot right near the back by the floating ribs. It's a narrow gap between the plates, about a quarter inch, but one that a skilled knifer can slip his wares clean through. That kinda death is a long, slow son of a bitch, too."

Rudensky's face lost the last traces of its usual ruddiness. He swallowed hard and tried to bleat out a response. "Back off already. You've made your point."

Cavell leaned to the side, removing his blade. "Not fully, but I won't hesitate to slice up you and your family if you pull any more shit like today." He moved in a little nearer. "Or if you do anything to compromise our operation."

Rudensky arched up, adjusting his shirt collar and huffing out a breath. "You keep sending people to an early grave, and it's going to start drawing attention. This is a small town. I can only sweep things under the rug for so long."

"Ah, but there's no shortage of deep holes in Arizona." Cavell watched a hawk circling before returning his gaze to the sheriff. "The newcomer. The one interested in Heller. He got a name and location?"

"Payne. Kyle Payne. Not sure where he's staying, but there's only three motels in town, or he could be over at Heller's place, so it shouldn't be hard to track him."

"That's your job, Sheriff. Call me when you pinpoint him." Cavell returned his blade to the concealment sheath under his jacket, then walked back to his Jeep. As he drove away, he watched the shrinking image of Rudensky in his rearview mirror, seeing the man slump against his vehicle and rub his pale cheeks.

Breaking men wasn't hard for Cavell. He'd been doing it most of his adult life. Or at least physically breaking them. But now, in the sheriff's case, he only needed to create additional fissures in the man's frail, blustering confidence to make him malleable.

And then, in another week, once the Tanners' drug operation was fully underway, he'd install a new sheriff.

CHAPTER 13

Amaretto's Café was nestled in the center of an outdoor courtyard within a Western-themed strip plaza.

Payne saw Lara sitting at a round table with one boot up on a chair like she was settling in to read a book. Her back was against a wooden post, and she had a full view of all the other patrons entering the courtyard.

After he sat down, a barista approached and took their orders. Both requested plain black coffees.

Payne felt uneasy having his back to the main entrance, and he lifted his chair and repositioned it closer to the woman. He rapped his knuckles lightly on the sole of her boot. "So, *Lara*, you come here often, or is it just in between breaking into people's cabins and stalking them at gas stations?"

The crow's feet deepened at the side of her mirror sunglasses, and she pursed her lips. "When people leave their windows open, it can invite trouble."

"Is that what you are, trouble?"

"I think we both have some troubles. And I think we can

both benefit from sharing information, starting with your connection to Heller."

"I'm just here to tie up some loose ends with John's estate and pay my respects; then I'll be on my way." He leaned back, resting his hands on his lap. Seeing Lara swivel in her seat allowed him to see the faint outline of a pistol under her shirt. "You know, I really like Arizona. All the women here carry firearms." He thrust his chin at an older couple sitting in the corner of the courtyard. "I bet you even that granny there is packing a .38."

"She strikes me more as a Derringer girl, but, yeah, our carry laws are far better than most states'."

He removed his sunglasses. "Though undercover cops don't have to worry about such laws. Or are you with the feds?"

Lara sat up, planting both feet on the ground and sliding closer. "I'm with the DEA out of Phoenix. I've been working on a case involving some individuals of interest in Pineland for the past few months. I was making some breakthroughs with a confidential informant by the name of Mike Portman when he went dark three nights ago just before we were supposed to meet. Said he was getting together with a John Heller to discuss some issues that would be of help in my case."

Payne slid his sunglasses back on and decided to trust this woman – at least a little. "Your tracks at John's cabin, they're the same ones I saw on the shoulder of the road by the mechanic's yard. Did you venture beyond the fence and get a glimpse inside John's vehicle?"

"No. There were a couple of blockheads on four legs roaming around."

He waited for the barista to put down their coffees and leave before continuing, while Lara went about emptying a dozen sugar packets into her cup.

Payne relayed his findings about the other impact site on the dashboard. But it was when he revealed the indication of a spike strip taking out Heller's tires that Lara nearly dropped her coffee in mid-sip.

She wiped the drop of spilled liquid off her hand and set the drink down. "So, no accident. I thought that could be the case, regardless of that bullshit report from the sheriff."

Payne nodded. Despite her claims, he was still unsure about her motivations, so Payne thought he would push her buttons for a bit. "Wonder what the sheriff would say about you breaking and entering a dead man's home?"

"Rudensky... pfff... he's a rent-a-cop. Bought and paid for by Tanner. He only sticks his neck out if there's profit in it for him, or if Tanner or Cavell yanks his chain."

He decided to feign ignorance. "Cavell? That's not a name I've come across yet."

"He's an ex-con with a penchant for extreme violence. He and the Tanner brothers were all in juvey together in younger days and have remained tight. It can't be a coincidence that Cavell shows up in Pineland with his little fiefdom of whackos. Levi Tanner may be an unscrupulous businessman manipulating local politics for his own gain, but Cavell is a true psychopath who rolls with the Serbian mob in Riverside, California. Or he used to until coming to Pineland."

"He's still with them. The Serbians only offer memberships that expire when you're dead. At least that's what I heard from business contacts overseas who have experience with them." He took a sip of his coffee. "When did Cavell arrive?"

Her eyes darted up along the flapping shade canopy. "About three months ago, shortly before my investigation into Pineland began."

"You think there's a connection to Cavell and Tanner and what happened to my friend John?"

She resumed sipping her coffee. "Not only yeah, but hell yeah. My informant said he had some photos of operations going on inside Tanner's meat-packing facility that would prove Levi Tanner was more than dipping his fingers into the illegal drug trade. That would also explain Cavell's sudden arrival in town, since he has the criminal connections to peddle such shit."

"What type of drugs?"

She suddenly gave him a startled glance. "Let's back up here a minute. Tell me who the fuck you are again, other than being Heller's BFF? I saw the photos of you two on the wall in his living room, and I did a little digging of my own."

"So you did break into the cabin."

"I didn't say that. You've heard of open windows, right?"

"You're a clever wrangler of words."

She frowned. "And you and Heller worked in Virginia for a security consulting company." She clawed out air quotes at the latter words.

"You're a sharp one and must have been top of your class, Agent Lara..." He dragged out the words, prodding her for a last name.

"Medina."

"And you don't approve of Mexico's largest economic force peddling dope across the border, so you joined the DEA to help stem the tide and *make a difference* in the world."

"That sounds like a good recruiting pitch. I might use it sometime." She leaned forward, propping her chin up with one fist. "But it seemed more like a comment by a cynic. And it was a nice try at diverting the conversation away from yourself."

He held his hands up. "Ask away, Lara. Aside from my line of work, what else do you want to know?"

"Your accent... you're not from here, but it's not East Coast either."

"Midwest. Grew up in northern Michigan. But you probably knew that already given you knew my name and you have access to a government database with the DEA. So, what else did your background search on me say?"

"Worried?"

"Not in the least. I haven't done anything illegal. Not in Arizona."

She gave him a coy smile. "Grew up in Ishpeming, Michigan, which probably makes Pineland seem like the epicenter of human culture. Your father was a game warden, so you were most likely a little redneck kid with a .22 in one hand and a fishing pole in the other."

"Not much sun in the Great Lakes region, so my neck was pretty pale, actually, but, yeah, Ishpeming is one block smaller than Pineland, except we didn't have a sheriff. Most people handled things on their own." He rubbed the stubble on his chin. "Did I pass your little character test, or you got more questions?"

She tilted her head at him. "So, what did Heller speak with you about the last time he called?"

"Our upcoming bike trip across Route 66, the weather in Pineland, and the Arizona Cardinals. It was a short conversation since I was supposed to be flying out this weekend so we could prep for our vacation and the fact that the Cardinals seem to think that turning their losing streak around means doing a three-sixty."

Her phone buzzed, and she plucked it out of her back pocket to scan the text. Then Lara stood and slid her chair back. "From the photos of you and John, you guys seemed close. I'm sorry for your loss. I still think we can help each other out."

Now she moved closer, sliding her hand over his. For a moment, he got lost in the features of her lovely face. With her other hand, she removed a pen from her jacket and wrote a number on the inside of his right wrist. "In case you decide collaboration is in your wheelhouse."

She turned and walked through the courtyard, and he watched as her sleek figure confidently strode away.

Payne got up and moved to the seat she had been occupying so he could have his back to the post and a clear line of sight to the entrance. He pulled out his iPhone and called a number that had remained dormant for months.

"Kyle Payne, I thought you'd forgotten how to use technology or were living in some cave in the Kalahari."

"Hey, Alisa. It's sure good to hear your voice."

"But you only need to hear it twice a year, I guess."

"Haven't been stateside much until recently. You know the drill. Or used to know it."

Alisa Fairbanks had once been the head intelligence analyst for Heller's covert ops team, and her voice had inhabited Payne's ear for many operations abroad. Since leaving the agency to work in the private sector, Payne got together with her during occasional visits to Virginia.

Before working at Langley, Alisa had served as a Navy cryptographer and later part of a government-sponsored Red Team Unit responsible for penetrating military cyber-defense systems to test for weaknesses.

"You in town, wanting to grab dinner, or is this a work-related call?"

"Things are on hold with work right now. Not sure I'll be going back, actually."

"Damn, I never thought I'd hear you say that. Figured you for a lifer, especially with that savior complex of yours."

He gave a slight chuckle as the thought of forming his next words cast a sense of dread deep within him. "I'm in Pineland, Arizona, right now. John and I were supposed to be saddling up for a trip, but he... um, he was killed in a car crash three nights ago."

Payne heard an audible gasp, followed by the phone growing silent for a long minute before Alisa responded, "John is dead. He's dead? He can't be."

"Rollover on the highway east of town. I know this is a lot to take in, but I don't think his death was an accident. I found puncture marks on the front tires of his 4Runner, identical to the type created by Stinger strips." He sighed. "And there's more but I can't get into it right now."

"Tell me what you need. You want me to fly out there and help, I'll be on a plane tonight. Just point me to the front lines, Kyle."

"I appreciate that but stay put for now. I could use some help tracking down the backgrounds of a few people."

"Fire away."

"Levi Tanner, the owner of the Tanner Steak Company in Pineland; ex-con Aiden Cavell; and a woman by the name of Lara Medina, a DEA agent out of Phoenix."

"You got it. I'll get back to you ASAP."

"Thanks, Alisa." He watched a couple of sparrows pecking at some crumbs near his boots. "Two more things. John had the numbers 3106 on a text that never got out. Does that ring any kind of bell for you from the old days? Maybe a code of some kind?"

"No, sure doesn't. I'll run it through my cryptography software, though, and see what turns up."

"Lastly, can you backtrack John's cell phone to determine his location during the past few days?"

"You're kidding, right?"

"Let me rephrase that: what would you need to get that done? Do I have to physically get you his phone, or can you do that remotely by..."

"Just get the SIM card and upload it into your laptop, assuming it's a new laptop with a card port. Otherwise, you'll need to insert it into a data card, which can then be put into your laptop. I can do the rest from there by..." Alisa sighed. "Just get your hands on the SIM card."

"OK, I'll be in touch shortly."

After Payne hung up, he thought back to the antiquated building that the sheriff's department was housed in and recalled seeing little in the way of a high-tech security system.

Looks like a recon trip is in order.

CHAPTER 14

PAYNE RECALLED SEEING A MILITARY SURPLUS STORE ON HIS WAY into Payson and stopped in to see if he could pick up a few items not likely to be found in a mainstream hardware store.

Certainly not in any store in Pineland.

The single-story brick building was located in an older section of Payson, but dilapidated not historic. It was nestled between an antique shop on the right and a veterinary supply store.

After pulling into the parking lot, he walked through the open front door, which was blasting a current of cold air. It was a two-room affair with the front counter facing the entrance, and it smelled like a musty cave. Behind the register sat a rotund figure in a faded plaid shirt, blue jeans and old cowboy boots, which stuck out beyond a stack of MREs piled next to the counter. He was wearing a faded blue Navy cap with various ceremonial pins on the side.

On the wall over the man's left shoulder was a poster of an armed man in a black mask and tactical vest, pointing his MP5 at the viewer. The caption below read *We're with the government, and we're here to help.*

"Good afternoon," said the man, who pulled his gaze away from a hunting magazine and lowered his reading glasses to stare at Payne. He was wearing a Colt Python .357 in a left cross-draw holster on his protruding beltline.

"Sure seems like it," said Payne. "Can't complain about the weather, and this is sure a cool little town."

"Used to be. Too many Californians decided they liked the land in Arizona better than back home. Now those avocado-lovers moved out here and think they ought to be telling me who to vote for."

Payne glanced around the room, which had every square inch packed with used military items and a plethora of survival and prepper gear. The pathway through the jumbled mess caused Payne to shuffle sideways, and he marveled that such a place had ever passed a fire inspection.

Then he peered through the next room, which was three times the size and tightly lined with camouflage garments, used boots, sleeping bags, water barrels, tents, along with several bookshelves.

He heard a whimper and searched amongst the stack of solar-powered batteries to his right. A second later, a caramel-colored Pomeranian emerged, moving alongside Payne's leg and inspecting his boots before glancing up.

He bent over, stroking the animal's ears. "Would've expected an Irish wolfhound to be the watchdog here."

The owner chuckled. "Five years ago, maybe. Used to bring my Great Dane in every day, but he would knock so much shit over, I was spending more time reshelving things than getting work done." He gave a low whistle. "Get over here, Charger." The dog scampered back to the man, hopping up on his lap. "Anything I can help you with, mister, or you just browsin'?"

"Looking around for now. You wouldn't happen to have a lock pick set, by chance? I read on a prepping forum that I should add such a thing to my bug-out bag in case there's ever a need."

"Oh, there'll be a need soon enough. An EMP or tactical nuke by them North Koreans could send us back to before the nineteenth-century real quick. Or things are gonna go to hell when there's a civil war on our own shores. You can't be too prepared." The man gave him a stern look. "You got enough ammo laid in?"

Payne held back a grin. "I have just enough to get more if necessary."

The man chuckled. "Never heard that one before. Pretty good." He extended a beefy hand. "Name's Ben."

Payne realized that he seemed to have checked the proper boxes on the conspiracy theorist's mental checklist, and he returned the handshake. "Kyle."

Ben stood, cradling the Pomeranian as he walked, his belly dragging against the back of the glass showcases. He maneuvered around the corner, walking to the far end and pointing down.

Payne followed a similar line of navigation through the mazelike stacks until he was opposite the owner.

"I got the standard twelve-pack of picks, if you're old school, and also several different kinds of battery-operated jigglers with inserts."

Payne pointed to a familiar-looking set of titanium picks in an open carry case. "Those will do."

The man placed the dog on top of the showcase, then unlocked the sliding glass door and removed the item. "Anything else?"

"Could use an air pistol in .22 if you got it."

The man retraced his steps back two showcases and pointed down. "Got the break-barrel type and the CO_2 models. They're sold as kits with the pellets and spare CO_2 cartridges."

Payne squeezed past a stack of empty .50-caliber ammo cans and examined the pistols. "I'll take that Crosman."

"Good choice," said Ben as he unlocked the cabinet and withdrew the bolt-action pistol in its box. "I've used this little baby for nailing woodrats near my back porch."

Payne shot a thumb over his shoulder. "That should do it, but let me just check out your other room."

"Sounds good. Just watch where you're walkin'. Charger likes to follow people around and gets stepped on sometimes."

"Will do."

His walk through the den-like retail room was like visiting a personal museum and brought back a flood of memories as he gazed over the poncho liners, folding shovels, spools of snare wire, water purifiers, jungle boots and mosquito head nets.

But it was the mini library that Payne found the most interesting. There were copies of the *Special Forces Counter-Insurgency Methods*, the *Green Beret's Guide to Improvised Munitions*, and the *Combat Tracker's Manual* along with books on poisonous plants and mantraps. He felt like he'd just glanced over his entire resumé with the agency.

"You ever worry about this stuff getting into the wrong hands?" he shouted back to the owner, who was reclining in his chair again.

"Nah. Hell, most of that's on YouTube, which is why those copies are all covered with dust."

"Fair enough." He bent down to give a shoulder rub to Charger, who was panting from the stagnant hot air in the place.

"Now, that being said, I'll give you a two-for-one deal on any of those books."

Payne kept his smile contained. "That's mighty gracious, but this kind of stuff scares me, so I'll pass."

He retraced his steps to the front room, grabbing a small hank of paracord, a box of infrared glo-sticks, cheap gloves and a knitted black cap that folded down into a ski mask.

Removing his wallet, he tossed down two fifty-dollar bills and told Ben to keep the five in change.

He glanced at the man's hat again. "When did you serve, if you don't mind me asking?"

"Not at all. I was a gunner's mate in the Navy for eight years, ending in '92. Wish it'd been four years instead, and I might've kept more of my hearing, but it is what it is."

Payne had noticed a VFW badge on the left side of the hat. "You wouldn't by chance know a John Heller out of Pineland?"

The man's face grew somber. "Yeah, tragic what happened. The coroner's a buddy of mine. He told me. You knew him?"

"I did. He was a good friend. That's what brought me up this way. Did John ever hang out with anyone at the VFW? I'd like to notify them."

"There's already a small informal ceremony for him going on there tomorrow night, so I think most of the members know already." He stroked the silver whiskers on his chin. "There was a guy John hung out with a lot whom I haven't seen in a while. Young fella, probably late twenties. Served in Afghanistan, as I recall. Mike something, don't remember the last name. He was a lost soul. Seemed like John had taken him under his wing, as many of us do with the younger vets."

Payne thanked the man and exchanged handshakes. He rolled up the items in the cap and headed outside to the fresh air.

Mike… was that the same guy Medina was talking about, Mike Portman? Has to be. If that's the case, then John may well have crossed trails with the wrong people.

Payne had countless scenarios running through his head,

but most of all he needed more information on what Heller had been doing on that lonely stretch of road at night. He thought about the missing climbing gear from John's garage.

Was the canyon below that guardrail the destination? He shook his head. *But why go there at night? He had to be heading somewhere else.*

Payne glanced up at the sun. Seeing he still had a few hours until darkness came, he decided he could recon the sheriff's station.

The canyon would have to wait until tomorrow.

Right now, he needed to eat, and he knew just the diner where he could get a burger and begin his surveillance of Rudensky's office from a distance.

CHAPTER 15

THE DRIVE BACK TO THE OUTSKIRTS OF PHOENIX HAD ONLY TAKEN ninety minutes, but Medina felt like she had been behind the wheel all day. Her body was worn out from the past few sleepless nights, lousy truck-stop food, and a headache that had stopped responding to ibuprofen.

And now her confidential informant was missing and presumed dead. Meaning that months of grueling detective work had probably been blown.

Pineland was the last place that Medina ever expected to be working. If it hadn't been for her taskforce busting Portman, the activities of Cavell and the Tanners would have gone unnoticed.

Portman was part of Cavell's crew, transporting stolen firearms to an emerging cartel northeast of Nogales that was planning an all-out war against the reigning Delgado family across the border.

The past few weeks of painstaking work had yielded little other than Portman revealing that Tanner had retrofitted his meat-packing plant with a state-of-the-art HVAC system in one of the little-used subterranean levels in the facility.

Portman also indicated that dozens of Cavell's men arrived for work each night and often wouldn't return to the compound in the woods for several days.

When she pressed Portman for more answers, the man was reluctant to provide further details. Medina was beginning to think she was being strung along until Portman called her three nights ago, indicating he had photographic evidence of large-scale fentanyl production at the Tanner facility along with offering details of an overheard conversation between Cavell and Tanner, who were discussing a cartel member who had been instrumental in their progress.

Then Portman disappeared.

Was Portman privy to information on Manny Torres? Is Torres connected with this venture? She ground her teeth. *Why did Portman think bringing Heller into the picture was a good idea?*

After reflecting on her conversation at Amaretto's, she had a strong feeling that Payne might be able to help put her back on track.

He doesn't seem to be interested in anything but nailing down what happened to his buddy... but who knows?

Her mind was swirling, and she nearly missed her exit, swerving off Highway 87 at the last minute and taking a series of secondary roads towards Fountain Hills. Out of habit, she kept tabs on the vehicles in her rearview mirror.

After driving a circuitous route for a few miles, she turned her Ford Explorer onto El Lago Boulevard and followed it to the parking lot for Fountain Park. She always thought it was bizarre to see an actual water fountain shooting up into the cobalt sky in a region that saw less than ten inches of rainfall a year.

Medina pulled her SUV in under the faint shade provided by a large palo verde tree. She got out, arching up in a stretch as she yawned. She put on a baseball cap and then went through a few stretches to loosen up her legs.

A short jog would be good for her soul, as well as her body, but this was also the designated location where her supervising officer had told her to meet.

She had already stripped off her Glock 17 and tucked it in the under-seat lockbox, preferring to run with her backup gun, a .38 Smith & Wesson that she kept in a bellyband under her baggy T-shirt.

Medina locked her car, then headed to the concrete pathway, jogging past two women pushing strollers and a couple getting walked by their designer dogs.

A few minutes later, she skirted around the disc golf area and headed for a park bench nestled under a box elder tree where a barrel-chested man was scrolling on his phone.

"Thought you said situational awareness goes to shit when you're on social media," she said, leaning one leg on the bench as she stretched.

"I said your brain and personality go to shit on social media. Besides, I was checking my emails in between watching you hobble over here like a worn-out racehorse."

"Geez, don't sugarcoat things, boss."

He tucked his phone away, leaning one arm back along the bench while looking at her briefly before returning his gaze to his surroundings. With his hulking frame, he nearly took up the entire bench.

Neil Strozzi wasn't just the man who oversaw her operation. He was the DEA bureau chief who pulled the strings for all drug interdiction operations in Arizona.

Strozzi was also a guy who had made a reputation as being a hardliner, having cut his teeth in younger days as an undercover narc amongst MS-13 gangs in southern California. He garnered respect from his agents but was always in the crosshairs of the political elite who saw him as a relic of the Old West.

"Anything from your guy Portman, or is he still MIA?" he inquired.

She blew a strand of raven-colored hair off her nose. "Pretty sure he's bottoms up in some arroyo by now. Whatever he uncovered must have been significant since he was in pretty deep with Cavell and his crew."

"Well, we knew he'd be a risk on many levels when we recruited him this winter. I just figured he would've had a little longer expiration date."

"I can't prove it yet, but I'm pretty sure he was the second victim in a rollover accident that happened three nights ago east of town, though the sheriff seems to have omitted that from his report. A local guy, John Heller, was the driver, but he didn't survive the crash."

"How are Portman and the driver connected?"

"Not sure yet, but the last call I received from Portman indicated he was meeting with Heller. He was scared shitless. Thought his cover was blown. Also said Heller was the only one in Pineland he trusted…"

"So, what did you learn about this guy Heller?"

She stood up, putting her hands on her hips. "The only thing he and Portman had in common was the VFW in Payson, where they both attended social functions on weekends. The more I dig into Heller's background, the more red flags I keep seeing. And now a buddy of his has showed up and has been poking around."

Strozzi leaned forward, rubbing his bristly black hair. "We need eyes inside Cavell's outfit, and without your CI, that's going to be a major challenge. From what you told me before about what Portman said, he thought there was a cartel connection, especially since Portman was originally busted along the border for running Cavell's stolen guns to one of the fringe cartels south of Nogales. If Torres is in Pineland, then he must have been there to help get a drug op underway, willingly or otherwise. I can only imagine Torres has outlived his usefulness, especially given Cavell is in the picture."

"Regardless, Cavell, with his Serbian mob connections back on the West Coast, is certainly the guy to set the wheels of drug distribution in motion. We just have to figure out how the Tanners and Cavell are going to pull that off, or there are gonna be a lot of obituaries piling up around the US in the very near future."

Strozzi smacked a fly on his neck. "It's a never-ending war just like last week and last year and the one before that."

"You still got surveillance on Davey Tanner?"

Strozzi nodded. "He's a tough one to follow full time since he works at the prison down here, and we can't get anyone on the inside to monitor him. The last report I got from my guys tailing Davey indicated that he met with Levi two weeks ago for dinner in Scottsdale. Not sure what they talked about, but they looked like they're still pretty chummy."

"*Chummy*, nobody says that anymore."

"At least not uncultured youngsters like yourself."

Medina muttered several curse words in Spanish. "I've got plenty of culture; just none of it's related to that garbage you're always telling me you watch on TV."

"The original *Magnum P.I.* show is not garbage."

She rolled her head around, trying to work out the kinks in her neck. "Say, you still have that contact over at Langley?"

He nodded. "Yep, Jason's been working with JSOC lately, but he's always been knee-deep in ops with the agency."

"Can you run the names of John Heller and Kyle Payne by him? See what turns up. I know Heller was former Special Forces, and I suspect he may have been someone the agency was sheep-dipping for their ops, but the only thing I could find on Payne was that he's originally from some Podunk town in the Upper Peninsula of Michigan. Raised by a father who was a game warden."

"You really think a couple of spooks are somehow tied up with Cavell and Tanner?"

"If they are, then things could get very complicated, or at least very ugly."

"Just remember, you run everything through me. No one else at the DEA."

"You're such a control freak, but, yeah, I hear you."

He stood up, grinning. "If by that you mean I have freakish amounts of control over others and my own destiny, then I concur." Strozzi stepped closer, lowering his sunglasses as he looked at Medina. "If at any time you want a team on standby near Pineland, you say the word. I don't like you flying solo on this one."

"We already agreed this is the way it has to be for now. Too many new faces in Pineland will draw suspicion. With me posing as a rep for Heller's insurance company, I can justify my presence there, at least for this week."

"Alright, but we're less than an hour away by helo, so if you get wind of something going down, you call me ASAFP."

"Copy that, sir."

Strozzi patted her on the shoulder. "I'll let you know what I find out from Jason. He's back stateside right now, so it shouldn't take too long."

Medina gave him a two-fingered salute and watched him walk off. She turned and headed in the other direction, continuing her jog and breaking it up with hundred-yard sprints.

She hoped the exercise would bleed off some of her tension.

But after the first loop around the lake, she knew it would be a long time before a day would come when her heart and her mind weren't racing.

CHAPTER 16

Templeton Federal Corrections Facility, Phoenix

DAVEY TANNER WAS GROWING IMPATIENT WAITING FOR HIS afternoon coffee to arrive as he sat at his desk. He could have easily walked down to the staff lounge and obtained it himself, but the pleasure came in seeing his voluptuous secretary saunter into his office. Plus, Davey was used to lording over his three hundred employees, people who were there to serve him, like a team of horses under a whip.

As warden of the maximum-security prison, he was responsible for overseeing the lives of twelve hundred male inmates at the desert facility on the northeastern outskirts of the city.

Unlike his last post on the bleak edge of Yuma, being near Phoenix meant he could enjoy a Diamondbacks game with his wife, meet friends for the Thursday night bowling league, or visit one of the nearby gentleman's clubs after work.

While his older brother, Levi, had opted to stay in Pineland to run the family business after their adoptive father's passing, Davey couldn't wait to live in the big city.

Any big city.

Having failed the police academy after high school, he applied to be a correctional officer at the Arizona State Prison near Casa Grande. Given the attrition rate, Davey eventually made senior officer two years later and transferred to various prisons around the Southwest, climbing the political ladder to grade 11 lieutenant by this thirtieth birthday and eventually becoming assistant warden a few years later.

But it wasn't until he applied to the federal prison system that his true grit was recognized as an asset by the new governor, who had a policy of reducing recidivism by avoiding the "bed and breakfast" approach used at most prisons throughout the country. Davey eliminated amenities like coffee, cigarettes and porn while keeping the crude meals hovering on the cusp of minimum caloric and nutritional requirements. And though it was known only to his inner circle of guards, each incoming convict had to earn their bed, pillow, blankets and toiletries by modeling proper behavior, as outlined by Davey.

A weakened and demoralized prisoner is far more cooperative.

It was a model gleaned from his days in abusive youth homes, and it worked just as well at his prison, dependent on that year's political administration and funding.

Despite all the certificates of achievement and awards for meritorious conduct lining his office walls, Davey viewed his role as little more than that of a professional zookeeper.

Get the beasts out on daily exercise in the yard. Clothe and feed them and maintain a rigid schedule of activities to prevent too much time for idle thoughts.

The whole system reminded him of a military-style summer camp in Prescott that he and Levi had attended a year after they were adopted. Only the food was better at his prison, and he had a sound-dampened room in the basement for inmates who became noncompliant and needed a reminder of how things worked.

A knock on the door was followed by his curvy, brunette secretary entering, holding a steaming coffee mug in one hand and a croissant in the other. "I thought you might want something extra to go with your cup of Joe," she said.

He barely noticed the food, his eyes drifting along her ample cleavage, which was the primary reason she'd been hired last week over more qualified applicants.

"That's perfect, Lisa. You're a gem."

"Anything for you, Davey."

His smile faded. "It's warden. Everyone behind the wire calls me warden."

She gave a firm nod, placing the food and drink on the desk, then stepping back. "Yes, sir. I mean warden, sir."

"Just warden will do, Lisa." He waved his hand towards the door. "You can go now. Get me those audit files I asked about before lunch."

"Yes, of course, Warden." Lowering her eyes, she scurried out of the room.

Despite her rush, Davey still managed a glimpse of her swaying hips hugged by the blue fabric of her skirt. He wondered how long it would take to convince her of a visit to the special room in the basement.

He felt his personal iPhone vibrate in his pocket. Davey removed it, then glanced at the number. He got up and walked to the door, closing it before answering.

"Yeah, what's up?" he asked.

"What do you mean..." Cavell's voice was a snarl. "You forget my text about calling you today?"

Davey checked the wall calendar. "Shit, sorry. I've got someone from DC coming here next week to look at my accounting systems, so my head's been elsewhere this morning."

There was an audible sigh. "You know, Davey, I expected this kind of bullshit from you when we were kids, but Levi assured me you were different, more responsible now. Hell, you're a fucking warden, which has to account for something, but your head needs to be in the game, or this whole operation is going to be at risk of going to shit."

Davey balled his fist, walking to the window and staring down at the inmates in the yard. "I know. I know. It won't happen again."

"I don't think you do know. I've put a lot on the line coming out here to this pissant town in the pines. My business associates in the syndicate sense any signs of weakness or lack of follow-through, they're going to eat us all alive. You, me and Levi will be a pile of ashes in some burn-barrel in the desert. The Serbs I roll with make all the prisoners at your big house down there seem like part-time juvey offenders... You hear me, bro?"

Davey slumped his shoulders forward. This was the only person in his life who talked to him in such a demeaning manner. It had always been this way with Aiden. One minute, the man could make you feel like an absolute asshole and break your nose; then he'd smooth things out in a microsecond to the point where he convinced you that he was your best friend as long as you played by his rules. As Levi had said when they were younger, *That guy is the nicest bully you'll ever meet.*

In the years since their youth, Aiden had somewhat managed to temper his bouts of rage, but the veneer of civility was something that could always be stripped away in a flash.

And Davey had no desire to ever be on the receiving end of that primal creature's anger.

"I swear, Aiden, as of this moment, I've got my head on straight, and there's only smooth sailing ahead."

"Alright, good. That's real good. Now, talk to me about the prisoner transfer on Sunday. Tell me everything you've got about inmate 3106."

CHAPTER 17

THE TIME PAYNE SPENT AT MONIQUE'S DINER, INTERSPERSED with several coffee breaks on sidewalk benches, had provided him with ample opportunity to carry out surveillance on the building where Sheriff Rudensky's office was located.

With the sun dipping below the treetops, Payne returned to his rental car at a nearby park a block from Main Street and removed a small fanny pack, which contained the Crosman air pistol, lock-pick set, gloves, ski mask, glo-sticks and a small spray can of lithium grease he'd bought at the local hardware store on the next block.

He strapped the pack on, then headed west along a manicured trail that led past the library and a large community garden carved out of the forest behind the sheriff's office.

Payne veered off the trail, heading towards a large pine tree he'd spotted earlier. Beneath it was a clump of young currant bushes that would provide ample concealment while he waited for the coming of darkness.

As he sat on the ground, a familiar feeling washed over him, and his mind drifted back to numerous layup positions during his missions in urban regions around the globe.

It was his sniper tradecraft that had taught him to have the patience and physical stillness of a puma. While the former trait was never a problem, the latter had become a challenge in recent years due to lingering knee, shoulder and hip injuries from decades of grueling fieldwork.

Such occupational issues were what eventually forced many case officers to throw in the towel, eventually leading to an early retirement or, worse, a deskbound job at Langley.

Payne had no desire for either. Until recently, he figured he would follow in the footsteps of Heller and other senior officers who holstered their weapons after thirty years or more on the job.

When he first began with the agency, there was a clear sense of purpose in what he and his colleagues were doing, and that was battling the war on terror. That was further bolstered by the senior management on the seventh floor at Langley, who were comprised of former case officers who'd come up from the field and understood the nature of asymmetrical warfare.

But something had changed in the DNA at Langley in recent years, brought about by partisan politics on the Hill, which had swept through all the intelligence agencies, undermining the link between the directives of the experience-driven men and women in administration and those, like Payne, who operated in the shadows and knew the realities on the ground.

Now there was a culture of fear and self-advancement permeating the decision-makers, and the more Payne thought about it, the less he wanted anything to do with the new order and its skewed ways.

His mind drifted in and out of recent events at the agency until the woods around him were shrouded by nightfall. The only ambient lights in the area were from a gas station a few blocks across from the sheriff's department and the occasional passing vehicle on the two-lane road leading into town.

With the trinket shops and diner closed, the night life in Pineland was nonexistent, and Payne figured all the tourists were back at their motels or vacation rentals. Even the lone stoplight in the middle of town had turned to flashing yellow for the night.

He pulled out his iPhone and turned on the camera, holding it up and slowly scanning the property and building. It was a little-known feature, but the internal light-sensing device for taking night-time photos also had the means of detecting the infrared signal found on security cameras.

As he and his colleagues at the agency knew all too well, modern phones were great for surveillance and tracking a target's movements, but that worked both ways.

He only identified a single minuscule light over the rear exit, which corresponded with the security camera he'd pinpointed earlier during an afternoon jog.

Payne slid his fanny pack around and removed the Crosman 2240 air pistol. He'd already expended a third of the box of ammo pellets he bought earlier, adjusting the iron sights and practicing with the finicky weapon at a gravel pit in the forest near Payson. It wasn't the most precise pistol, but it would be suitable for what he needed.

Earlier, he had replaced the small CO_2 cartridge, which would provide the force to send the tiny projectile down-range. Payne slid the bolt back and placed a single .22-caliber pellet into the chamber, then pushed the bolt forward.

He leaned his right shoulder against a tree stump to steady his arm and extended the pistol, focusing the sights on a wall-mounted spotlight fifteen yards away over the back door of the building.

With everything ready, he waited for the sound of a passing vehicle on the main road. A few minutes later, a U-

Haul truck rolled by, and Payne squeezed the stiff trigger of the pistol. The lightbulb shattered, sending some faint shards of glass down onto the pavement.

He returned the pistol to the pack and removed the small can of lithium grease. Then he examined the parking area again before glancing back along the trail to his right. He donned his gloves and lowered his ski mask, then stepped out from the woods.

Payne sprinted towards the side of the building that was far enough out of range of the security camera over the back door. He crept closer, staying just underneath the angled camera, and quickly sprayed the lithium grease onto the lens. Next, he moved towards the rear door and sprayed a tiny rivulet into the keyhole. Finally, he removed the two lock-pick tools in his shirt pocket. The grease would help the pins inside the lock glide easier, a trick he'd learned from a former professional thief brought in by Heller years ago to teach urban tradecraft and vehicle-acquisition skills.

Payne placed the long end of the L-shaped tensioning tool in first at the bottom of the keyhole. Next, he inserted the rake, or snake rake as it was known in the industry, which had a sawtooth pattern across the top, which slid over the various pins. This was the most frequently used tool of a thief and one he'd practiced with thousands of times until he could employ it quickly on padlocks and deadbolts under a variety of field conditions.

By the flaking grey paint and patina on the edges, Payne figured this particular lock hadn't been updated in years. Two minutes later, the tensioning tool clicked the lock to the right, and he pulled open the door.

He entered, slowly easing the door closed. Payne scanned the hallway floor and walls with his phone but didn't see any infrared signatures from other cameras. He moved down the passage towards Rudensky's office on the left. He turned the handle and found it locked. Applying the same lock-picking technique as earlier, he had the hollow-core door open in under sixty seconds, which was fifty-nine seconds longer than it would have taken him to kick in the cheap barrier.

Wonder if he and his deputies even have bullets in their pistols?

Payne paused in the entrance, examining the room. There was a security camera in the corner that he recalled seeing during his initial visit with Rudensky. Its faded and grimy plastic lens made him wonder if it was even operational.

Just to be sure, he pulled out two infrared glo-sticks, which had a ten-foot section of cord tied to one end. Payne activated them and tossed the duo on the floor under the camera. The soft white light, which appeared innocuous to the naked eye, had the effect of disrupting the internal camera software that recorded images.

A scent of cheap cigars and body odor emanated from the couch on the left, and Payne wondered how often the man shacked up here after hours.

Just hope he's not planning to sleep here tonight.

He walked past the angled pole with the Arizona flag and proceeded to the drawers on the left side of the desk. Kneeling down, he put the tensioning tool and snake rake to use one last time.

This lock made the other two seem like platinum editions, and the simple pins inside quickly succumbed to the raking action of Payne's implement. Sliding open the drawer, he removed the clear evidence bag and fished out Heller's phone. He removed the SIM card and slid it into his shirt pocket.

He found himself staring at the other objects in the bag.

Why'd you have to leave this world so soon, John? We were gonna go on a helluva bike ride.

He forced his mind back to the present, stowing the phone in the bag and returning it to the drawer. Payne glanced down at a metal box at the bottom, flipping open the lid. Inside were a few bundles of fifty- and hundred-dollar bills. The thick rubber bands around the bundles were inscribed in black marker with the words, Widows & Orphans Funds. He figured there must have been a few thousand dollars. Given his gut feeling about the sheriff, he wondered how often Rudensky dipped into the funds for personal reasons.

Payne closed the lid and shut the drawer. He backtracked to the door, then grabbed the line attached to the glo-sticks and yanked them quickly across the floor before stepping into the hallway. He shut the door and used the rake and tensioning tool to reset the lock before heading to the exit.

The fresh smell of pines in the parking lot was welcome after Rudensky's stifling, sweaty office. He left the grease on the external camera lens, knowing that most of it would melt off in the morning hours, then relocked the door and trotted back to the edge of the woods, turning to surveil the area.

The diminutive SIM card in his pocket suddenly felt like a barbell weight. He just hoped it would provide some breadcrumbs on Heller's final hours.

CHAPTER 18

AFTER HAVING A LATER DINNER AND TAKING A SHOWER IN HER motel room, Medina got dressed and checked the weather report. Tomorrow's forecast indicated daytime temps in the mid-seventies, but she still decided to pack a windbreaker.

She had learned long ago that Arizona was a land of extremes where it could go from triple-digits during the day to below freezing after sundown. And here at nearly seven thousand feet in Pineland, it had even been known to snow in the spring and fall.

She was pleasantly surprised to see a text from Payne. He wanted to meet at Heller's cabin in the morning.

Nothing like going back to the scene of my break-in.

Medina replied she'd be there in the morning after her jog and picking up coffee at the truck stop. She finished getting dressed in shorts and a tank top and plunked down on the bed to watch TV.

A few minutes into scanning through the barrage of choices, her phone rang.

It was Strozzi.

Unusual for him to already be calling me since we just met. This has to be juicy.

"Sorry to wake you, kid."

"Ha-ha. I probably keep later hours than you."

"Not likely." He cleared his throat. "So, I spoke with Jason, my friend who's worked with the CIA for years. He didn't find anything specifically about a guy named Kyle Payne, but he did know about John Heller. Apparently, Heller was involved in black ops for over two decades, mostly 'wet-work, and had a reputation as being a helluva operator. A few years ago, he started a unit composed of seasoned operators to work in asset recovery. These were guys he pulled from Ground Branch."

"Never heard of it."

"Me neither until Jason mentioned it. Ground Branch is made up of CIA case officers who have already cut their teeth in field ops. You don't even get asked to join Ground Branch until you have years of covert missions under your belt. The Ground Branch agents are some serious motherfuckers who play by their own rules and are beyond skilled in sniping, munitions, bare-handed fighting, guerilla warfare, you name it. When they were recruited into Heller's new unit, their sole job was to rescue compromised agents or assets from behind enemy lines using any means necessary. They mainly operated alone, getting in and out like ghosts while eliminating any threats along the way."

"Damn. Did Jason think Payne was connected to this outfit?"

"Again, spooks like that probably aren't on any official roster back at Langley, but he did say that there was a guy, mid-thirties or so, who was like Heller's protégé. And Jason said he remembered this dude because he taught a man-tracking class a few years back for Jason's crew. This fella had some old-school fieldcraft skills… which, get this, he said came from having a dad who was a conservation officer who tracked down poachers. That sound like this guy Payne to you?"

"Sure does. Can't be too many people who had that kind of upbringing."

"There's one other thing Jason told me. Apparently, this person we're talking about is on disciplinary leave. Rumor has it that he went rogue on some recent op and killed an innocent civilian overseas." Strozzi's voice deepened. "Lara, if you see this guy Payne again, watch your ass. He could be a loose cannon and about to unleash his own private war upon Pineland when he finds out who was behind his friend's death."

Medina chewed on a fingernail as she paced. "Payne's presence could work to our advantage, actually. If push comes to shove and one or two of Cavell's goons need to be removed from the picture, or even Cavell himself, it's better to have blood on Payne's hands than on the DEA's."

"You're talking about walking a very slippery slope. While I agree about not having fingers pointing back at us, orchestrating something like you're describing involves too many variables beyond your control to guarantee the right outcome… and an outcome where you walk away with your head intact."

"I'd run anything like this by you first, boss."

"You'd better," said Strozzi in a paternal tone. "But you also have a knack for flying off the cuff sometimes. A trait that has served you well in the field, but this op in Pineland seems to have more tentacles than we anticipated. So remember – observe and report before taking any action."

"Will do, boss." Medina hung up, feeling like tossing her phone under the tires of an eighteen-wheeler that was rumbling along the two-lane highway outside.

This whole fucking operation just keeps getting murkier by the hour.

Instead, she slid back onto the bed, replaying Strozzi's words about Payne killing an innocent, and wondering if meeting him alone at the cabin was a wise choice.

CHAPTER 19

THE NEXT MORNING, CAVELL HAD RISEN BEFORE DAWN AND RODE out from his secluded compound in the forest.

After driving his Harley-Davidson for twenty-four miles, Cavell pulled off Highway 87, south of the minuscule town of Sunflower, and headed east for a further three miles to an abandoned hangar that was once used for a small airfield.

The elevation drop from Pineland to this part of the cactus-studded Sonoran Desert was around three thousand feet, which meant the daytime temps sweltered to triple digits. It was only 6:30 a.m. and the temperature was already nearing ninety-five degrees, so today was going to be a cooker.

He drove through the open bay whose doors had long ago been hauled off by locals, pulling into the right-hand corner, where a blue Dodge Ram was parked alongside a black Land Rover.

Killing the engine, Cavell dismounted and removed his sunglasses. He walked towards the two men leaning against the Ram, both of them extending hands. Cavell pulled them in closer, giving them bro-hugs instead. "Sure is good to see you boys," he said.

"Likewise," replied Davey Tanner with a smile.

"Seems like old times, brother," said Levi Tanner.

While Aiden knew people threw about the familial term, to him it struck a deep chord. The Tanner boys were as close to family as he'd ever had and probably would ever have.

While he was in prison, he had been taken in by the Serbian crime syndicate, whose protection had enabled him to survive that hellish pit. But it also meant he was permanently indebted to them, though Cavell thought indentured was a more accurate term.

"Nice wheels," said Davey as he thrust his chin towards the motorcycle.

"Yeah, sure is a sweet ride, and this is the right state to own a chopper," replied Cavell.

"You remember when we stole those ten-speed bikes off them ninth-grade girls when we were kids?" said Davey with a huge grin.

"After we pelted the shit out of 'em with apples from that old guy's yard," said Levi.

Cavell let out a belly laugh. "Damn, they never saw it coming either. We just kept popping up from that ditch like gophers. They were damn near unconscious by the time we rode off on their bikes." He pursed his lips. "If I had to do it all over again, I would have dragged that redhead into the grass and had some fun with her."

Davey folded his arms. "The cash we got from those bikes let me buy my first set of boots and a cowboy belt. No more fucking hand-me-downs. I finally had something of my own."

Cavell nodded. "I bought a Buck folding knife that I had for years and a jimmy-tool for breaking into cars."

"I put my money on a boxing match in Phoenix," said Levi. "First time dealing with a bookie, but the way that fight went, it seemed like you guys were the only two who came out ahead."

Their laughter filled the small hangar as they recounted a few more tales from their youth.

Cavell returned to the Harley, removing a water bottle from the leather saddlebag and swigging down some of the warm fluid.

"I thought it best to meet one more time to make sure we've got all of our bases covered with this last leg of the operation before things go live on Saturday," said Cavell.

Levi dragged a shirtsleeve across his moist forehead. "I'll be glad when we don't have to meet in this blast furnace again. Maybe we can find a more suitable location near Pineland in the future."

Cavell shook his head. "Too many inbred motherfuckers who are into everyone's business in that town. That's why you and I can't be seen together, Levi." He thrust his thumb towards a case strapped on the rear pannier of his motorcycle while looking at Davey. "Before we leave here, I'll get you the industrial-grade drill along with a few high-speed cobalt drill bits that'll do the job for boring the sniper holes in that storage container along the interstate. Just make sure to police the area outside afterwards to clean up any metal debris and erase your tracks."

Davey nodded. "I'm going to take care of that right after we're done here." He shifted his weight, glancing beyond Cavell. "You bring the rifle?"

Cavell nodded. "There's a .308 takedown rifle in the other carrier on my hog. That beauty has a three-thousand-dollar scope on it too. She'll take care of business."

Davey licked his lips. "Sounds good. That's the same caliber rifle I used in Wyoming last fall for dropping antelope nearly a mile out."

Cavell nodded. "I already broke it in at my place. And most importantly, like the firearms we've been running down to the border, this one doesn't exist in any databases." Cavell returned to his bike, unlocking one of the metal panniers on the rear. He extracted a fiberglass gun case and handed it to Davey.

The younger Tanner brother placed it on the ground, kneeling over it like it contained a priceless artifact. He flipped open the latches and lifted the lid, examining the Beretta BRX1. Davey wasted no time in assembling the rifle.

When he finished, he stood and walked to his truck, removing a set of hearing protection and a small sandbag from the back seat of his truck. The latter was a handmade item consisting of two gallon-sized Ziploc bags filled with fine sand that were duct-taped on top of one another. This would provide a stable surface to rest the rifle barrel on while also absorbing some of the shock of gunfire.

He walked to the right bay door and placed the sandbag onto an old stack of chest-high pallets he'd arranged before Cavell's arrival, while eyeballing an empty red gas can on an earthen berm two hundred yards away.

The two men moved up alongside Davey, with Cavell handing the younger brother a box of .308 full-metal-jacket rounds.

While Davey donned his hearing protection and inserted the first round, Levi and Cavell stepped back, speaking between gunshots after removing their hands from their ears.

"Everything's on track for the first convoy of deliveries," said Levi. "That will put a truckload of product in the hands of your contacts."

Cavell nodded. "That should be a good first run. After that, it'll be best to stick with bimonthly shipments."

"That's assuming your colleagues can move things that fast."

"They'll move it alright," said Cavell. "Pretty soon, our product will be in the hands of college kids from San Diego to Seattle. Once the West Coast network is up and running, then we can look into slowly spreading east. And this new liquid form of fentanyl that Torres developed for us will be far easier to disguise during transport and for our dealers to handle while selling the product."

Cavell shifted his attention to the younger brother, who paused from shooting and walked back to the others. "Of course, this all hinges on you coming through on your end," he said.

Davey rubbed the back of his thick neck. "I should have the exact route of Vincent Delgado's transport from my prison to the border on Sunday, just a few hours before the guards pull out. We have to coordinate with the Border Patrol and the Federales who will be taking custody of Delgado. Once I know that, I'll have a two-hour lead to get out to the sniper's den and get ready for the shot."

Cavell narrowed his eyes. "Remember, half of the success of our operation in Pineland depends on developing and delivering the product; the other half depends on getting the cartels out of the way. You kill Delgado and it'll allow my West Coast crew to muscle their way into the vacuum that's gonna be created by the coming cartel turf war."

The Tanner brothers gave each other knowing glances before Levi spoke. "God damn, you think of everything, Aiden."

He shuffled forward, resting a hand on their shoulders as a grin filled his unscrupulous face. "Speaking of God, by this time next month, we're all going to be richer than the Almighty himself."

CHAPTER 20

AFTER UPLOADING THE SIM CARD FROM HELLER'S PHONE TO Alisa, Payne closed his laptop and secured it in the safe in the cabin bedroom. It was nearing nine o'clock, and he needed to fuel up with a good breakfast before Medina arrived, so he locked up the place and drove to Monique's Diner.

Connie seated him in a corner booth, which he appreciated, as it gave him a clear line of sight of everyone entering from the front parking lot.

After ordering a ham and mushroom omelette, he sipped on his coffee. The exceptionally bitter taste made him wonder if it was from yesterday's pot.

Maybe that truck stop is worth looking into.

He glanced at the other patrons, who were mostly older couples whom he'd seen before during his last visit and a handful of cowboys sitting on circular stools at the front counter. Absent were Phoenician tourists or wood-smoke-tainted campers.

Payne watched the line cook head into the walk-in freezer and remove some meat patties from a crate adorned with the Tanner Steak Company logo and wondered how much beef flowed into people's fridges and freezers in this town. He saw the man remove a floppy covering of frozen gel packs, recalling a similar-looking item he'd seen in Heller's gun safe.

Payne's attention was abruptly diverted to the back door, where three men had just entered.

By their scraggly appearance, they definitely weren't ranchers. The lead figure was wearing Mexican-style cowboy boots with pointed tips while the other two had on military-style footwear. From growing up with a father who was a man tracker, along with his operational years hunting down insurgents, Payne habitually found himself noticing such seemingly mundane details.

By their unshaven looks and slovenly garb, he wondered if they were living in some ten-by-twelve shed in the boonies.

His sight was interrupted by Connie's smiling face as she set his plate of food on the table. "Those three dudes who just waltzed in the back door… they regulars?"

She didn't turn to look, but her smile faded. "Thankfully, no, especially that gutter trash with the mustache, Aiden Cavell."

"So that's him," said Payne as he cut up his food.

Connie pursed her lips. "He and his maggots show up here every now and then, and afterwards I reach for the Lysol and flea spray."

"Don't hold back." Payne chuckled. "Tell me how you really feel, Connie."

She patted his hand. "About you, I feel pretty good, but those fellas are trouble, and the sheriff won't do nothing about 'em, so just watch yourself, hon."

As Payne polished off his meal, he kept an eye on the three trolls in the corner, who likewise maintained a perpetual gaze on him.

Cavell waved off Connie from replenishing their coffees and got up, heading for Payne's table. He stopped short of the opposite seat and leaned a leathery hand on the backstop. "You must be the new guy in town I've been hearing about."

Payne thrust his chin at Cavell's two lackeys. "If you and your girlfriends who crawled in here with you are looking for showers, you should try the truck stop."

Cavell emitted a grin bordering on irritation. He waved a finger in the air. "Now I remember where I first heard about you… you're the pal of that old fuck John Heller, who bit the dust along the highway. Damn terrible tragedy."

Payne crumpled the napkin in his hand, then tossed it on the table. For a second, his eyes drifted over Cavell's carotid region. A region that he'd seen spurt out arterial blood count-less times over the years from close-quarters blade work when silencing an enemy was required. From the look of Cavell's twisted nose and scarred hands, he was pretty sure the man had also done the same. Payne had kept his other hand on his folding knife in his right pocket, ready to fling it open and start the dance he was sure was coming.

He glanced down at the couple two booths away, who were seated with a little girl, and reconsidered his intentions.

Again, he gazed at Cavell's men, who were nervously fidgeting in their seats like two poodles waiting to piss. He stared into Cavell's eyes. "Only two guys… is that all you have left these days?"

Cavell was silent.

"Where's the rest of your crew? Surely a tough guy like you needs groupies to follow him around."

Again, Cavell said nothing. He stood upright, briefly stroking his mustache.

Payne could tell by the man's body language that he was exerting considerable effort to control himself, but his eyes remained dead and unmoving.

A stone-cold killer.

Payne knew the predatory look. He'd witnessed it

numerous times in Heller and his fellow teammates over the years. And if there had been mirrors present, Payne would have seen it in his own reflection in desert caves, jungle hides, and urban hellholes around the globe.

Cavell reached into his pocket and pulled out a twenty-dollar bill, flinging it on the table. "This is my town. Just like the Apaches and the Hopi have their tribal lands, you're on mine now. But it's good to have a full belly for your road trip back to wherever you came from."

Payne leaned closer, removing the blade from his pocket and keeping it concealed under the table. "*Kud puklo da puklo.*"

Serbian for *Whatever happens, happens.*

He let the saying percolate in Cavell's brain for a second.

The man scrunched his eyebrows together. His cheeks were taut for a moment before he let out a bronchial laugh. "Indeed, we will see what happens next, Kyle Payne." He turned and walked towards the back door, motioning for his men to follow.

"Dear Lord, I thought there was going to be a four-alarm fire in here," said Connie, who had moved up alongside Payne as he slid out from the booth.

"He's all bark for now, but it's probably best I head out the side exit." Payne removed a twenty-dollar bill and placed it alongside the other one from Cavell. "Hope this covers your concerns."

"Oh, don't you worry. Take his money with you. I ain't touchin' that thing."

He chuckled, slipping the bill in his back pocket and winking at her as he walked by. "Connie, you are truly one of a kind."

CHAPTER 21

At the far side of the parking lot, Sheriff Rudensky and his junior deputy, Ron Lehane, were sitting in their cruiser. Rudensky had backed his vehicle in a few minutes earlier and was waiting for Payne to exit.

"How long does it take a guy to down a fucking omelette?" said the sheriff, who was chewing on a toothpick as he watched the side entrance nearest to Payne's rental car.

"How do you know what he's eating?"

"Brother-in-law's the owner here and sometimes cooks in the mornings. Gave me the heads-up when Payne arrived and told me what he ordered."

"Brother-in-law, eh… does that mean you get a reduced price on your meals, beyond the LEO discount, that is?"

"Hell, you'd never catch me eating off this menu. The packaged food at the truck stop is better than this shit-rag of a diner."

"Apple pie is sure good. Me and the wife come here once a week just for that."

This level of conversation was what Rudensky had to

endure given that Lenny Firth was boots up at the bottom of a canyon. For now, he had explained his deputy's absence as another one of Firth's drunken benders, and Rudensky wasn't surprised when no one in his small circle at the sheriff's department barely raised an eyebrow.

And while Lehane was a capable officer, he was still too starry-eyed after graduating from the academy in Casa Grande last fall. Plus, he was born and raised in Phoenix, having only spent weekends in Pineland as a youth at his grandmother's place west of town. As far as Rudensky was concerned, Lehane was just another dumb Phoenician.

The toothpick slipped out of Rudensky's mouth at the sight of Aiden Cavell exiting the back door. Behind him were two of his men.

"What the hell are those guys doing here? Cavell usually heads to Payson."

"I seen 'em grabbing coffee before, mainly on weekdays though. Don't think Connie likes them much, which is why they never stick around for breakfast or lunch. She run 'em out of here once, from what I heard."

"Not surprising since Connie's as grumpy as an old rattlesnake."

The two men watched as Cavell mounted his Harley-Davidson and drove away.

A minute later, Payne left the establishment. Two of Cavell's men were leaning against his rental car.

"Damn, that city boy is about to get his clock cleaned." Lehane reached for his door handle.

"Steady." Rudensky grabbed his deputy's arm. "Let's see how this plays out."

———

Payne stepped out the side door slowly, palming his car keys and scanning both directions. Turning towards his car, he saw Cavell's two goons leaning against the hood.

They stood there with smug grins and arms folded, trying to flare out their biceps.

"You mind getting off my car. I've got enough to do and don't need to degrease the surface."

"Cavell said you were a smart-ass," said the younger man with fuzzy blond hair that made his head look like a Q-tip. He spoke with an accent, and Payne figured he was one of the Serbs in Cavell's outfit.

"You guys really want to make a scene with the sheriff sitting in his car over there and all these folks inside?" He nodded towards Rudensky's cruiser parked near the back corner of the lot.

The bigger man remained silent, staring through Payne, while his partner fielded the question. "The sheriff won't interfere. As for the sheep inside, our boss wants to teach them a lesson by showing what happens to those who cause trouble."

Payne moved to the side of his car so they would have to follow, allowing him a confined space to control their movements better. "Seriously, this is how you guys do business in this town… just wait for your target and telegraph your intentions? You must be the B-Team. If I were in your shoes, I would have jumped me the second I walked out the door and jimmied a blade into the ribs. Quick and dirty, and you can be on your way."

"See that in a movie?" asked Q-tip.

The other man didn't talk. He had a pug-like face with broad shoulders and numerous scars on his chin and cheeks. Payne would have to drop him first.

Payne angled his body to the quiet man, then raised a

hand and waved towards the back door as if he was talking to someone. "I got this, Connie. Just go back inside."

The big man half turned towards the door.

Payne took the advantage, sliding forward and shooting out a spear hand at the throat, followed by a vicious groin kick. Immediately, he pivoted to the left, sending a right hook into the jaw of the man's sinewy partner.

He chambered his right leg for a shin kick to the man's quadriceps, but Payne felt his body violently compress as the big man slammed into his waist, driving him into the side of the car.

Damn, that fella can take some punishment.

Payne swung his elbow into the man's face, crunching the nose and causing a stream of blood to rush down the chin. Payne followed up with another groin shot but with the tip of his boot, causing the goon to groan and recoil into the other car. Next, Payne shuffled forward, sending a combination right hook and an uppercut that toppled the big fighter.

A blur of something shiny shot toward Payne's face. He unconsciously parried with a double-forearm block. He was surprised to see a pair of brass knuckles on Q-tip's hand and shot a finger strike into the guy's right eye. A heel kick to the left knee came next, which snapped a tendon. The man shrieked and collapsed next to the front tire.

Payne pivoted and sent a shin kick into the pug-faced man, who was now trying to stand, sending him flying onto his back.

When he was sure the two men were no longer an immediate threat, Payne leaned over and retrieved the brass knuckles from Q-tip. "Thanks. I haven't had a set of these in a long time."

He stepped around the bodies, seeing Connie and several patrons standing like slack-jawed mannequins in the diner's window. He returned to the Honda's driver's side and got in, groaning from his bruised ribs.

Payne backed out, noticing the sheriff's vehicle still stationary at the far end of the parking lot. The sun's reflection on the windows prevented him from determining what Rudensky was going to do next, but he figured he'd know soon enough.

CHAPTER 22

TEN MINUTES AFTER DRIVING AWAY FROM THE DINER, PAYNE SAW the sheriff's vehicle racing down the road behind him. In his rearview mirror, he could see Rudensky's face getting closer as the man tailgated him, then turned on his car's flashing lights.

Looks like I'm on everyone's shit list today. What the hell does this stooge want?

Payne drove on for another half mile before locating a gravel shoulder large enough to pull onto. Since it was the only pullout for what appeared to be miles of blacktop, he assumed the sheriff had chosen this particular time instead of just talking with him in the diner parking lot.

Payne lowered his window, watching Rudensky approach while his deputy remained in the vehicle.

Odd. Unless he wants to throw his weight around and doesn't want any witnesses.

Rudensky rested one hand on the door while the other sat atop his Glock 17 service pistol. "Mr. Payne, I'm glad I caught up with you. A few more miles east and you'd be in another county, and I'd have a real headache dealing with the paper-work for hauling your ass in."

"For what? You mean those two cretins outside the diner. Those guys came at me first and…"

"The sun was in my eyes back at the diner. I don't even know what you're talking about." Rudensky pulled out his iPhone, retrieving some video footage, then turned it around towards Payne. "But what I do know is that I had an intruder in my office last night who not only broke into the building but removed evidence from an active investigation. You see, I have one of those nanny cams on the Arizona flagpole by my desk. Guess you missed that one, idiot."

Payne felt his sides constrict. "All I see is a guy in a black ski mask who looks like he was fishing for things he could pawn for a few bucks." He rested an elbow on the door's armrest. He tried to channel the growing tension in his face into a grin so he could shift the focus back on his accuser. "Doesn't look good, Sheriff, being the man in charge of main-taining order in Pineland and you just had the rug pulled out from under you, and in your own place."

"Thought you might say some shit like that." Rudensky scrolled to some still images. This one was grainy and showed a man removing his ski mask near the edge of the woods.

Payne maintained a poker face while silently chiding himself for underestimating the surveillance capabilities around small-town business premises.

Shit, that must be from the gas station across the street. That type of camera shouldn't have that much reach.

The facial recognition was barely clear enough to know it was Payne if you stared hard enough. Payne knew from the lack of clarity that it was taken from a low-tech camera and that any attempt to enhance the image would only result in his face becoming distorted beyond recognition.

He also knew that while Rudensky's attempt at intimidation was anemic, the man could seriously interfere with his personal investigation in Pineland. And right now, he didn't need any more hassle.

Payne knew Rudensky could have arrested him at the diner but had instead chosen this approach so no one at the sheriff's department or the diner was privy to their conversation. This was a delay he could live without right now, so he decided to feed into the sheriff's arrogance.

"I got you, you son of a bitch." Rudensky shoved the phone back towards Payne's face.

Payne lightly shrugged his shoulders. He gazed in his rearview mirror at the deputy in the vehicle, who was scrolling on his phone.

The sheriff grinned. "You're quite a dumbass. The bottom drawer had over three thousand dollars in cash for the widows and orphans fund for fallen officers."

"Want to tell me what this little interrogation is about?"

"Yeah, you smug prick. I'll tell you. And I'll speak slowly so you're real clear about what I expect from you, if you want to avoid being tossed in a cell." Rudensky put his phone away, then rested both hands on the vehicle door. The man's fierce gaze shifted, and his eyes darted along the highway for a moment as if he hadn't determined his next move.

Payne decided to push things along. "You want something, or you and your vigilant deputy back there would have hauled me to HQ. So what is it?"

"From the little I learned about Heller's background, and what you were able to do at the diner to those guys, along with breaking into my office, I'd say you have a unique skill set… a skill set that I could use to solve a problem of mine."

Payne raised his sunglasses onto his head. "Go on."

"Levi Tanner, you know him?"

"Heard of him. Seems to be the moneyman in this town."

Rudensky glanced back at his deputy, who was now laughing at something on his phone. "Tanner has a flash drive he keeps in the safe in his office. It contains photos that, if they were made public, could become a serious problem for me."

Payne chuckled. "So you're going to hold grainy photos of some thief over me to get photos of your shady activities back."

"Yeah, don't you love the poetic justice in that?"

"It's irony, actually. Poetic justice is where virtue is rewarded and misdeeds are punished."

Rudensky slammed his open palm down on the top of the car. "Enough, asshole. I want that flash drive. You get it for me; then you can be on your way out of Pineland, forever."

Payne raised an eyebrow. "Just to clarify, you want me to sneak into a secure building and snag something out of what I'm guessing is a high-dollar safe?"

"Bingo." Rudensky tapped on the iPhone in his vest pocket. "Then you're free and clear. But you try to write me off or skip town, then I send out a nationwide APB about a professional thief who broke into a law-enforcement office and made off with critical evidence and the cash box for the widows and orphans fund."

Payne decided to play along, choosing his words carefully to avoid implicating himself in last night's theft. "But you indicated that money was untouched."

"Not how I see it, and that kind of sympathetic BS in the news gets the public riled up so they really wanna see justice served."

Payne tapped his fingers on the steering wheel, contemplating this fresh revelation about the dirt that Tanner must have on Rudensky. More importantly, the sheriff must know the layout inside Tanner's facility, and that could prove to be worthwhile intel. "From what I hear, Tanner's building is pretty spacious. Hypothetically, a floor plan of the place and the number of security guards there would sure speed things along if a person were to consider such an undertaking."

The sheriff removed his iPhone again. "Give me your number. I'll text you the details. And I'll even add in the security code for the keypad on the rear entrance. I've been in that way enough times to know it like the back of my hand."

"What type of alarm system does Tanner have?"

"Dyson."

"That's the name of a vacuum cleaner brand."

Rudensky smirked. "I think it's Dayton. Yeah, it's Dayton like the city in Ohio." The sheriff watched a Volkswagen camper van with a young couple at the helm drive past. "We clear on how things work, Mr. Payne?"

"Crystal clear, Sheriff."

Rudensky put his hands on his hips. "And I shouldn't have to stress this, but everything we just discussed stays between us. You get caught inside Tanner's place or blab about any of this to anyone, I throw you to the wolves and send out the photos of you robbing my office."

Payne gave a faux salute, bowing to the man's inflated sense of his own authority. "One thing before you leave, Sheriff: you wanna tell me who was behind my friend John's death? I saw the puncture marks on the front tires of his 4Runner. It sure as hell wasn't an accident. Somebody wanted him silenced."

Rudensky rolled his tongue around the inside of his cheek. "Unfortunately for both you and me, I can't prove anything, but I would encourage you to direct that question towards the guy on the motorcycle leaving the diner. Aiden Cavell."

"Tanner's really got your hands tied behind your back despite that badge, eh? He probably convinced you that his agenda wouldn't hurt anyone while expanding the size of your wallet."

Rudenksy didn't respond, averting his gaze.

Payne pivoted towards the man. "You know there's an old saying that selling an idea works best when those being manipulated are confident that they're acting of their own free will."

The sheriff's left eye twitched. He kicked a stone across the pavement. "Just get me the fucking flash drive."

Payne watched Rudensky return to his vehicle, sliding into his seat with a deflated look. The two officers sped off as quickly as they had appeared. He leaned his head out the window, inhaling the smell of spruce trees and feeling like he was descending further into an inky abyss.

CHAPTER 23

AFTER RETURNING TO HELLER'S CABIN, PAYNE CALLED TO CHECK on Wheeler, but his phone went straight to voicemail.

Hopefully, he's cleared out of this region for a while. Wonder what ever became of those bodies back at his house?

He figured Cavell and Firth would have cleaned up, and the dead bikers were now serving as coyote food.

His text to Medina last night had received a favorable reply, and she had indicated that she would be over after showering and grabbing a breakfast burrito at the truck stop.

Payne thought of her athletic figure wrapped in a towel. Her dark hair cascading over those tan shoulders and those fierce brown eyes holding his gaze.

Most of Payne's relationships since his time in the agency had been fleeting. Getting involved with other agents always meant an intense, short-term fling until one, or both, of them were reassigned to a distant part of the globe, perhaps never crossing trails again.

And he'd once made the mistake of becoming romantically entangled with a civilian, which involved a web of lies, cover stories and bogus excuses. In the end, sharing only a sliver of yourself with someone was like a slow death to the soul, and he swore to stick with work-related relationships, however fleeting.

Still, Medina's blend of toughness and independence, coupled with her alluring looks, was appealing, and he found himself pleasantly surprised to run across her in Pineland of all places.

But then there's nothing normal about this town.

He sat on the back porch, enjoying a cup of coffee and the sunshine flittering through the spruce trees along a nearby ridge. The silence was interrupted by an incoming call from Alisa.

"Hope you got some sleep," she said.

"Not much of that these days."

"So, I'll be accessing John's SIM card after I hang up and will hopefully have something of use. I also delved into those three individuals you asked me about." He could hear typing on her laptop as she continued speaking. "Levi Tanner is, on paper, considered a well-respected businessman throughout Arizona with the cattle industry and the culinary world along with being buds with the governor, a few US senators, and he has even rubbed elbows with several celebrities over the years. He has a very polished public profile online… which, in my experience, means he's got someone scrubbing his negative reviews and erasing the slightest hint of a business complaint."

"He's probably got the cash to make that happen."

"And then some. His Tanner Steak Company has a net worth of nearly half a billion dollars, a far cry from when his father ran the company. He's also got a younger brother, Davey, who is not connected with the family business, at least not outright. He's a warden at a federal prison in Phoenix."

Payne leaned forward, resting his elbows on his knees. "Interesting. He certainly went off in another direction."

"Not really… he's just in the human cattle industry."

Payne chuckled. "You stay up all night thinking of that one?"

"Shut up. At least I have a sense of humor."

"You should use it some time."

"Careful, Kyle, or you might find your bank statement a little short this month."

He pursed his lips. "You'd hack into my account just to spite me. That's a statement not a question, by the way."

"My guess is you only spend your cash on motorcycles and hunting rifles."

"Ah, there's so much more to me, but people just don't see it."

"Maybe you don't ever let them."

"Anyway, back to your ultra-professional briefing… what's the story on this guy Aiden Cavell?"

Alisa took in a deep breath, and her voice became serious again. "He's been a hard one to track down. Real name is Aiden Cavelosivec. He goes way back with the Tanners. For years, they bounced around group homes together until they were fifteen when the two Tanner boys were adopted and moved up to Pineland. Aiden wasn't so fortunate and remained in the system. Four months later, he was busted for grand theft auto. Ended up in juvey and repeated the same pattern for the next few years until one of the attempted thefts saw an innocent bystander being killed by one of Aiden's crew members during a gunfight with the cops."

"How old was Cavell at the time?"

"Just a month shy of eighteen."

"Let me guess, he was tried as an adult given his history?"

"And sent to prison for ten years. Normally, a kid like that would have been eaten alive, but my research indicated he was taken in by the mob, but not the usual suspects. Cavelosivec… Aiden's father was Serbian."

Payne thought back to the tattoo on the chest of one of the thugs beating on Wheeler. "The Serbian crime syndicate is tight. Those guys always look out for their own and will spill blood at the mention of anyone screwing with them or their reputation."

"After being released from prison, Aiden rose up to become an enforcer for the Serbian mob's West Coast operations. During that time, there were dozens of execution-style murders associated with them, but nothing was ever pinned on Cavell other than a few racketeering charges, which amounted to nothing."

"He must be setting up shop in Pineland to expand their network in Arizona. But why not Phoenix or Tucson?"

"Tanner's company is pretty sizeable," said Alisa. "Maybe Cavell and the two brothers are using that for a staging area."

"But for what? The Serbian mob in this country mostly have their hands into opioids and prostitution."

"Not sure. This was as far as I could go."

"Thanks. That's a big help."

"You're not getting rid of me just yet. There's still Medina."

He rolled his thumb around on his temple. "Bring it on."

"Lara Celeste Medina. Born in Santa Ana, Mexico. Father was a truck driver in Mexico who was killed in the crossfire of a cartel turf war when Lara was twelve. After that, her mother packed up her and her three siblings and moved in with an aunt in Phoenix. Following high school, Medina went through the police academy in Casa Grande, then joined the Pinal County Sheriff's Department. Following six years working anti-cartel busts, she got her federal certs, then signed on with the DEA. She was involved in drug-interdiction along the border for two years, but the strange thing is that there's not a lot of information in her personnel file after that. Nothing of consequence."

Payne drummed his fingers on the table. "Undercover work, I'm guessing. She definitely struck me as someone comfortable working solo and outside of a uniform."

"Her bureau chief is Neil Strozzi. He's a real ballbuster and would probably be lynching criminals if he could. He's a throwback to another era of justice. You'd like him."

"I thought guys like that died off in this country a generation ago... or were forced into retirement. If Medina is on his payroll, then she may not be as hamstrung in her reach as I thought."

"That doesn't mean that she or Strozzi are going to do what is necessary to exact payback for John's death."

"Yeah, but she could be a useful ally."

"One other thing, when I probed deeper into Medina's recent cases with the DEA, there was mention of someone called 'the Chemist.'"

Payne nodded to himself as another piece started to slot into place. "Medina did indicate she had an informant in Pineland. Went by the name of Mike Portman. Pretty sure that guy was with Heller in the vehicle just before he died."

"I think we're talking about two different people," Alisa said. "This individual was probably Manny Torres. He was someone on the DEA's watch list for years. Torres was *the* cartel chemist, known for formulating his own high-grade brand of fentanyl and other drugs. He literally went to college to become a chemist, so he's not some stoner concocting shit in a basement like most of those guys."

"And Medina was after him specifically?"

"Not sure, but there were months of entries in her messages to Strozzi about this chemist. She must have been tailing him, which might also mean she was working undercover along the border since there are plenty of references to ops in Nogales."

Payne took a sip of his coffee, sifting through the revelations. "Thanks again, Alisa. I can tell you must have burned the midnight oil on this."

"Anything for you… and John, you need me again, you call, no matter what time it is."

———

Thirty minutes later, while Payne was packing a small rucksack with some provisions for the day, he heard the porch steps creak and saw two shadows float across the thinly veiled front windows.

A dainty knock on the door followed along with the sound of a dog whimpering. "Kyle, it's Heather and Zoe from down the road. Are you around?"

Payne reholstered his pistol, lowering his T-shirt and heading to the front door. After welcoming them in, a repeat performance by Mochi ensued as the dog trotted past him towards the recliner, then circled back to the girl.

Heather thrust out a large Tupperware container. "We thought you might like some pulled pork from dinner the other night, so I brought over a bunch, along with some buns that are wrapped separately inside."

"Wow, I can smell the wood smoke already. This is going to be a hundred times better than the sliced turkey I bought at the grocery store. Thank you, Heather."

"My pleasure."

The sound of crunching gravel emanated from down the road, and a second later, a blue Ford Explorer pulled in beside Payne's car. Medina stepped out, sauntering towards the porch. She paused inside the entrance. Payne noticed an expression of surprise on Medina's face at the visitors, especially at the sight of Zoe.

"Hi, hope I'm not interrupting anything," Medina said.

Payne waved her in, then introduced the women to each

other, both of them giving each other cordial but scrutinizing gazes.

Heather put her hand on her daughter's shoulder while smiling at Payne. "Well, we should get back home. Zoe's got homework to do still, and I've gotta feed the chickens."

"Thanks again for the fine food. I'm sure looking forward to it," said Payne. He walked them to the door, then kept his eye on the pair, with Mochi trotting obediently alongside, until they arrived back at their small house.

"You got a thing for soccer moms, or you just being a sheepdog?" asked Medina, who had plunked down on the recliner with a grin.

Payne headed to the fridge, placing the smoked meat inside. "You sure like to say what's on your mind. Are you one of those people without any filter?"

"Sure. Which leads me to my next question: are you a spook like your pal Heller?"

Payne leaned back against the counter, folding his arms. "Yes. You definitely don't have a filter."

Medina stared into his eyes for a long moment. "You see, someone I know who does freelance work for Langley from time to time said Heller was a legend at the agency. Apparently, he had his own team of guys who did off-the-books jobs overseas. And he also had someone fitting your profile. Thing is, when I did an open-source search on you, your online presence seemed pretty" – she rolled her eyes up at the ceiling – "sterile, to be honest. The few details I could find struck me as being manicured. And if we're going to put our heads together on what's going on in this town, I'd like to know who the hell you are."

"So you think we're partners now, is that it? Your informant here is AWOL, and you need my help because your little undercover op is on life support."

"I'm not looking for a partner, trust me. I'm used to

working things alone." Her eyes widened, and she waved a hand at him in reference to her original question.

"I'm pretty boring. Grew up in the Upper Peninsula and mostly spent my youth in the woods, so not much excitement there. Afterwards, I bounced around the world working in security, consulting for Fortune 500 companies who had their staff in hot spots overseas."

She leaned forward, a clipped smile creeping out. "You're going to stand there and tell me you and your buddy Heller were just some regular dudes working in the private sector, showing corporate suits how to avoid getting roofied at nightclubs in Dubai or Jakarta or wherever?"

He flared an eyebrow. "You know, I did some research of my own, Agent Medina. Seems like you've had an exemplary career in law enforcement with practically every working day devoted to bringing down the Mexican cartels. Very impressive."

Medina gazed at his face for a long moment. "You did this shit at the coffee shop yesterday... your default mechanism is to immediately redirect any attention from yourself back onto the person asking the question. Seen it done a thousand times with professional cons during interrogations. Only your lines float out of your mouth like you were born with the ability."

"You can never turn off the cop in you, can you? It's your prism for seeing the world."

"And what's your prism, Kyle?"

"It used to be more one-dimensional. Lately, it seems like there are too many facets." He felt surprised at the admission. He turned and grabbed his daypack off the counter. "Anyway, I contacted you because I'm going to drive out to the crash site by that canyon and see what I can see. Thought you might want to join me. But if you're having second thoughts, then we can say adios."

Medina stood. "I'll go, but I'll follow you out in my own

car." Again, he noticed her analytical gaze as if she was deciding if she could trust him.

And why would she?

She was a woman about to follow a stranger into the backcountry, and she'd known him less than twenty-four hours. And then she was a streetwise undercover narc whose instincts were raising red flags about his shrouded past.

"How long we gonna be gone?" she said.

He pointed to a folded topographic map on the kitchen counter. "Not sure, but if we have to hike down to the bottom of Deer Canyon, it could be a six-mile trek one way, so I'd bring along some extra water and food." He thrust his finger over his shoulder. "I can get you a pack from the garage."

"No need. I've got a seventy-two-hour bag in my rig."

Payne didn't need her company, but he sure welcomed it all the same. She had a pleasing edge about her that was more than a little appealing, but he mostly wanted to pick her brain about recent undercover work along the border and anything else he could pry out of her regarding the DEA's operation in Pineland.

And prying was what he figured was in store for the afternoon since she was as interested in peeling back his own carefully constructed professional façade as he was hers.

In the past, he would have avoided such things, but Payne was looking forward to the verbal chess match that was about to unfold. And, frankly, he wasn't entirely sure how much longer he wanted to be in a career that centered around continually circumventing disclosure of his own life and having his personality perpetually concealed under a well-constructed, flawless veneer.

CHAPTER 24

DAVEY TANNER FINISHED THE TORTUOUS DRIVE ALONG THE rocky jeep trail that led down to a dry gulch halfway between Phoenix and Tucson. Just before descending, he took notice of the forty-foot shipping container a mile distant. He parked his Ford F-250 pickup near the only cottonwood tree for miles.

He gazed with disdain at the digital temperature reading on his dashboard, which indicated 112°F, knowing that it would be another stifling twenty degrees hotter inside the metal container. He let the engine run for a few minutes longer, enjoying the blast of air-conditioning before the unpleasant job ahead began.

Why the hell did Cavell want me to do this job?

Davey already knew the answer. Everything with Cavell, and even his brother Levi, was a power play. They had both been intimidating and manipulating people for so long it was second nature, and Davey surmised this situation was no different.

They want to make sure I'm completely invested in this operation. He rubbed his smooth chin. *And why the hell wouldn't I be? It was my idea in the first place, but Levi takes all the credit as usual.*

What began last fall as a crudely hatched scheme over beers at Levi's estate in Pineland had mushroomed into their current plan thanks to Cavell's muscle and connections.

But it was Davey who first brought attention to the fact that the cartel inmates at his prison spoke in whispers about a skilled drug designer named Manny Torres. After digging into the man's background on both sides of the border, it became clear to Davey that Torres was the common thread laced through the rise and fall of numerous cartels during the past decade.

After Davey inflicted a brutal interrogation upon one of his senior inmates to reveal Torres' whereabouts, he then relayed the information to Cavell, who orchestrated the abduction in Tucson a few months later.

Now, as Davey turned off the engine and stepped into the sweltering heat, he longed for the end of this leg of their new business venture.

Gonna take my payout from Levi in a few months, then get the hell out of this country. He and Cavell can run things. It's not my scene, man.

He thought of the images of mountaintop villas in Switzerland that he'd come to enjoy online every evening after work.

Davey punted a young cylindrical cactus by the side of his truck, then scowled as he saw all the spines jutting from his boot.

Fuck this desert and this state.

And the wife. And the job.

Gonna start over soon, far from all this horseshit.

He drove the tip of his hiking boot into the sand and twisted back and forth to dislodge the spines. When he finished, Davey walked to the back of his truck and popped open the rear hatch. He removed a green duffel bag with the drill and cobalt bits, along with a gallon jug of water that was strapped to the bed. After locking up his rig, he trudged up the embankment, heading towards the lone storage container.

After thirty minutes of weaving through clumps of prickly pear cactus and shoulder-high mesquite trees with his cumbersome load, he arrived at the Conex container. He could hear the steady rumble of traffic along Interstate 10 and paused to watch the stream of vehicles a half mile to the northwest.

The rusty steel box had been put here by the US Bureau of Mines in the 1960s for storing monitoring equipment, then later transferred to the Arizona Department of Transportation when the interstate was being built. It had been there so long it looked like a geologic formation that had sprung from the dusty ground.

He glanced down at the packrat nests in the drainage channels that ran underneath, grateful they had enough instincts not to venture out in this heat.

Wish I could say the same right now. He chortled, thinking of an expression from the prison: *It's hotter than a stepmother's kiss.*

Davey unzipped the duffel bag, removing a six-pound sledgehammer and a large pry bar. He placed the hooked end of the pry bar onto the old, galvanized lock on the Conex door, then slammed the hammer down several times until the lock broke apart.

He swung open the creaky door, wondering how many years had gone by since anyone had been inside. A blast furnace of dusty air rushed around him. The piercing odor of bat urine, coupled with baked metal, caused his eyes to water.

Davey gazed at the far left-hand wall, which was where he planned to drill the hole to accommodate his sniper rifle.

Peering into the dead-end structure, he grabbed the duffel bag and forced his boots forward, already feeling like his heatstroke meter was inching into the red.

Just remember Switzerland. And those snow-covered mountains.

CHAPTER 25

DESPITE REVIEWING THE MAP EARLIER AND THE COORDINATES from the accident report, the crash site was farther out than Payne thought and much more remote.

He periodically glanced at Medina's SUV in his rearview mirror.

During the past twenty minutes of driving, he'd only seen two other cars on the road, and those were people speeding past him, most likely heading towards the casino on the Apache reservation.

His phone's GPS indicated the area was one mile ahead on the right and he slowed, taking a narrow turn, which descended a hundred feet before leveling out.

"This is it," he whispered, in words laced with sorrow as he gazed at a canyon below the guardrail on his right.

Payne drove on a hundred yards before parking on a gravel shoulder that was barely large enough to accommodate their vehicles. He exited, taking a long swig of water, then donning his pack while Medina gathered her things from her SUV.

"Why the hell were Heller and Portman out this way?" she said.

"Hopefully, we'll find out soon enough."

They locked their vehicles, then walked along the narrow shoulder, gazing at the precipitous cliffs below the guardrail. The bottom of the canyon was obscured by angled rock walls, dense vines clinging to the sides, and its sheer depth, which Payne figured to be around three thousand feet.

They paused at the curve in the road. Payne's head swiveled around, gazing at the descending blacktop they'd just driven, then at the woods across the road, and finally up at the ridgeline of rocks hugging the east side of the highway.

Medina pointed to two parallel skid marks that spanned a hundred-yard section of the highway, blotting out part of the yellow line in the middle. "That must be where Heller tried to brake just before the rollover."

"You mean once his tires were blown by whoever staged the attack," said Payne.

They spent a few minutes gazing over the guardrail. The foliage was so dense at this point that there wasn't much to see, so they crossed the highway to examine the skid marks.

Payne moved into the forest along the shoulder, pacing back and forth while frequently glancing at the line of sight up and down the road.

"What are you doing?" Medina enquired.

"Setting up a spike strip is a two-person job. You need a spotter keeping tabs on the approach route. That guy will usually be at least five miles up from the staging site. Assuming that Heller was driving fifty miles per hour until a mile before the switchback, it would take him six minutes to get here, so the other guy would have ample time to place the spike strip." Payne pointed to his boots. "The other guy rolling out the strip will be waiting about where I'm at now so he can spring into action as soon as he gets the call from his buddy."

He pointed to where she was standing. "That curve in the road is ideal for obscuring the spike strip since any incoming vehicle will have a temporary blind spot until they come around the bend and straighten out. By then, it's too late."

She gave him a hard stare. "You speaking from experience?"

He didn't answer and continued to study the ground. He paused beside a large aspen tree, motioning her over. "See these imprints in the soil?"

She squatted down, staring at a bare patch of dirt a square foot in size. "Um, no. I don't see anything."

"Look closer and with your eyes open this time. If you examine the triangular tip, you'll notice these are extremely narrow cowboy boots. Exactly the type I saw Cavell wearing at the restaurant."

"That style is pricey and not what a working cowboy uses, given the flared tips, which get hung up in the stirrups."

"True." Payne nodded. "Exactly what Cavell had on, and to a tracker, a person's footwear is their signature. This has to be his. And since I know Firth is involved and was the first one at the crash site, it wouldn't be a stretch to think he was Cavell's spotter a few miles up the road."

She smirked, leaning forward, nodding towards the boot mark on the ground. "This isn't exactly solid evidence that it belongs to Cavell or that he was here. To play devil's advocate, it coulda been some tourist who stopped their car to take a leak."

"Not a tourist. Look, I understand the law-enforcement officer in you having the need to obtain reliable evidence from a crime scene, but my gut tells me those are Cavell's tracks." He pointed a stick at the inside of the boot print. "In man-tracking, there's this term called 'dwell time.' It refers to prints that have greater detail and more depth since the individual stood or squatted in one spot for a considerable length of time compared with the type of shallower track that someone leaves when they're merely walking. Or stopping to take a leak."

Medina glanced at the road, then back at him as he continued talking. "And the details of the track pattern are still crisp and well-defined, which means that those prints were made within the past four days since it was windy as hell before that. I checked the National Weather Service reports last night. Otherwise, the details of the boot shape and the edges of the tracks would have eroded away."

She craned her head towards the skid marks on the road.

"That means advance planning. Whoever did this stood here for a while, waiting for Heller and Portman to head this way. Only question is where were they going?"

Payne fixed his gaze on the guardrail again. "Something's been bugging me since I arrived here. When I was in John's garage, I noticed that the climbing rope and harnesses on the wall were gone. I also found a carabiner under the seat of his vehicle in that mechanic's yard, and Wheeler told me he saw Deputy Firth toss something resembling a small duffel bag into the canyon after Wheeler arrived. Maybe this spot was chosen for more than its tactical advantage in taking down the vehicle. I have to wonder if John and Portman were going to rappel down into this canyon."

"You think they were seriously going to head down there at night?"

"We're assuming it was night since that's what Rudensky's report indicated." Payne rubbed the back of his neck. "It didn't occur to me when we initially spoke, but Wheeler said something about getting the call to come here in his ambulance *after* working the night shift."

Medina's eyes darted up at the clouds. "Now that I think

about it, my last message from Portman was immediately after he left the Tanner facility. If Cavell or Levi Tanner suspected him of being an informant, then they would have had him followed to see if he was working with anyone."

"Which led them straight to John."

They both stared at the open maw of the chasm beyond the highway as if expecting a response.

Finally, Medina stood. She cinched down the shoulder straps of her tan pack. "Looks like we'd better see what's at the bottom, then."

"My thoughts exactly." He thrust his chin back in the direction of their vehicles. "I noticed a game trail that skirts below the rim. With any luck, we can make it down below by midday."

————

Earl Hedley rolled out from under the chassis of an old Ford Bronco, setting aside a wrench and arching up his head to work out a kink in his neck. He glanced around the three-bay garage, wondering where his two assistants were.

Since taking a beating from that stranger enquiring about Heller's vehicle, the two young men had been drinking more than usual, and he figured they were drowning their shame in the travel trailer out back.

Hedley dragged his greasy hands across the side of his coveralls and stood up. Heading to the mini fridge under his workbench, he plucked out a cold bottle of Miller and removed the top.

Before he could enjoy the beer, a beeping sound emanated from his open laptop on the right. Hedley shuffled to the end of the workbench and scrutinized the images.

"Oh, shit." He bit his lower lip, clutching the beer bottle tightly before slamming it down and grabbing his cell phone.

"Come on, damnit. Pick up." He paced around the garage, coming to a halt as soon as he heard Aiden Cavell's voice on the other end.

"Those trail cams you had me set up a few months ago on the highway near Deer Canyon just went bat-shit crazy. They're showing images of that guy Payne and a woman heading down below."

There was a long pause before Cavell replied, "Good, then we won't have to look for a new place to ditch their bodies."

CHAPTER 26

PAYNE NOTED THE TRACKS OF MULE DEER, JAVELINA AND porcupine on the narrow trail, pausing on occasion to step over fallen aspen trees or brush aside the thick vegetation that cloaked the path. The switchback trail had a precipitous descent for the first mile, then levelled off at the bottom, where it merged with the main artery of the boulder-strewn canyon.

Though Payne had surmised the vertical depth of the canyon to be around three thousand feet, the precarious switchbacks turned the trek into a two-hour jaunt that tested their knees as well as their balance. He pulled out the folded topo map from his BDU pocket and matched up the terrain features around him with the contour lines on the map while Medina scrutinized the region.

"It's that way," said Medina, in a sarcastic tone, thrusting a spear hand to the right. "There's only two ways we can go, and the area below the highway guardrail is in this direction."

His voice took on a sarcastic edge. "Thanks for the clarification. I'm actually looking for a few side canyons so I have some visual handrails to tell me where I'm at while we're hiking."

"You know, there's this thing called GPS."

"Love GPS when I'm driving, but, in my experience, those devices only work well in open country and forests, not in narrow canyons. Plus, I never have to worry about my map shutting down or running low on batteries."

She glanced at the sheer vertical walls of basalt. "Makes sense. In the desert, I rarely use a map and instead triangulate my general location based on the peaks or mesas in the region."

"You mean when you're navigating the tangled corridors of Scottsdale?"

"Ha-ha… I spend time in the backcountry once in a while. Did a lot of that when I first started with the DEA, busting meth heads at their hideouts in the sticks." She glanced at his tan hands and the scars on his knuckles. "Not all of us grew up as gully jumpers, eating squirrel tacos for dinner every night."

He folded the map and tucked it away. "You say that with envy. And it was raccoon tacos, by the way."

"Gross."

"It's actually delicious meat. Tastes like roast beef due to the amount of brown fat in it. You should try it sometime."

"Yeah, I'll DoorDash that when I get back to my motel tonight."

He pointed to a distant fissure in the cliffs on the right as he led the way. "It's two miles off, so it'll be a good landmark. After that, it looks like the drop-off below the guardrail is a quarter mile beyond that."

"Didn't seem like it should be that far."

"Canyon country is always snaky, making you move like a snail, especially if you're in terrain potentially laced with mantraps."

"Walk through booby-trapped areas on a regular basis, do you?"

"My old man does on occasion when he's pursuing poachers. Those guys have some nasty traps and trail deterrents, so he taught me how to spot 'em."

"So you grew up learning all that survival and tracking stuff?"

He nodded. "I had the wilderness as my playground, and some experienced woodsmen like my dad to show me the ropes. When I was in my early teens, I would sometimes take off for days with just my .22 rifle, a wool blanket and a cooking pot and live like a mountain man. I wouldn't have traded it for anything."

"And your mom was OK with you disappearing into the wilds like that?"

Payne's face grew taut. "She was lost in her own wilderness, you could say. Had a drinking problem that she couldn't shake." He could feel Medina's eyes on his face but kept his attention focused on the canyon walls.

"If I were a psychologist, I might ask if your taking off into the woods was to escape life at home."

He paused, studying the ripples in the tawny cliffs. "More like a refuge or therapy, even. You always know where you stand with Mother Nature. She works on a pass-fail system, and there aren't any grades. Either you have the skills to live on her terms, or you suffer the consequences quickly, and sometimes fatally."

Medina gave him a clipped smile. "Kyle Payne, the philosopher. Who knew?"

He pressed on, moving around clumps of willow thickets. "And what about you? You must have grown up between worlds as well, alternating between US and Mexican culture." He recalled that he'd only learned of her heritage from Alisa's earlier briefing. "I assume, anyway, with a name like Medina."

"Correct, but Medina is also an Arabic word, as you must know, being the international *consultant* you are."

He kept his face forward, concealing his grin at her prodding. "True enough… Mecca and Medina. Two of the sacred cities of Islam. Or so I'm told. Never been."

He pushed back the memory of extracting a Saudi asset in Medina last summer. Payne sighed, mildly displeased at himself for so instinctively floating more lies out of his mouth, and he wasn't even on the job. It was a default mechanism hardwired into his being from years of applying tradecraft where your true self was layered so thickly with cover stories that the line between reality and fiction became blurred.

Been doing that bullshit for too long.

He paused to examine some bobcat tracks. "So, do you identify more with this country or Mexico?"

"More like Mexican and Southwestern culture, which has become blended together in recent years. I'm not convinced the US, as a whole, has a one-size-fits-all identity, given how regional things are with places like Texas, New York, Santa Fe, LA and elsewhere."

She paused to take a swig of water from her pack's hydration tube. "We moved to Arizona when I was a kid, but I still have dreams about our old home in Mexico with its adobe walls, garden out back, and my chickens."

"Get back there much to visit?"

"No way. Too risky. Last time my sisters and I went down there to see family a few years ago, there were grenades going off in the distance after some skirmish broke out between two cartels. And that was only three miles south of the border."

Payne and Medina continued their discussions for the next two miles of slow going through the car-sized boulders strewn along the canyon bottom. Pausing just beyond the rock fissure Payne had indicated earlier, they took a shade break.

They had only been there a few minutes when he lifted his head up to the indigo sky, watching a cluster of ravens circling. A second later, he began sniffing the air, turning his head in the direction they were traveling. "Smell that?"

Medina nodded. "Dead animal."

"Damn, it stinks like Satan took a piss around here," said Payne. "And ravens and crows circling overhead usually means a bear or cougar kill site."

He recalled a similar gut-wrenching odor in a Somali coastal village a few years ago after a tribal warlord butchered the occupants of a rival pirating outfit. For weeks, Payne couldn't get the smell of rotting flesh out of his nose.

He turned back towards her. "Or a dead person, possibly."

Almost certainly.

After hiking another thirty minutes, his suspicions were confirmed.

Except it wasn't just a single corpse they found.

CHAPTER 27

PAYNE AND MEDINA RAISED THEIR SHIRT COLLARS OVER THEIR noses to cut back the stench of rotting flesh.

The body count was staggering, with at least eight human skeletons along with three newer corpses in varying states of decay. Scattered around the area were a half-dozen skulls, ribcages and assorted bones that had been picked clean by the local rodent population.

Payne gazed through a small opening in the thick canopy of ancient cottonwood trees, then up at the cliffs to a ledge cloaked in wild grapevines, which was sixty yards away. Beyond that, the view was obscured by the angle of the rocky slope, which curved like a slide, creating a natural overhang that sheltered the bodies. The smooth cliff walls he'd seen from the guardrail weren't visible, and he surmised that this particular site had been selected for precisely this reason so the corpses wouldn't be spotted from above.

Payne squatted down, poking a stick at a bleached-white human femur. "Someone has been using this area for months, if not more. These remind me of the gnaw marks I'd see on wolf-killed deer up in Michigan when the mice and squirrels were grinding away on the bones."

They walked around the dreadful canyon graveyard, which was spread out over an area of a hundred feet. Some of the bodies lay where they fell, picked apart by rodents, while others appeared to have been dragged off a short distance and consumed by larger animals, given the bone-crushing marks.

Payne stopped beside a body whose face had been chewed off. The figure was still clad in cowboy boots, denim jeans and a blue plaid shirt. "Looks like what the locals in town wear." He examined the faux-gold belt buckle glinting in the sun. It looked like a custom design with a man riding atop a bucking horse. He leaned closer to study the inscription. "Rodeo winner or maybe competitor."

"God," Medina exclaimed, stepping around a crushed ribcage to the right and pausing before a man's remains whose shattered legs resembled pretzels. Medina donned her gloves and turned over the body. "This is him. My informant, Mike Portman."

Payne stood and moved closer, staring at the mangled face and the empty eye sockets, which had been pecked clean by birds.

"You sure?" he said.

"Positive. He always wore this leather flight jacket. Said it reminded him of his Air Force days." She pointed to a metallic sliver jutting out beyond the jeans on his left leg. "And he'd had a knee replacement a few years ago."

Payne glanced up towards some blue fabric swaying on the edge of a low-hanging tree branch jutting out from the rock face. "Damn, is that what I think it is?"

He set down his pack and moved towards the rock face, deftly climbing up thirty feet to a ledge and shaking the tree branch. The blue duffel bag fell by Medina's feet.

Payne retraced his route down, watching her with anticipation as she unzipped the bag. She ran her hand past the contents, revealing a bundle of climbing rope, two red helmets, a Petzl braking device for controlling descents, a dozen carabiners and two Black Diamond harnesses.

Medina set the bag on a rock slab. "Looks like you were right about Rudensky altering the accident report. They must have driven out at sunrise to rappel down here, once Portman found out about this being a dumping ground for Cavell." She glanced around the macabre scene. "Seems pretty risky to dump all these bodies here and just hope no one ever comes across it."

"According to the map, this canyon feeds into two other canyons a short ways down. A flash flood in here would sweep away all this evidence in one storm. Problem is that it's a drought year, according to the weather report I heard on the drive up from Phoenix."

Payne walked past her, standing beside another body whose flesh looked like it was shrink-wrapped to the bones. The man's eyes were intact, and the macabre sight reminded Payne of a funeral he'd witnessed in rural Thailand where the locals used a pickling method to preserve the corpse. "This would be the other, most recent arrival. Strange that the coyotes and birds haven't consumed any of him."

"I used to see that along the border when some drug addict died," she said. "The critters wouldn't come near him. They'd be repelled by the toxins in his system, especially if fentanyl was the culprit."

Payne nodded, then used his boot to push on the left hip and roll over the gangly figure. He kneeled, pointing to the scars on the chest. "This guy was tortured. Those are burn marks, probably a section of rebar, by those groove marks." He pulled back, a chemical odor overwhelming his nose.

Medina moved up beside him. "OK, it's a little unnerving

that you even know that kind of detail." She pointed to deep striations on the wrists. "Looks like he was restrained too." She narrowed her eyes and quickly dropped to one knee, running her hand along the man's rawhide-like neck. "It's faded, but tell me what you make of that."

Payne leaned over, examining a faded tattoo, which showed a spiral image with a beaked figure of some kind in the center. "Is that an eagle or maybe a hawk?"

"Thank God you see it. I wasn't sure if I was imagining things or not." She removed her phone, taking several photos of the image, then the face and body. "You're new to the Southwest, so I'm assuming you haven't heard of Manny Torres?"

"You'd be right." He feigned ignorance, not wanting to divulge the knowledge gleaned from Alisa's probing.

"Torres was a cartel chemist. He designed and cooked up the juice that was then sold on the streets, each one a unique product to whichever cartel he was employed by at the time. Torres was a sharp guy with an actual degree in chemistry, so his particular skillset was very coveted by cartel kingpins like Vincent Delgado. Torres' body being here confirms what Strozzi and I have suspected all along: that Cavell abducted him in Tucson a few months ago. This is the proof I was looking for to connect the Tanners to what Portman told me about them getting into the drug trade."

"So they force Torres to give up his formula for the drugs and probably even had him refine the process to meet their particular requirements, then discard him."

"Probably," she agreed, "but this still doesn't explain how the Tanners plan to move a large amount of fentanyl. And it doesn't explain what Portman was doing with Heller on the night they died."

"That's been giving me a headache since I arrived. I just don't see a connection between the two men, but I have a friend running a records search on Heller's cell phone locations in the days leading up to his death, so that will hopefully provide some answers."

Medina shot him a look of mild scorn. "Someone with the actual phone company or a hacker friend?"

"Exactly."

She shook her head, standing up and brushing past him while taking numerous photos on her phone.

Payne did the same, moving around the remains. He paused suddenly, glancing back at Torres' body. "I just remembered that when I arrived at John's cabin, I found a gel pack in his safe."

"That's weird."

"I thought so too. At first, I figured it was the type of thing John was using on his old injuries. You know, like an ice pack, but why have it in the safe? The thing is, it smelled exactly like the odor coming off Torres' body just now."

Medina put her hands on her hips, her eyes darting along the ground. "What did it look like… the gel pack?"

Payne wove a picture with his hands. "A dozen or so small pockets with clear fluid, each one about one-inch square inch and clustered in rows of four by eight or so."

"Jesus. At the last big DEA bust along the border this past winter, they found evidence of fentanyl being manufactured clear instead of the usual blue. It was intended to be used in liquid form for micro-dosing and was far more potent than the pill version. Strozzi and his forensics guys figured it was Torres' work but could never prove anything."

"So, you think the sports gel packs are being used to conceal the fentanyl? That doesn't seem like a practical way to move a ton of drugs."

She gazed down at Portman's decomposing body. "When I last spoke to Mike, he said he'd obtained proof of the Tanners' drug production setup. He made it sound like he had just left the steak company warehouse. This was shortly before meeting up with Heller."

Payne stepped closer. "I wonder if that 'proof' was the gel pack in Heller's safe. They would have needed to stop at the cabin to get Heller's climbing gear." He thought back to his breakfast at the diner. "The line cook at Monique's pulled out some patties from a Tanner steak crate in the freezer. When he pried off the lid, he removed a gel pack just like the one in John's safe. The Tanners must ship out thousands of pounds of meat a day, using those temporary ice packs to keep the steaks cool until the shipment arrives at its location. That's how they're going to move the fentanyl. Only, thanks to Torres, it won't be thousands of pills that they have to conceal."

Medina stood still for a long while before speaking. "The smell of the steaks and meat inside the shipping crates would help mask any residual odor from the frozen fentanyl in the gel packs."

"Then once the Tanner steak orders arrive at their destination, the ice packs are discarded. That's when Cavell's crew comes in and retrieves them. All they would need to do is separate out the individual packets and sell those as is. There'd be no need to turn the fentanyl into pill form. The buyers could use it for micro-dosing, exactly like cannabis and psychedelics."

She shook her head, almost in disbelief. "It's actually brilliant."

"Torres was the key, though. And once Portman discovered that he had been in Pineland and how he had produced clear liquid fentanyl in the shipping packets, his number was up."

She looked at Portman with sorrow. "I should have pulled him out sooner or been closer to Pineland. He was barely twenty-five years old. He didn't deserve this."

"You were too far away, and he needed someone nearby he could trust," he said, holding her gaze now. "So he called John. They shared a bond through their military service. And John was the kind of person to always offer a hand up from the darkness."

They spent the next few minutes meandering around the thick swaths of shoulder-high willows, searching for other bodies and taking photos.

It was when Payne leaned forward to sift through the pockets of another corpse that he heard the raucous sound of jays in the trees down the canyon from the direction they'd come.

Bird alarms of the forest. Not good.

The sound of crunching gravel and breaking branches came next. He waved to Medina to move towards the cliff face.

Both of them kneeled in a cluster of shoulder-high willows, their pistols removed.

"Bear?" whispered Medina.

Before he could answer, six heavily armed men appeared along the right side of the canyon.

CHAPTER 28

PAYNE RECOGNIZED THE PUG-FACED MAN FROM THE DINER parking lot. He was following immediately behind the leader, a barrel-chested thug in a black biker vest, with a red beard.

Their rifles were a mishmash of UZIs, AKs and shotguns.

"Cavell's guys," he murmured. "We need to drop a few now before they get the jump on us."

Medina nodded, leveling her Glock 17 at the approaching group.

The leader had moved out of sight as he passed behind a large boulder.

"I've got number two." He rested his front sight on the pug-faced man and squeezed the trigger.

Medina did the same, dropping the fourth man, who was clearly visible.

The other guys scattered into the brush, unleashing a barrage of gunfire along the entire floor of the canyon.

Payne and Medina slid back behind a vertical cleft of rock as bullets ricocheted off the cliff walls.

"Four against two, I sure like those odds better," he said.

"Except we're just as trapped as before and massively under-equipped."

He gazed up at the canyon, which was around a hundred feet wide. A quarter mile ahead was a fissure emanating from a side canyon. He'd noted it as a prominent feature on the topo map, and it appeared to be a narrow slot canyon.

That might provide the tactical advantage we need.

He nudged Medina's elbow. "We need to get some distance, and then we can tip the odds in our favor. I'll provide cover fire while you head through the boulders. Once you get to that bend in the canyon, wait there on the left. I'm going to head up that side canyon on the right and wait until they pass me; then I'll come up behind."

She nodded, leaning forward and preparing to sprint through the thick stands of saplings.

Payne crept out a foot and scanned in the direction of their enemies. He caught a sliver of movement forty yards to the right where someone was slowly snaking through a patch of young cottonwood trees.

Payne patted Medina on the leg, then squeezed off a burst of rounds towards the creeper.

Medina crouch-trotted in the opposite direction to the first rock formation, a finger-shaped slab of sandstone jutting defiantly at the sky.

Another barrage of gunfire erupted from down-canyon as Cavell's thugs opened up. This time Payne had to drop to the ground to avoid the rock slivers slicing through the air from the spent rounds.

He lay on his side, dropping out the HK's half-spent magazine and replacing it with a fresh fifteen-rounder from his BDU pocket. He only had one more stick of life insurance left, so he'd have to avoid any more diversionary shooting.

When he was done, he crept through the brush, trotting from boulder to tree trunk to sandstone slab until he caught up with Medina. He squatted beside her, both of them pressing their backs onto a fallen log as they peered through the tangle of rock formations. "Now, we stage the playing field to our advantage and take them out one by one," Payne said.

He pointed his thumb over his shoulder. "See that side canyon. I'm going up it a short ways, being careful not to make any obvious tracks. They're going to see it's choked with vegetation and won't venture in. Meanwhile, you're going to continue down the main canyon, but I want you to leave some obvious tracks in the soil. Once you've walked for five minutes, find a place with good cover and make your way to it, without leaving any signs this time."

"A kill box?"

He nodded. "We'll squeeze them in, but since I'll be coming up the rear, just be damn sure of your shots."

"Copy that."

He watched her venture off, then crouch-walked to the slot canyon. The entrance was laced with agave, also called shin-dagger because of its spear-like leaves. He stepped around these, being careful to place his boots on rock and not on the surrounding patches of sand. Then he ducked around the gnarled branches of scrub oak whose twisted trunks had been shaped by life in a place with sparse daylight. The canyon was S-shaped, and he ventured another fifteen feet before finding a suitable hiding spot in a small alcove carved out by the wind and rain over countless centuries.

He was only thirty feet from the main canyon, which would afford him a slim line of sight while enabling him to hear approaching foot traffic.

He didn't have to wait long.

The first brute was stumbling over the rocks, his AK pointed along the main canyon as his eyes darted nervously along the cliff walls. Payne only caught a glimpse, but it was clear from his pigeon-toed walk that the lanky figure was unaccustomed to traversing anything but concrete.

He leaned back out of sight as the man paused near the slot canyon before continuing.

Payne waited thirty seconds until he didn't hear any further movement. He stepped out and hunched low, stalking back to the mouth of the ravine. He waited near the entrance, scanning the main artery ahead. The redheaded leader was in the middle, while two others were farther ahead to the left, and the pigeon-toed man was thirty feet to the right of Payne.

I've gotta cut this band in half if Medina's going to have a chance at taking out those other two shooters.

Payne holstered his pistol and picked up a softball-sized rock. He waited until there was another blast of wind before following the lanky man, who was slowly weaving through some manzanita bushes.

Payne crept forward until he was fifteen feet away. He waited until the redheaded leader in the distance ventured behind a boulder; then he lunged forward, flinging the rock at the scrawny man's skull. It was an imperfect throw and landed at the base of the neck, but the violent force smashed several cervical vertebrae, making the sound of cracking twigs and unhinging the thug's head. He dropped where he stood, folding back on himself.

Payne ducked down, watching in the direction of the leader and the other two men. A few seconds later, he crept forward, retrieving the dead man's AK and spare magazine along with a CZ 9mm pistol.

He pulled the AK's slide back partway to check the chamber before returning to the manhunt. The redhead was weaving between a cluster of jagged rock spires, and Payne maintained a parallel path, picking up his pace.

The leader was pausing to study the tracks, his suppressed UZI pointing at the ground as he waved to his men. The other two thugs converged on his location, presenting Payne with a shooting gallery.

He leaned his left shoulder against the trunk of a tree and unleashed a volley of bullets at the trio, aiming at the man in the middle. The bald-headed man dropped immediately, after his neck and chest sprang leaks from the 7.62 rounds. The goon to his left took a hit in the left shoulder before darting out of sight while the redheaded man ducked and swung around, spraying the canyon with his UZI.

Payne dropped around the other side of the giant cottonwood tree. When the shooter stopped to reload, Payne trotted to the left, making his way towards Medina's intended location, then buttonhooked back towards the two remaining shooters.

Payne saw the wounded man pressed against a tree, applying a bandana to his bleeding shoulder. Payne set his rifle sights on the man's head. At the point of squeezing the trigger, he caught a sliver of movement to his right.

The redheaded man had made a beeline for his path, hoping to intersect his attack line.

Shit.

Payne dropped fast as a spray of bullets strafed the trees around him. He heard the bullets zipping by his head. He dove on his side, angling the AK towards the two blue legs in the distance. The bullets cut through the leader's jeans like ribbons, splintering apart the man's knees and shins.

The redhead hollered in agony, collapsing to the ground.

Payne sat up, sending two more bullets downrange that blew off the side of the man's skull.

A second later, he heard gunfire up ahead. He squatted, scanning the tangled canyon floor. Payne crept forward, relieved to see the last shooter lying slumped on the ground with two holes in his chest.

Medina stepped from the shadows of the cliff a second later and moved towards Payne.

"That's all four," he said.

Medina brushed her fingers along his face, removing some flecks of stone and dust by his right eye. "You good?" she asked in a soft voice.

"Yeah, you?"

She sighed, gazing down the canyon. "Just hope there aren't more of Cavell's hoods on the way."

"Me too. But let's assume there are and gather up the weapons and ammo in case. After that, we should push on in the opposite direction."

"Agreed."

They spread out, collecting the dead men's rifles, pistols and magazines, jamming what they could carry into their packs.

Let's hope that'll be enough for the second wave.

CHAPTER 29

AFTER AN HOUR OF HIKING ON OR AROUND VAN-SIZED BOULDERS, Payne and Medina managed to cover just over a mile. The sunlight was fading from the cliff walls, and Payne stopped in the bend of the canyon, slurping down some warm water from his pack's hydration tube.

He scanned the unforgiving terrain ahead. The canyon had widened from the narrow confines of their starting point along the highway, and the geology had changed from basalt to outcroppings of sandstone that were pockmarked with overhangs and ledges undercut by millennia of flash floods.

Payne pointed to a series of small caves a hundred yards to the left. "We should probably hole up for the night. No sense in trying to hobble around all these boulders and risk busting an ankle or worse."

"How far is it back to the vehicles this way?" Medina said, dragging a shirtsleeve across her sweaty brow.

He didn't feel like pulling out the map and recalled the one in his head from studying the features earlier. "Three miles to the confluence of two other smaller canyons, and then there's a slope we should be able to use to head up to the rim. After that, it'll be another two miles or so back to our rigs." Payne saw the fatigue on her face turn to apprehension as she stared at the caves. "It's our best option and beats staying out in the open," he said.

"I'm sure the snakes have figured that out too."

"Nah, they'll be out hunting for rodents, so we'll have the place to ourselves. You'll be fine."

At least I hope so.

Payne didn't wait for further objections; instead he simply turned and pushed past a cluster of small willows.

A few minutes later, he trekked thirty feet up a small slope to the row of caves, which resembled the mouths of immense fish. Most of them were nothing more than divots with long shadows, giving the impression they were much deeper. But after walking along the faint pathway, he found one that extended back enough to require his flashlight.

"This should do." He turned on his headlamp and cautiously moved inside, ducking slightly to accommodate the five-foot ceiling. The air was cooler, but there was the faint odor of animal droppings, and his light revealed generations of bat guano along the floor skirting the right wall.

After moving twenty feet back, he discovered a knee-high rock partition across the bottom half of the floor along with a dusty pile of firewood stacked against the side. There were some crunched cans and faded cigarette butts beside an old firepit, and Payne wondered how many cowboys had found refuge in this primeval place over the years.

He removed his pack and cleared away the cans to provide some spots to sit down.

Medina plunked down across the firepit. The sound of their breathing echoed off the walls. Both of them faced the entrance, watching the final rays of dusk slipping from sight.

"You're a helluva shot with that pistol," she said, glancing in the direction of the concealed HK under his T-shirt. "I was thinking about those first two guys we dropped. For every three rounds I got center mass, you got in a single headshot at forty yards, and on someone who was moving."

"Well, HK pistols are quality guns. Better than that stock service Glock of yours."

"Uh-huh. And what about the guy who had his head twisted back like a PEZ dispenser?"

"What I've come to learn since being out here is that canyon country is dangerous as hell."

"You're such a bullshit artist." She tilted her flashlight towards the stacked branches. "I'm gonna get a fire going."

He shook his head. "Smoke and flames are never the friends of someone on the run. Night vision can pick up a Bic lighter from a few miles off, and smoke will saturate our clothing to the point where we'll be smelled long before we're seen."

"And you know this how?" She shot him a glare. "Oh, yeah, that security job of yours, training people how to stay safe in urban environments."

"And don't forget I mentioned growing up in the woods."

"With a dad who was a game warden, right?"

Payne nodded. "Kudos for that sharp memory of yours."

"You remember how I said earlier this morning that someone I knew at Langley indicated Heller was a spook? Well, he also said that Heller's Number Two was someone with exceptional fieldcraft skills. In fact, he taught a man-tracking class for the dude I'm talking about and his unit." She swiveled around to face Payne. "And the Number Two had been raised in the woods by a father who used to track down poachers for a living."

Payne's eyes momentarily darted along the ground, then back towards Medina. "Imagine that."

"Yeah, imagine that."

He pointed to the charred stubs of firewood in the center of the stone ring. "Hey, clear those out for me."

She gave him a puzzled look, then plucked out the sooty logs while he rummaged through a side pocket in his pack.

A second later, Payne removed three glo-sticks. He bent each one until a popping sound occurred, then shook them. Tying them at the top with a short strand of paracord, he arranged them tipi fashion in the middle of the rock ring.

The blue-green glow emanated a few feet beyond the rocks. "There, you can have your campfire after all, Agent Medina."

She smirked, holding her outstretched hands over the tipi. "Now, we just need some marshmallows and life is good."

He smiled and leaned back, watching the wind outside whip some leaves along the cave entrance. As he did so, he canted his head up, the red light of his headlamp illuminating the jagged ceiling, which was painted black from past camp-fires where others had taken shelter over the centuries. Now, it was providing respite to two weary survivors of a gun battle.

He folded his arms, realizing that once the sunrise came, they could be engulfed in a much more savage fight with dozens of Cavell's thugs who might well descend on the region.

As had happened many times before, the future seemed obscured. Only this time there wouldn't be any intel on enemy numbers, drone support or a quick-reaction force on the way.

Payne felt like he was standing on a diving board over a blacked-out chasm, unsure of his immediate future. Hell, just his future in general, but one thing was clear.

And that was that with each passing day, his desire to return to the agency withered.

Beyond the fatigue from the day's grueling events, he was

tired of the ingrained habit of putting up walls with everyone he encountered in his life.

After a long bout of silence contemplating his next words, he glanced over at Medina, whose brown eyes seemed to have a supernatural hue to them in the artificial light. "This cave reminds me of one I was in with Heller years ago in another part of the globe. Back then we were doing security work, you could say, but not for a private company.

"Our orders came from the seventh floor of Langley. We were the ones taking the fight to the enemy, who had just raided an encampment of locals in western Afghanistan. The makeshift village was set up as a med station, providing vaccinations and whatever else was needed for the children in that impoverished valley. A few dozen tents, a chow hall, latrines and an area for daily prayers. Most of the people there were widows and orphans, who were wearing little more than rags for clothing."

He stretched out his legs. "Heller and the rest of our team had been hunting down these insurgent groups that were plaguing the mountainside. Mostly small guerilla units that would sweep in and wipe out a village, then disappear for a week into the wilderness before repeating the same thing in another valley."

"Sounds like the Apaches out here during the 1880s," she said.

He nodded before continuing, "One morning, we got intel that the insurgents were only eleven clicks to the northwest of our location. So we saddled up and made a beeline around the southeast of this cluster of hills, planning to strike them at nightfall."

He glanced up at the rock ceiling again as his eyes narrowed. "Before we got halfway to our destination, we got a call on the radio from one of the medics at the encampment. Three RPG strikes had slammed into the cliff walls above the site, causing a massive rockslide that took out a huge portion of the refugee tents below." He shook his head as a grimace formed. "Three fucking guys who had snuck up to a nearby ridge with their weapons, just waiting for us to leave."

Payne pulled his knees in closer to his chest. "We hoofed it back to the encampment to help with rescue efforts while we waited for the helos to arrive. It turned out to be a recovery operation. There were so many kids under the rubble. All that rubble. It took days to remove them all." He swallowed hard. "I can still see their faces."

"God, I can't imagine the horror," said Medina.

Payne pursed his lips. "When the last of the bodies were buried, we headed back into the mountains. I was the most experienced tracker, so I ran point, pushing hard with our unit for three days until we caught up to the insurgents." He turned, gazing into the faux campfire. "We could have taken down their outpost in a matter of minutes or even called in a drone strike, but we took our time, sniping them one by one."

There was a pregnant pause. Medina slid back a foot from the ring of rocks. Payne's attention shot to the sound of the howling wind outside, which seemed to keep pace with the anguish in his soul.

Medina broke the silence. "Seems to me that something like that would either drive a person to hang up his spurs and go into another line of work, or make him more committed than ever to the cause."

"If by cause, you mean doling out justice, then I agree. But if you're referring to Langley's cause, then I would strongly disagree."

"That why you have this jaded side of you that keeps rearing its head? Because you don't buy into the company vision anymore, is that it?"

He shrugged his shoulders, gazing at her. "You've been on that side of the fence too. Anyone who's been in the trenches as long as you have, dealing with the garbage of the world, knows there's black and white and then there's that blurry line slapped down upon those opposing forces by the cake-eaters on the Hill who dish out the cash and ultimately decide which way your rifles point."

She didn't voice an opinion, but Payne could see the response in her momentarily disenchanted eyes. "So you and Heller got out after that and started your security consulting business, or is that just a front?"

"We made a lateral move within the agency, you could say. Something involving less bureaucratic entanglements and with more actionable meaning, or so it seemed until recently."

"Well, that's not nebulous at all."

"Heller was tasked with creating a personnel-recovery unit to extract high-value individuals around the globe who needed immediate rescue from whatever hell was raining down upon that particular city or region. That type of thing was formerly reserved for a cadre within Ground Branch, but the agency wanted to create something more streamlined and with a single purpose."

"And what happened recently to change your perspective?"

Silence. Payne stared into the ring of stones before Medina spoke again. "This have anything to do with a civilian death?"

He pivoted, giving her a hard stare. "You or your boss have some surprising access. Another reason why I'm reconsidering my career path… the word 'covert operations' used to mean just that."

"My boss' contact heard some whispers. Said that this number two of Heller's was being investigated for the murder of an innocent bystander."

Payne balled a fist, his eyes narrowing. "She was a fourteen-year-old kid. I was going to try to get her out from a trafficking ring, but it only ended up with her getting killed by the very guy I was trying to extract, who saw her as nothing but a plaything. This scumbag said my superior at Langley had arranged for her to join him, which was news to me. Come to find out that that little detail was left out of my pre-mission briefing."

He rubbed his chin. "But the reality-disabled guys at Langley, who saw me as a throwback to Heller's days, decided to place the blame for the girl's death on me so their shiny new asset wouldn't look like the garbage he was to the higher-ups."

She chuckled, breaking the mood of sadness slightly. "'Reality-disabled,' that sounds about right. How do shit-nuggets like that get a pat on the back? Thank God for the boss I have, or I would have left this job a long time ago."

"You mean Neil Strozzi?"

Medina scrunched her eyebrows together. "Of course, you've been poking around in my background. You got my phone and vehicle bugged too?"

He thrust his chin at her shirt. "Just your garments. I put a tiny tracker on you the other day."

She angled her head down at her clothing.

Payne laughed, tossing a twig at her.

"You asshole," she said, flinging a pebble at his arm.

"Why, Agent Medina, beyond that pretty face, you have a violent streak in you I wasn't aware of."

"You can stop calling me that. It's Lara."

"Yes, ma'am, Agent Lara."

"I mean it, or I'll drop a lizard on you while you're sleeping."

"Good luck sneaking up on one. You move like a thirsty elephant who just spotted a waterhole."

She frowned. "You musta been an only child, or maybe your siblings ran away when you were born."

"How's that?"

"Because if you had sisters, they would have kicked you around and made you more respectful of women."

He let his gaze linger on her face for a moment and then lay on his side. "I'm respectful. I'm even going to give you first watch, and I'll take the midnight shift."

"How thoughtful," she said, in a voice laden with sarcasm, as she dragged her pack away from the makeshift firepit and turned towards the cave entrance. "Just don't get any bullshit ideas later about needing to press your body against mine to fight off hypothermia."

He turned on his back, lowering his cap over his eyes. "The thought had crossed my mind."

Medina grinned, leaning back on her pack and resting an AK across her lap.

Payne raised the brim of his cap slightly to gaze at her beautiful black hair and athletic silhouette before closing his eyes.

CHAPTER 30

At dawn, plum-orange fingers of sunlight stabbed through the foliage outside the cave, creating a dappling of shadowy figures that danced on the limestone walls.

From his sentry position near the mouth of the cave, Payne watched the glow alight on Medina's face, her eyes slowly opening as she stretched out her legs. He turned away but was sure she had caught him staring. If she noticed, she didn't say anything. Instead, she sat up, completing her stretch by arching her back.

"The very kind gentleman at the concierge desk downstairs said they'd have your omelette and espresso up in a few minutes," he said, moving back into the center of the cave.

"I'm a lightweight in the mornings. An orange will do."

He grabbed his pack, removing two protein bars and tossing one in her lap.

She glanced at it, then threw it back. "Thanks, but hard pass."

"Suit yourself, but it could be quite a long trek out of here."

Medina stood up, adjusting her ponytail. When she finished, she removed a water bottle and Ziploc of trail mix from her pack. The M&Ms inside had lost their battle with the heat in her vehicle long ago and turned the entire concoction into a globular mass of nuts, seeds and melted chocolate.

"Wow, you're tougher than I thought," said Payne, looking askance at the sight of the goopy mess.

"Better than that synthetic tube of chemicals you're consuming."

"And that bag of slop has been sitting in your vehicle for how many years in the Phoenix sun?"

She finished her last handful and washed it down with water. "You gonna lecture me about my diet, or are we going to get the hell out of this canyon?"

He extended his hand towards the entrance. "Lead the way, *chica*."

She waved at the opening. "You're the tracker and woodsman."

They slid on their packs, keeping their recently acquired rifles at a low-ready position. He motioned towards her AK. "Alright, I'll lead the way, but always remember, Agent Lara, that muzzle safety is essential and to keep that thing pointed away from my ass."

"What about your head?"

He choked back a laugh.

Despite the uncertainty of the coming trek and the precarious firefight the day before, he sensed the tension ease up in his neck. Payne had enjoyed their banter last night, and as they set off, it felt like he had known Medina far beyond his time in Pineland.

———

Three hours of arduous hiking over more boulders and they stopped before a sheer cliff. Below the sixty-foot rock wall was a sizeable pool of water, and Payne dropped to his knees and splashed his face repeatedly, washing away the dust that had mingled with his sweat.

Medina was more cautious, brushing away some floating plants with her hand and carefully dipping her baseball cap into the water before pouring it over her upturned face like she was showering.

"Looks like this is as far as we go in this canyon," said Payne, canting his head towards the sandstone rock face. He waved his hand to the right where a narrow path wound up through clusters of cactus to the rim. "That game trail should do the trick."

"If you're a billy goat."

He scanned the surroundings on either side of the canyon. "Not much of a choice, and backtracking the way we came isn't on my agenda today."

"What is your agenda, today, tomorrow… as long as you're in Pineland?"

"Probably not much different than yours, except a higher body count."

"That's what worries me. You go after the Tanners and Cavell, and Pineland is going to become a war zone. A lot of innocents could get caught in the crosshairs. Plus, there's this thing called the law, remember."

He gave her a scrutinizing gaze. "And you're going to be the enforcer, making sure my weapon stays holstered, is that it?"

"You don't strike me as the kind of person who can be kept on a leash. I think we have similar agendas, but mine involves shutting down the Tanners' drug operation before the fatality rate of kids in this country skyrockets."

He glanced up at several cumulus clouds passing over.

"My father always said that if a man has the ability, then he also has the responsibility." He walked on, continuing with his original thought. "Look, I'm all for eliminating the Tanners' little fentanyl empire, but that's a secondary objective for me. Taking down Cavell and those behind John's death is what matters, and the reason I'm still in this town. Seems to me that if you let me do my job, yours will get a helluva lot easier. I've done this sort of thing before, and once the muscle of an outfit like this is removed, the foundation starts to crumble."

"I think you underestimate the Tanners. Those boys may have been adopted into a wealthy family and be considered respectable businessman, but they were forged on the streets in their youth, which means they have fangs."

He glanced at a scar on her forearm. "You sure you're talking about the Tanners?"

Medina frowned, thrusting her chin at the animal trail. "We should get moving. Once we reach the top, we'll still have a heck of a walk back to our vehicles."

He hoisted up his pack. "You mean what's left of our vehicles. Cavell's crew probably saw to it we couldn't drive off or even have them towed away by that shady mechanic in town."

"What worries me more is whether there's going to be an armed welcoming committee waiting there for us." She removed her iPhone, taking it off airplane mode and holding it up to search for bars. "Maybe I can get through to my boss when we're on the rim. It'd sure be nice to have a tac team heading our way."

"You really want that kind of presence around Pineland?"

"No, but I also have this thing about wanting to collect retirement one day."

Payne smiled, following behind her as they trudged up the diminutive trail that zigzagged along the rocky slope.

"You don't seem like the type to ever hang up your gun and badge. You've got fire in your blood for what you do."

"That a bad thing?"

"Never. It's to be admired. This world needs people with passion, especially in your line of work."

She glanced back over her shoulder. "And what about you, Kyle… you have passion for your work still, or has cynicism undercut that?"

He pulled his eyes away from her hips, pondering her question.

For years, he'd always had such a crystal-clear perspective on what he did for a living and an equally crystal-clear feeling that he was making a difference.

He gazed up at the cobalt sky. "Ask me again when this is all over."

CHAPTER 31

AFTER CRESTING THE RIM OF THE CANYON AN HOUR LATER, Payne and Medina hunkered down under the shade of a large juniper tree, finishing the last of their water and snacks.

When they were done, they resumed the hike, covering the two miles back to the turnoff by their vehicles by noon. The flat terrain was a welcome relief, but the temps were rapidly climbing, and it felt like it was going to be another ninety-degree day.

Once the two-lane highway was in sight, they walked a parallel route through the woods for a few hundred yards until their rigs were visible from their vantage point above the switchback by the guardrail.

Payne and Medina crept through the brush, pausing at a large fallen pine sixty yards from the parking area. "Damn, you were right," she said as they stared at the slashed tires on both vehicles.

"I don't see any movement in the forest beyond the road, but you never know who could have their rifle scope on the area."

He pulled out his iPhone, powering it on. A few seconds

later, he motioned for her to follow him away from the over-look and into the woods. "We need another way out of here. Let's head a half mile back the way we came and wait there. I'm gonna call a guy who should be able to come get us."

Her eyes widened. "You've been here a couple of days, and you know 'a guy' who's going to drop what he's doing and drive out here to get us?"

"Yeah. This guy owes me, big time."

CHAPTER 32

THREE HOURS LATER, PAYNE AND MEDINA CLIMBED INSIDE AN old Jeep Cherokee driven by Garrett Wheeler.

As they sped off, Wheeler glanced at Medina in the rearview mirror. "So, insurance agent from Phoenix, eh."

"She's an undercover narc with the DEA," said Payne.

Medina shot them both a repellent glare. "And how are you connected with our little spook friend here?" she asked, settling her gaze on Wheeler.

"'Spook,' nice," said Wheeler as he shot a sideways look at Payne. "I figured you were something along those lines, given those bodies you stacked up at my place."

"Wait, you've killed more guys besides the ones in the canyon?" inquired Medina.

Wheeler shook his head, chuckling. "You wasted some dudes in the canyon too? Man, you're gonna keep the vultures well fed around here."

"Anyone else?" snapped Medina.

Payne licked his chapped lips. "Well, there were two bikers at the diner, one of whom was with the group we encountered in the canyon, while the other will probably be eating soft food for the rest of his days."

"Goddammit, Payne," she snapped.

"I've been demoted to my last name. Not good," he said to Wheeler.

"This isn't funny," said Medina. She slid back in her seat, pulling out her phone. "And I need to check in before my boss rolls into Pineland with a fleet of black SUVs."

After several futile attempts, she thrust the phone back into her pants pocket. "Where the hell are we going, and when can I get reception?"

Wheeler glanced at her again in the mirror. "Sorry, but this region is pretty spotty. We'll be back at the ranch in a half hour, and you'll be able to get out a call from there."

"What ranch?" she asked.

Payne chimed in, "I thought you told me on the phone we could lie low at a buddy's place for a while."

"The D Bar O Ranch *is* my buddy's place. It's sixty-two miles northeast of Pineland. I practically grew up there, working as a hand during high school before joining the army. Backs up to thousands of acres of wilderness. No one will mess with you there."

"And your friend owns it?" asked Medina.

"Miles Dennehy has had the property in his family's hands for four generations. Currently, he owns a three-hundred-acre spread. The rest of the land he leases from the Forest Service."

"And he won't mind a couple of strangers showing up like this?" asked Payne.

"Nah, I already told him what happened at my house and how you intervened." Wheeler dragged out the last word as he looked at Payne. "Miles has no love for the Tanners even though he used to run his cattle over to their slaughterhouse back when old man Tanner first started his steak company.

Once Levi took over, he decided to cut out the smaller outfits like Miles' and just do business with the big three ranches on the other side of Pineland. Well, that, and let's just say Miles has some history with the Tanners."

As they sped along the blacktop towards a lone mesa in the distance, Wheeler glanced between his two occupants. "So you're welcome to stay at the ranch as long as you need, but I'm sure curious about what's coming down the pipeline." He looked directly at Payne. "You got something in mind, or you just hiding out for a while?"

"A little of both, but I won't be around too long. My business is back in Pineland. There's a growing number of people who keep getting added to my list, but I think I know a way to tie up all the loose ends at once."

Wheeler thrust his chin towards a cluster of structures below the mesa. "Well, you two get some food in you and a shower, and we'll talk later."

Payne watched a lone raven circling to his right. "I appreciate you coming to get us, and your friend's hospitality, but this fight that's coming doesn't involve you."

"Like hell. Cavell's guys came into my house and tried to kill me. They killed your buddy and have been infesting Pineland for months with no end in sight. If this doesn't get handled now, my friends are going to be overrun, and the town will resemble Kingman in a few years."

Medina leaned forward again. "Not to mention the fentanyl crisis that's about to flow out of Tanner's facility."

Wheeler's grip on the steering wheel became white knuckled. "Philanthropist, my ass. He always struck me as a FIGJAM."

Payne laughed. He noticed Medina's puzzled expression. "Fuck I'm good, just ask me."

She flared her eyebrows. "I can think of a few similar expressions in Spanish for him." She glanced at her phone as a barrage of text messages came in. She patted Wheeler on the shoulder. "Pull over. I need to make a call."

"We'll be at the ranch in twenty minutes," he said.

"Pull over now. It can't wait."

Wheeler came to an abrupt halt along the gravel shoulder.

Medina hopped out and walked off behind the vehicle. By her body language, Payne could tell it probably wasn't a standard check-in with Strozzi.

Payne stepped out, making a quick call to Heather. It went to voicemail, and he left a message about recent developments with Cavell's guys and how she might want to vacate Pineland with Zoe for a few days. When he finished, he tucked away his phone and moved up alongside Medina, who was staring at the horizon. "What's happening?"

She put her hands on her hips. "Strozzi is pissed at me for being radio silent for too long. When I told him about finding Manny Torres' body in the canyon and our little shoot-out, he really went off the rails. He's recalled me back to Phoenix so we can discuss what happens next."

Payne stepped closer to her. "Don't go yet. I know of a way to get inside Tanner's facility. I've got the security access code to the rear entrance. I need some eyes inside there. At the very least, you and Strozzi need to know what's going on in there, if he's considering launching an assault on the place." He rested his hand on her arm as she looked at him, unconvinced. "The head of the snake is in Pineland. You'll be able to do a hell of a lot more up here than sitting at briefings back in Phoenix for days on end. Stick it out for one more day, and we'll see what we find at Tanner's place."

Medina glanced down at his hand. "You getting sweet on me, Payne? Trust me, I don't need to be swayed to take the fight to Tanner. I just have to convince my boss to let me stay a little longer, and that'll require some effort."

"Just Facetime him so he can see that wolfish grin of yours. That'll convince him."

She smiled. "Is that all it takes?"

"That sounds like a trick question." He stepped back, heading towards the vehicle. "Make the call, Medina. You know I'm right about this."

CHAPTER 33

TANNER PACED AROUND HIS OFFICE, ALTERNATING HIS GLANCES at the cloudy sky outside his window with intermittent glares at Cavell. "This can't be good. If your guys never came out of Deer Canyon, then that must mean they fucked up, and Payne and the woman are alive."

"Relax, Levi. If either of them knew anything at all about what we were up to, there'd be a platoon of SWAT guys descending on this place. Plus, the trail cams set up by that canyon indicate that they never returned to their vehicles and were picked up by Wheeler."

"The medic? Seriously? Wasn't he the other headache you were supposed to deal with? These failures are becoming epic, and I have too much on the line."

"You mean *we* have too much on the line. You forget that I have to answer to my boss with the syndicate in California. You think there's a lot of bodies at the bottom of that canyon east of town... this is a guy who has mass graves in both Europe and the US, so spare me the doom and gloom act."

Tanner thought about that statement for a second, his face turning even paler. "If they found Torres' body in that canyon, then the DEA is going to think he was connected with us, especially since that guy Portman must have been their informant."

Cavell shook his head. "Won't matter. The first shipment of drugs will be rolling out soon, and your lab below has been cleared out of all the processing equipment and sent to the new facility up north. They come searching around here, they won't find a thing to connect us to any of it."

"Still, there could be a lot of heat in Pineland and at my place," said Levi.

"If necessary, we'll let things settle for a few weeks before beginning at the new lab. Besides, the DEA will be knee-deep dealing with the cartel violence in the streets of Phoenix once Delgado is eliminated."

Cavell glanced out the window again, then at the clock on the desk. "Davey will take care of Delgado in forty-eight hours, which will take the DEA's eyes off Pineland."

Levi ruffled out a breath. "This plan of yours had better work."

CHAPTER 34

ONCE EVERYONE WAS BACK IN THE VEHICLE, WHEELER PUSHED on. Fifteen miles later, he turned right off the main dirt road, heading down a compacted gravel driveway and onto the ranch.

The deeded property was fenced with barbed wire, and Payne marveled at the irrigated hay meadows on the right, which were in stark contrast to the desolate high-desert terrain they'd been driving through.

Payne gazed a mile into the distance where there was a cluster of log and stone buildings along with two large barns beside a corral.

"How big is Miles' operation?" asked Payne.

"About three hundred and fifty cows, a couple of bulls, and thirty-two horses. It's down quite a bit since when I worked here in high school, but Miles has managed to hold on."

"What caused the downturn?" enquired Medina.

Wheeler glanced at her in the rearview mirror as he clenched his jaw. "One word… Tanner. Levi's old man, Jacob, decided to cut out Miles after an incident about six years ago when Levi sexually assaulted Miles' niece."

"Shit, that bastard," snapped Medina. "Why isn't Levi already in a grave in the outback somewhere?"

"It almost came to that, from what I know. I was in the military then, so I only caught snippets of what happened when I came back for visits. The whole thing was swept under the rug by the sheriff at the time, and Tanner's army of lawyers were cooking up bullshit environmental damage claims against Miles, planning to bankrupt him so he'd lose the ranch if he pursued action against Levi. Or I should say *further* action since Miles broke Levi's jaw when he first learned what had happened."

"Sure seems like Pineland has a core of rot that needs to be cut out," said Payne.

Wheeler slowed the vehicle as two cattle dogs ran up, then escorted the rig as he drove. "After that, Tanner terminated Miles' beef contract. Miles ending up having to lay off half his staff and reduce his herd and horses by nearly the same. It's been rough going ever since, but he's still making it work."

He pulled up under the inviting arms of an immense elm near the buildings. Wheeler swept his hand from left to right, explaining the layout. "There are two bunkhouses near the barn, which are used by the cowboys. Next to that are the barn for the horses and the tack room. The main house is that two-story log cabin there. That's where Miles and his wife, Bee, live and where we'll be having dinner in a bit." He swiveled back towards Medina. "And it's where you'll be staying tonight. They have a bedroom downstairs."

He shot a glance at Payne. "And behind the barn is a small historic cabin made out of local sandstone. That's where you'll be at. It's a cool place and one of the original buildings from when Miles' great-grandfather settled the place."

"Any streaming TV services?" quipped Payne.

"Yeah, along with a Jacuzzi and room service," said Wheeler as he stepped out of the vehicle.

Medina patted Kyle on the shoulder. "Payne doesn't need room service... he only eats yummy protein bars."

Wheeler greeted the two dogs, then led the party along the wood-chipped pathway. "Let me walk you up to your respective places so you can grab showers before dinner. Note that I've been repeating that suggestion since you first got in the vehicle."

On the way past the barn, they paused and watched six cowboys returning on their horses. The dust-covered men gave tired nods, the ranch foreman, Clem Stuart, stopping to talk to Wheeler and meet the newcomers.

Payne noticed the wooden crates lashed on either side of Clem's horse behind the saddle. He saw a familiar hazmat symbol on the side. "What's the dynamite for?"

Clem shot a thumb over his shoulder. "Had to blast a truck-sized boulder in the canyon so our cattle could get to the natural waterholes below. Damn thing crashed down from the side of the cliff a few nights ago. Heard it over the music in the bunkhouse. You'da thought a cannon went off."

Payne glanced at the cattleman's weapon of choice sheathed in a leather rifle holster alongside the saddle. Payne had heard that ranchers had switched over to ARs for helping to keep the coyote population in check. The rifle company's logo was faded, and the buttstock was coated with fine grit from the trail.

"Looks like a trusted tool," Payne said.

"Yep. She does the job better than my old Marlin."

He noted the buttstock extended from the sheath farther than normal. "You got a suppressor on that?"

"Heck yeah, it'd be cruel to shoot a rifle without a can around my horse or my dogs."

Payne was surprised he didn't mention his own hearing and had to admire a man who put his animals above himself.

Clem tipped his hat, then turned his horse towards the barn. "Well, my day is only half over, but y'all have a good evening."

"Likewise," said Payne. Other than the sight of the AR, he felt like he'd stepped back a century in time.

CHAPTER 35

WHEN PAYNE ARRIVED AT THE MAIN HOUSE TWO HOURS LATER, he would have thought the meal in front of him was intended as a family banquet. The handmade wooden table filling the dining room was lined with plates of roasted venison, corn on the cob, barbecued quail and an assortment of fresh vegetables from the garden. He deeply inhaled the welcome aroma of spices and home-cooked food, grateful to be in a home filled with character.

"Hope you got room for all this," said the voice of an older man behind him.

Payne turned and saw a sixty-something cowboy with a furrowed face that resembled driftwood.

"Miles Dennehy. Welcome to my ranch." The man was a foot shorter than Payne, but his calloused hand seemed as big as a bear's paw. The two men shook, and Miles pointed to a seat on the far side. "Best get settled in before the other vultures arrive. My two grandsons are probably gonna wrestle us for those venison back straps."

Payne moved to the seat. "I can't thank you enough for putting us up here and for this incredible feast." He pointed a thumb at his neatly ironed long-sleeve shirt. "And the loaner outfit."

"Any friends of Garrett's are welcome friends of mine." Miles sat down, easing himself into the chair as if one of his bones might break. Payne had spent time with Bedouins in the Sahara and remembered how days spent out in the wilds on camelback had been the source of many of their aching joints.

He was about to ask Miles about his property when his eyes widened at the sight of Medina entering. She was wearing a blue floral-print dress that extended just below her knees, followed by a pair of brown cowboy boots. Her black hair was hanging loosely on her shoulders and accentuated by her tan complexion. He briefly traced his gaze down to her waist, his appetite shifting away from the food.

Both men stood as she approached the table, Miles walking around and pulling out her chair. "Glad you could join us, Ms. Medina. It's always nice having the fine company of a lovely lady at the table. I mean, besides my wife, that is." Miles winked at her as she sat; then he returned to his chair.

Payne remained transfixed, finally reaching for his glass of water to soothe his suddenly parched throat. "You're Lara Medina, right?" he enquired as he gazed into her eyes.

"Same as before, yes."

Not exactly.

The tough, battle-hardened DEA agent seemed to have melted away, revealing a stunning feminine side he'd only seen hints of on the trail.

She glanced at his shirt. "You cleaned up nicely. Who'd have thought you'd look good in something with pearl buttons."

Miles shifted his gaze between them. "You two worked together a long time by the looks of it."

Not long enough.

"Seems like a long time," Medina replied with a grin.

The crackle in the atmosphere between Payne and Medina was interrupted by the sound of the back door slamming. A second later, Wheeler appeared along with two cowboys in their early twenties.

Miles introduced his grandkids, then went into the kitchen to help his wife bring out the rest of the trimmings. Beatrice Dennehy came out with a large bowl of gravy and biscuits, followed by Miles, who was carrying a tray of baked potatoes wrapped in foil.

Miles set down the tray near Wheeler, then waved his hands towards his wife, who settled into her seat at the other end of the table. "And the star of the show, my wife, Bee, who holds the reins on what happens under this roof and in the kitchen."

Payne had briefly met her earlier upon arriving and noted her stately presence. "Bee, this is simply an exquisite dinner." He smiled. "Thank you for all of your hard work."

"My pleasure, Kyle." She averted her eyes, shyly reaching out for Wheeler's hand on the right and her grandson's on the left while beginning a prayer.

When she finished, the solemnity turned to a flurry of movement as bowls were passed, ladles filled, and tongs began liberating the grilled steaks from their trays.

Payne couldn't remember the last time he'd had a meal in such pleasing company. For most of his career in black ops, he had been eating some kind of primitive gruel from a canteen cup in an impoverished setting while keeping his eyes trained on the potentially dangerous surroundings.

He savored the food as much as the moment, the homely marrow of both being a welcome respite.

———

Following dinner, Payne accompanied Miles and his friends out to the back porch for a glass of bourbon.

The old rocking chairs were as creaky as the wooden floorboards, and Payne opted to stand and enjoy the sight of the sun setting over the buttes seventy miles to the north.

"Heck of a spread you have here, sir," he said to Miles, who had just stuck the end of a hand-rolled cigarette in the corner of his mouth.

"It ain't bad, is it? As long as a man can see far and has a good woman by his side, he's got all he needs."

Payne glanced at Medina, who gave him a coy smile as she rocked in her chair like a kid, her boots swinging in the air.

Garrett leaned forward in his seat, looking at Miles. "I hope you don't mind, but I told Kyle and Lara about some of the problems you had in the past with the Tanners. Figured they should know the big picture for what they've got in mind next."

Miles removed the cigarette from his mouth, a grimace forming. He stopped rocking and cast a gaze at the sunset. "They say when there's no more room in Hell that the devils will walk this Earth. Heard that in a class in high school decades ago, but I always remembered it. Always figured it was just a clever saying, but the Tanners proved me wrong." He ground the tip of his boot onto a pine cone, then kicked the crushed remains off the porch. He looked over at Payne. "So what exactly you got in mind, son?"

Payne folded his arms. "Burning the Tanners' empire down to the ground."

———

After a three-hour discussion with Miles, Medina and Wheeler about the exterior layout of the Tanner facility and other tactical considerations, Payne bade goodnight to Miles and Bee, heading back to his small abode.

He sat at the round table against the wall, part of him grateful that his cell phone didn't have reception in this corner of the ranch. Payne thought of walking to the top of the driveway and checking if there were any messages from Alisa, but decided it could wait until morning.

He was tired, an exhaustion that extended to his bones and beyond. But there were still things to be done before he could put Pineland in his rearview mirror.

Violent, bloody things.

He was no stranger to delivering that kind of punishment. But part of him wasn't sure how much longer he wanted that as the dominant element of his DNA.

Payne got up, walking to the window and parting the thin white curtains. He stared up at the crescent moon, a white fang in the cloudless sky. Somewhere in a nearby arroyo, a pack of coyotes sang their territorial tune.

The sound was interrupted by a knock on the wooden door. "It's open," he said, figuring it was Wheeler checking to see if he needed anything.

Payne was pleasantly surprised when he turned to see Medina walking in.

"I would have figured you locked your doors and set up traps around the entrance before you slept." She stepped into the center of the one-room cabin.

"Who says I sleep?"

"Oh, you sleep like a black bear in hibernation." She flared her nose up, grunting. "And snore like one too. You should have heard the echoes in that cave last night."

"And you whimper softly like a wind-up doll, only cuter."

Medina lightly punched him on the arm. "I do not whimper."

She leaned a hand on his shoulder, raising one leg and

easing out of a cowboy boot, then repeating the same action with her other foot. When she finished, she took another step towards him, sliding her arms around his neck. "But I didn't come here to talk about sleep."

"No?" He put his hands on her hips.

She undid the top button on his shirt. "This looks good on you but seems a little warm for this place."

He smiled, pulling her closer. "Why, Agent Medina, are you trying to seduce me?"

She patted his cheek. "You're a sharp one, Kyle Payne. You must have been top of your class." Medina put her hand in the center of his chest, pushing him back until he sat on the chair. She lifted her floral dress slightly and then straddled him.

He leaned forward, wrapping his arms around her and pulling her in for a kiss. Medina pressed into him, holding his neck with both hands for a moment before sliding them down to the buttons and coolly undoing them.

Payne deeply inhaled the aroma of her hair, kissing her neck and sliding the dress off her right shoulder as the outside world disappeared.

CHAPTER 36

W<small>HEN</small> P<small>AYNE</small> <small>AWOKE THE NEXT MORNING, HE FELT A SENSE OF</small> peace he hadn't known in years. He lay beside Medina, their legs intertwined beneath the sheets. He brushed a strand of black hair from her cheek, watching her eyes slowly open.

He wanted to bolt the door closed and stay here all day. But the outside world beckoned. A minute later, he heard footsteps approaching his dwelling.

A knock followed, and Wheeler's voice filled the air. "Payne, breakfast in twenty."

"Roger that."

"You see Medina around, tell her the same."

"Copy that," she shouted with a giggle.

"I figured as much. See you both soon."

Payne tickled her ribs. "Nice job. You sure you've done undercover gigs before?"

She kissed him, then flung the sheets over their heads. "I prefer this kind of undercover work."

Medina ran her hand along his side, pausing on a comma-shaped scar above his right hip. "I noticed a few of these last night. More than a person should have."

"I have friends who'd put me to shame."

She glided her fingers around the other scars and pock-marks. "That makes six. Not good, Kyle."

"Eleven, actually."

"Jesus. That's a lot of mileage." She looked straight into his eyes. "Ever think about getting into another line of work?"

"Just lately, yeah. Not sure what that should be. Hell, I could ask you the same thing. Or are you a lifer like your boss, Strozzi?"

She leaned up on one elbow, pursing her lips. "For now, I'm all about putting a dent in the drug traffic along the border and in places like Pineland."

He sat up on the edge of the bed, sliding on his clothes. "Speaking of that, we should grab breakfast and head back to Heller's place. I need to grab some tools that punch holes in people."

"You still want to get inside Tanner's facility tonight?"

He nodded. "It's the best play. Actually, the only play right now."

CHAPTER 37

FOLLOWING A LATE BREAKFAST AND A FINAL REVIEW OF PAYNE'S recon mission to Tanner's warehouse, Wheeler drove them back to the outskirts of Pineland. They planned to stop at Heller's cabin to retrieve the weapons from the safe and wait for nightfall.

"Not a good idea to head straight up the driveway in case Cavell has more of his goons near the place," said Wheeler.

"I happen to know a back way in through a deer trail behind the garage," said Medina with a coy grin.

"You mean from when you broke into John's place," said Payne.

"You need to rethink your interpretation. I told you, there was no breaking of anything involved since I went in through an open window."

Wheeler glanced at Payne. "Can't argue with that."

A mile before the turnoff to Heller's cabin, Medina pointed to a dirt road on the left. Wheeler headed in that direction, following the old logging road around the base of the hill behind Heller's place.

After parking, the two men followed Medina up the trail,

arriving ten minutes later behind Heller's garage. They sat and watched the cabin and the surrounding woods, and when Payne was sure no one was there, he stepped out and headed around the front, keeping his HK pistol in a low-ready position.

He was about to head up the porch steps when he paused, hearing a muffled barking sound coming from Heather's vehicle beside her house. Payne proceeded along the road, eventually stopping at a Nissan pickup truck under a large elm tree. Mochi was inside, barking frantically and scratching at the steamed-up windows.

Payne had a sinking feeling in his stomach.

He noticed the front door of Heather's house was ajar. The screen door was torn off the hinges and lying amidst shattered glass on the porch.

"Damn it." He released Mochi, the dog bounding around Payne, panting like he'd been chasing deer.

He held onto the dog's collar while Medina and Wheeler circled around the perimeter of the dwelling, then cleared the inside. When they finished, Payne filled Mochi's water bowl from a hose by the garden.

"From the tracks in the driveway, it looks like another vehicle was here," said Medina. "And there are two sets of drag marks leading down from the porch."

"I left a message with Heather yesterday to clear out of here for a while, but I must have been too late." He balled a fist. "Shit. I should have come here right after we left the canyon."

Wheeler handed him a flip-phone that had a sticky note with Payne's name on it. "This was on the kitchen table."

They gave each other nervous glances.

Payne flipped open the burner phone and went to the menu for the address book, which only had one number. He pressed the call button and waited.

On the second ring, Cavell picked up, answering with a smug tone. "Payne, we need to meet."

"I've already met up with your crew a couple of times, and it didn't end well for any of them."

"Yeah, you've won a few minor rounds, but shit like that happens in the big leagues. Acceptable losses. But I doubt you want Heather and Zoe ending up like your pal Heller." Cavell growled as he spoke. "I was the last one to see Heller alive. Let me tell you, I enjoyed that look of terror in his eyes when he knew his number was up."

Payne clutched the phone. "I'm looking forward to reciprocating when I see you. For now, it'll have to wait, as I'm about to meet up with the DEA Rapid Response Team that's just arrived. They've got an army of guys about to storm your place. Or should I say your buddy Tanner's place, since you're just the hired help."

"Sure. I bet they parachuted in a few minutes ago. Send 'em on over. They can join the little party we're about to have with these two sweet ladies."

Payne knew a predator like Cavell was waiting for him to reveal emotion or empathy so he could relish the moment before continuing the verbal match. Payne kept his voice level, but it didn't help that he could hear Zoe crying in the background.

"Hang on. I need to move a ways off," said Payne. "One of the DEA guys is briefing the strike team, and it's hard to hear."

"Bullshit. It's just you and that woman you were spotted with by the canyon. My guess is she was the one holding Mike Portman's leash. DEA, probably. Regardless, bring the bitch along. More the merrier and all."

"Time will tell how many are here with me." He knew Cavell already had a clear advantage by having taken possession of two hostages, but he figured it wouldn't hurt to try to unbalance the man's tactical mindset.

"You think this is funny? You need to show up at Tanner's facility at nine o'clock tonight, or I'll dice up these pretty faces and then toss them into the meat grinder. After me and the fellas have some fun with them first."

"I show up there and you'll shoot me in the back of the head before I get twenty feet from my vehicle."

"I'd be thinking the same thing, but, like I said, we need to meet. There are some things to discuss. I get my answers; then you and the whores can go."

"I think you're confusing me with someone who cares. I barely know those women. Ran into them once while driving up to the cabin. For all I know, they've been working with you all along, keeping an eye on my friend Heller's whereabouts."

Cavell scoffed. "You wouldn't have called if you didn't care. Plus, if you're anything like Heller, then you're a proper Boy Scout, always trying to help out the underdog like he was doing with his buddy Portman. You'll come."

"I'll need to convince the agent here to stand down his tac team. They're chomping at the bit."

This time there was a longer pause before Cavell replied, "You know the location of the warehouse… be in the back parking lot at nine o'clock sharp. Just you and that hot DEA chick."

"You said that just you and I need to meet. Now you want her along. Sounds like you're making this up as you go."

"See you soon, Payne." Cavell chuckled. "Don't be late, and make sure to tell that strike team, imaginary or otherwise, to stay clear of the warehouse."

The line went dead, and Payne turned around, actually hoping there was a full-blown tactical detail, but instead he just gazed into the faces of Medina and Wheeler.

Six hours and counting.

He'd faced worse odds before, but it was always on foreign soil, where the rules of engagement were more flexible. And despite his best efforts, he kept seeing the distraught face of the young woman in Romania whenever he thought about Zoe and her mother being held against their will.

Payne tamped down the memory and clutched the phone as he looked at the lone members of his ad-hoc rescue team.

"That didn't sound very good," said Wheeler.

"Let me guess... Cavell and Tanner just gained some much-needed leverage," said Medina.

Payne gave them a brief nod as he headed towards the cabin to retrieve the weapons. "For now. But I'm planning to tip that scale by this evening."

CHAPTER 38

"THIS IS CRAZY. YOU CAN'T JUST SHOW UP AT TANNER'S PLACE and hope to blast your way in there to get Heather and Zoe," said Medina as the three of them stood in the living room of the cabin. "I'll call Strozzi and get a rapid-response team up here by nightfall."

Payne shook his head. "This whole town is under surveillance by Cavell and his crew. They see anyone new arriving here that raises their hackles, and it's game over for Heather and Zoe."

She raised her hands. "You just bluffed that you had a strike team here."

"Just to throw him off balance," said Payne.

Wheeler leaned against the knotty-pine wall beside the hearth. "Payne's right. Tanner has a lot of people on his payroll here, in one form or another. It's going to be hard to sneak in a twelve-man tac team in company Suburbans or a helo." He pulled out his cell phone, heading to the rear bedroom. "But I do have an idea that could even things up."

Medina shuffled closer to Payne, who was doing a visual inspection of the pistol and rifle mags on the coffee table by the couch. "Look, I know you came here for Heller's sake, but this whole thing has blown up into a much bigger scenario, and innocent lives are on the line. I'm not sure marching into that parking lot in a few hours is such a good idea. My people have the personnel and surveillance capabilities to efficiently breach that facility, far beyond anything you and I alone can do."

"You know as well as I do that by the time Strozzi and your colleagues get here and establish an incident command post… and assemble an assault plan… and get into position, the clock will have run out on Zoe's and Heather's lives. You and I *are* the front lines, Lara. We do this my way and there's a chance that we all walk out of it in one piece."

She folded her arms, stepping back a few feet and pacing beside the fireplace. "You're asking me for a lot, Kyle. Part of me agrees with you, but the other part says to call in the cavalry." She stopped on the other side of the couch, putting her hands on her hips. "I'll ride in there with you, but I'm going to give Strozzi an update first."

Payne glanced at his watch. "Go ahead, but wait two more hours so he's not storming up from the Valley with sirens blaring before we head into the warehouse. And tell him I'm going in alone. No need to put your head on Tanner's chopping block."

She gave him a surprised glance before heading out to the porch. "Alright. I'll relay the spirit of that message, but don't take that to mean I'm not accompanying you."

"Good news," said Wheeler, returning from the rear bedroom. "I have a few more comrades in arms to help us."

"Miles?"

"Miles and three of his cowboys. It didn't take much convincing when I told him what's happened to Heather and Zoe."

"They'll be a welcome addition," said Payne.

Wheeler picked up the Remington 700 rifle. "Amen, brother."

Payne watched Medina's silhouette through the curtains of the front windows. "Let's pack all this up and head out in thirty minutes. You'll want to notify Miles that the timeline has been moved up. I want to be in position on the outskirts of that facility in ninety minutes. That will give us plenty of time to recon the site and get into position before dark. After the sun goes down, you can put your sniping skills to use while Medina and I, along with Miles and his guys, head inside."

"Arrive early and control more of the variables," said the medic. "I can live with that."

Payne glanced at the bolt-action rifle in the man's hands. "When's the last time you put any lead downrange?"

"Couple of months ago, during a late spring deer hunt. Dropped a buck at six hundred yards with my Winchester."

"How many shots?" asked Payne with a grin.

"Fuck you is how many shots."

Payne stepped closer, patting Wheeler on the shoulder. "You know, for a Ranger, you're alright. I don't care what other people say about you."

"Yeah, and for a spook, you're not the unprincipled savage I figured you'd be."

Payne glanced at the arsenal of weapons in Heller's living room. "The day isn't over yet."

He felt his iPhone vibrate and pulled it out, seeing it was Alisa calling. "You're a welcome voice in my ear," he said. "I wish you were here right now."

"You've refused my presence twice, so this can only mean things have taken a nasty turn, or am I off?"

"Not entirely off, but I assume you're calling about Heller's SIM card? Find anything of significance?"

"Just one thing that was an anomaly. Most of his locations

were in and around Pineland except for two in Phoenix. One was a federal prison. The first time was a week ago, and the second was thirty-six hours before his death."

"A prison, why there?"

"I'm not so sure that place was his sole focus. On both occasions, he also went to the Viper Lounge, a gentleman's club a few miles south of the prison. I hacked into the security cams there and searched the interior and exterior feeds. He went inside for about an hour both times. The only thing I found on the camera footage of interest for both visits was a license plate on a Dodge truck belonging to a David Tanner, the warden of that prison."

"Looks like John was doing his own surveillance work. I wonder if he was trying to get close enough to Tanner to clone his phone?" Payne put it on speaker as Medina returned from the porch. "Some interesting developments," he whispered to her while Alisa continued.

"And that four-digit number that was in the text John was trying to send you, that corresponds with an inmate at Tanner's prison. Number 3106 is assigned to a Vincent Delgado, who, according to my probing into the federal prisons database, is scheduled to be handed over to the Mexican Federales tomorrow sometime."

Medina's eyes widened. "Tanner would know the exact time and even the travel route of that transfer."

"Who the hell is that talking?" asked Alisa.

"Lara Medina," replied Payne.

"That DEA woman out of Phoenix?"

"And hello to you too," said Medina. "You must be Payne's mystery friend from the keyboard jungle?"

"How things have changed since we last spoke," said Alisa.

"Oh, you have no idea the storm that has swept through here lately. But there's still a tornado coming. Thanks for everything." He left off her name. The less Medina knew, the less would eventually make it back to Strozzi when this was all over.

"Keep me posted on how things turn out, and the offer still stands about joining you there on the ground if you need another shooter."

Medina leaned in. "Not sure the coroner has enough body bags for another person like Payne."

Alisa replied, "So you've already gotten busy scratching names off a kill list. John would be proud."

"We'll see," said Payne. "I'll keep you posted, but right now I've gotta run."

"Take care, Kyle."

"Likewise."

After he hung up, Medina leaned her hands on the table. "If Delgado was on Cavell's radar, then that can only mean one thing: he's being targeted. Maybe that's why Cavell was running guns to the other cartels along the border, so they could take out Delgado during the transfer across the border."

"If Delgado's the kingpin you've described, then eliminating him will cause a war between the other cartels vying to fill his spot in the drug trade. That's a clever business move that would pave the way for Cavell and Tanner's fentanyl operation to carve out an opening in the distribution chain once the cartel supply lines are disrupted."

Medina gave him a nervous look. "And if they play things right, they could eventually become the new kingpins while the regions along the border are engulfed in a bloody battle for years to come."

"The Serbian mob is playing the long game." He glanced over at Wheeler.

The medic had finished packing up the weapons in two large backpacks. "Ready when you two are. It's normally only a twenty-minute drive to Tanner's warehouse, but it'll take at least an hour on foot from the trails behind his place."

Payne gazed into both their faces. "Last chance to reconsider. What we're about to do is going to have ramifications for this town and your lives in the months and years to come."

"This mean you're not sticking around after it's over?" she said.

"I haven't decided yet."

Wheeler hoisted a pack onto his shoulder. "You said before that there's a lot of *rot* in Pineland, and you were right. It's time to get rid of it before it consumes this place, so I'm in."

Payne rested his gaze on Medina. "Heather's and Zoe's lives are the most important thing," she said, "so let's remember that this is a rescue op and not an extermination campaign."

He gave a weak nod. "Agreed."

For now, anyway.

––––––––

Levi Tanner stepped into the warehouse office on sub-level two, tossing some bottles of water and granola bars onto Heather Ryland's lap. She and Zoe had one hand shackled to a water pipe against the back wall as they sat on the floor beside some old filing cabinets.

"Just a few more hours and you can both go free."

Heather handed a bottle and the snacks to Zoe, then motioned her to slide on the headphones for the tablet that Tanner had provided to keep her occupied.

She fixed her gaze upon Levi. "You're as full of shit as the cows you run through the yard out back. We've already seen you loading all the drugs onto your trucks a few hours ago. I

don't expect that you're gonna let us walk out of here alive."
Heather glanced at Zoe to make sure the girl hadn't heard her
words.

Tanner smiled. A cold smile. "You're right. I shouldn't lie.
I thought it best to spare your daughter the terror of knowing
what was coming. I remember being filled with terror my
entire childhood, and it's no way to live." He waved a hand
at the photos of his adoptive father on the wall. "Why, if that
ornery old fuck hadn't pulled me and Davey out of that
group home, we would've ended up in the same penitentiary
as my buddy Cavell." He leaned forward. "You know, the
guy who dragged your asses down here."

"Yeah, I can still smell his foul odor." Heather tried to kick
his leg, but he slid back. "You and Davey and Cavell are all
the same. Don't matter if you wear a suit and your brother
wears a warden's uniform, you're all gutter trash."

He brushed some lint off his shirtsleeve, then readjusted
his blue silk tie. "A wolf in sheep's clothing, as it were. And
you are not about to get in the way of my new empire."

He glanced over his shoulder as the door opened.

A scruffy man in blue coveralls entered. "Trucks are all set.
We're gonna head out."

"Very good. Call me once you arrive in Winslow for the
transfer."

"You got it, boss."

Tanner stood, watching the eight semi-trucks pull away
from the open doors of the loading docks at the rear of the
warehouse. He turned towards Heather. "It won't be long
now for you and your precious daughter. And you can even
thank Mr. Payne for getting you and Zoe involved in all of
this. Him and his friend Heller. They're the ones to blame for
your fate."

He exited the room, closing the door and waving at them
from the window before departing. He needed to call Davey

and go over tomorrow's hit on Delgado. It would be the last time they spoke until the cartel leader was dead since Davey's prison would be in the spotlight for a while.

Levi was just grateful that his brother's shooting skills far outmatched his minuscule IQ.

Thank God that buck-toothed bastard has one redeeming quality.

CHAPTER 39

AFTER WHEELER DROVE THEM TO A DEAD-END ROAD IN THE forest a half mile from Tanner's facility, the former Ranger led them in on foot along the old horse packing trail that had once been used for driving cattle down to the slaughterhouse. The pathway was choked with wild raspberry bushes and mountain mahogany, slowing their travel.

Thirty minutes later, Wheeler stopped a few yards from a short ridge behind the rear of the Tanner warehouse. He kneeled as Payne and Medina did the same.

Payne lowered his pack, removing a pair of binoculars and glassing the property. The three-story building was immense, covering ten acres with a parking lot half the size. At the right rear corner were four loading docks for semi-trucks.

The large bay doors were closed, and Payne spotted two armed guards walking around the back. By their faded camouflage garb, they looked like Cavell's guys, and he wondered how many more were out front and inside.

The sound of footfalls behind them caused Payne to spin around. The sight of Miles and three of his cowboys was a welcome relief, and it suddenly felt like this assault upon the facility might actually work.

He glanced at the men's weapons, which consisted of an AR-10 rifle and the semi-auto rifles Payne and Medina had acquired from the thugs after the canyon shoot-out.

"No Winchesters or Bowie knives?" Payne said to Miles with a hint of disappointment.

"Pff, what century you livin' in, son?" The weathered rancher snickered as he patted Payne on the shoulder.

"Welcome to the arena, boys," said Wheeler while the four cattlemen hunkered down beside him.

"Woulda been here sooner but got hung up helpin' a young couple who got driven off the road by a reckless truck convoy that was coming around the bend on Highway 79."

"Miles finally got to pull someone's vehicle out of a ditch with that sparkly new winch on the front of his pickup," said a bearded cowboy on the end.

Miles carefully removed the saddlebag off his shoulder and handed it to Payne. "Here's the dynamite you asked for. Got two long fuses in the batch like you requested, along with four sticks with regular fuses. And there's a lighter and some duct tape in the front pouch too."

Payne slid the bag over by his pack, then gazed at Clem, the ranch foreman, who was holding the AR-10. "These aren't coyotes you'll be hunting tonight. How do you feel about turning your skills towards two-leggeds?"

"As long as it's Tanner's inner circle, don't bother me a bit."

The other cowboys mumbled similar comments between themselves.

"Clem, you remain here with Wheeler and take care of the two varmints walking at the back of the building, while Medina, Miles and the others make their way down to the rear entrance and head inside. I already gave Medina the security code for the door. I'm going to skirt around towards the front of the building and use the dynamite to disable the power grid, then create a distraction, while the rest of you get Zoe and Heather out."

Payne glanced at his watch, then looked into Miles' hardened face. "Heather and her daughter are the priority. Once they're safe, then you are welcome to leave, or you can unleash Hell upon the place."

"Hell and then some," said Miles.

"Any questions?" Payne said as he glanced into the eyes around him.

No one responded and just went about cinching down their packs or doing a quick inspection of their weapons.

Payne was quiet, staring at the warehouse, then leaning back towards Medina. "You know, something that's bothered me from the get-go: why did Cavell want us to wait so long for the meet-up? He could have told us to show up here right after the call."

"Cover of darkness, maybe," replied Medina.

Payne gazed out at the spacious grounds surrounding the remote facility. "I don't think so. Tanner already has this place isolated from prying eyes."

"Unless they needed time to load the eighteen-wheelers," said Wheeler. He thrust his chin towards the loading docks. "There's a lot of black silt on that pavement. Probably from the surface roads in this region, which were resealed with fresh blacktop in the past week."

Payne scrutinized the corner of the lot with the binoculars. "There's been quite a bit of vehicle activity here recently." He turned towards Miles. "Those trucks you mentioned earlier, tell me about 'em."

"Eight semis. Two groups of four spread out a mile or so. They were the usual Tanner rigs, used for shipping their steaks around the country."

"Loaded with gel packs filled with fentanyl," said Medina with a look of disdain.

"The first shipment of drugs heading to Cavell's West Coast crew," said Payne. He shot a look at the immense warehouse below. "And since Cavell was brazen enough to tell us to come here, he and Tanner have probably already relocated their drug operation to another location."

"Except Miles came in from the east, so those trucks weren't going to California," said Wheeler, his face thoughtful.

"Why send them to New Mexico unless he's got some kind of distribution ring set up there?" said Medina. "Except it's a long way to Gallup or Albuquerque, which are the only sizeable cities."

Payne slid back, gazing at her. "Remember that other body we found in the canyon... the one that wasn't as badly decomposed as the others? He was wearing a bronze belt buckle from a rodeo. I looked up a few things on my phone back at the ranch this morning. Last year's rodeo winner in northern Arizona was a guy named Jimmy Begay from Winslow."

"So?" Medina queried.

"Lot a ropers around here have those buckles," said Miles, cutting in. "Hell, there are even fake ones you can buy online to make out like you're a rodeo champ."

Payne nodded, but quickly dismissed the notion and turned back towards Medina. "It didn't make sense to me at the time, but in the online news photo, Begay was standing next to his wife outside their rental truck company in Winslow."

"Tanner's going to transfer goods from the big rigs to the smaller rental trucks." Medina moved in closer. "Dozens of those rentals will then be bound for different cities along the

West Coast rather than risk having eight huge targets on the interstate that are subject to commercial truck inspections."

"Tanner probably installed one of his puppets at Begay's business in Winslow after eliminating him," said Payne. "He's tying off all of his loose ends."

Medina removed her iPhone, texting furiously. "This is something Strozzi will want to get a jump on. Winslow's a bit of a drive from here for those trucks but a helluva lot closer for one of our helo teams. And I need to see what he can track down about Delgado's prison transfer tomorrow."

The last rays of sunlight were piercing the treetops. Payne squat-walked closer to Wheeler's position. "I've got an idea that might buy us a little wiggle room and draw attention away from this part of the building."

"Yeah, what's that? You got an RPG in your pack?" said the medic.

"How well do you know Sheriff Rudensky?"

"We go back a few years, mainly through his brother, who is a horse vet. I liked the sheriff better when he was a deputy, though. Since becoming the head honcho, he's a real dick. Plus, given all the shady shit that has gone on in Pineland since Rudensky got elected, he's gotta be on Tanner's payroll."

"Oh, he is. No doubt about it. But, my only question is, how far does his conscience extend beyond his bank account?"

"Money has a funny way of eroding morality, so I wouldn't put much faith in your theory."

"Normally I'd agree, but Rudensky's got skin in the game and needs me to obtain something inside that's in Tanner's possession. Something of great value to his reputation."

"How the hell did you get dirt on Rudensky?"

Payne decided to forgo recounting the story about

breaking into the sheriff's office. "Not as hard to do as you might imagine, if you're in the right place at the right time."

He slid back, moving farther into the forest as he removed his iPhone.

Rudensky picked up on the second ring. "Hey, asshole, you have what I want?"

Payne sighed, hoping his gut feeling about the man was right. "I'll have it shortly, but I could use some help on your end."

"Yeah, how's that?"

"Cavell kidnapped Heather and Zoe. He's holding them at the Tanner warehouse and is going to kill them unless I show up in an hour." He let that information percolate in the sheriff's brain for a few moments.

"What the hell? Those crazy bastards," snapped Rudensky. "Look, if you think I knew anything about…"

"Relax. This isn't about you. It's about getting those two out of there alive." Now came the part about turning the emotional screws on the man. "Look, I think you were once a good lawman, but you got mixed up with the wrong people, who probably told you your job was just to keep things quiet. Except a lot of people have died lately. I'll get that flash drive so Tanner no longer has any sway over you, but if you want to do the right thing, then help me get Heather and Zoe out of there. He'll kill them otherwise."

There was a long and weighted pause. Rudensky cleared his throat, his voice tremulous as he spoke. "Of course. What do you need me to do?"

"In ten minutes, pull up to the front of Tanner's company with your sirens blaring. Make a big splash. When Tanner or Cavell come out, give them a story about how you spotted me on foot a mile to the east."

"And then what… that's all you want? What about Zoe and Heather?"

"I'll handle it from there."

"I can help. But you're not a one-man army, Payne."

He glanced back at the rest of his eclectic team. "Just do what I asked and our mutual problems will all go away."

Rudenksy ruffled out a sigh. "Alright. Ten minutes and I'll be there."

Payne slid the phone in his pocket, then moved back between Medina and Wheeler.

"Everything good?" said Medina.

Payne nodded. "The fireworks show begins in mere minutes." He grabbed the suppressed UZI, gently placing the saddlebag on his shoulder, then made his way behind Miles and his cowboys. "Let's roll, fellas. Time to turn that former slaughterhouse back into its namesake."

Payne glanced at the rest of the party. "Give me two minutes to take out the circuit breakers. Once you see the big bang, then it's game on."

He waited for the armed guard on the right of the building to finish his sweep and head back to the loading docks; then Payne headed down the slope towards the distant edge of the parking lot, hugging the tree line until he was at the side of the building.

Payne trotted up to the circuit-breaker box on the wall, removing a stick of dynamite and sticking it to the metallic box with a piece of duct tape. He glanced at the long fuse hanging down, figuring he would have three minutes.

CHAPTER 40

THOUGH HE WAS ONLY DRIVING THIRTY MILES PER HOUR DOWN the road that led to Tanner's facility, Rudensky kept a white-knuckle grip on the steering wheel.

This whole thing has gotten out of control. Levi and his brilliant scheme. How did I get sucked into this fucking mess? And now Cavell has Zoe and Heather. If that fucking animal touches them, I'll put a bullet in his thick caveman skull.

He rounded the last bend in the road, turning on his sirens and flashing lights. His headlights illuminated the front of the building, where three armed guards were standing. By their grungy appearance, they appeared to be Cavell's goons and not the usual Tanner security personnel.

Levi, what the hell are you doing?

He parked the car, quickly exiting and walking to the lobby.

Cavell pushed past his men. "Nobody called you, Sheriff, and I'm in the middle of something, so just turn around and…"

"I caught sight of Payne in the woods about a mile east of here. He had a rifle on his back, so I assume he's headed this way. You really started a war with this guy, didn't you?"

Cavell's eyes darted towards the forest. "He's on foot? Was he alone?"

"How should I know? I got word from one of the neighbors on Crocket Lane that some guy with a sniper rifle was sneaking through the damn woods. When I did a drive-by, I saw Payne bounding off."

"He's probably gonna try to pick us off one at a time," said Cavell. He backed up, motioning for his men to follow him inside. "Let's get to the conference room. He can't reach us in there."

Payne heard the dry woodchips near the front corner of the building crackle. Suddenly a guard doing his rounds appeared a few feet away. A third man they must have missed earlier. The guard froze at the sight of the intruder, trying to remove the pump shotgun on his shoulder.

Payne was bad-breath distance from the thug, but his UZI was slung around his chest. He rushed forward, removing his folding knife and jamming it into the goon's stomach, then driving the blade up until it hit the sternum. Blood and entrails spilled out, the man's eyes becoming saucers.

Payne thrust his hand over the guard's mouth, then shoved the blade into the throat, twisting down and slicing out a section of trachea. A second later, he stepped aside, letting the blood-drenched body tumble down the slope.

He returned to the circuit breaker and pulled out the lighter, turning his attention to the main road. A minute later, the flashing lights and sirens from Rudensky's vehicle grew obvious.

He heard Rudensky shouting to some guards near the

front lobby, followed by Cavell, who told everyone to get inside and lock the entrance.

Flicking the lighter, Payne ignited the fuse, then trotted up the slope towards the back of Rudensky's cruiser, waiting for the coming blast.

———

Rudensky had left his flashing lights on, which helped to conceal Payne's presence behind the sheriff's vehicle. Payne pulled out three sticks of dynamite and taped them together, then lit the short fuse. He leaned out from the bumper and tossed it at the lobby doors.

The resulting explosion took out the entrance and part of the empty reception room, sending a hailstorm of glass and debris into the air. A second later, the dynamite on the breaker box ignited, thrusting the exterior grounds and inside of the building into darkness.

Payne stood and trotted through the smoky entrance, leveling the suppressed UZI at two of Cavell's brutes rushing up from the stairwell on the right.

———

Medina, Miles and three of the cowboys remained hidden by the dumpsters near the loading docks when the fireworks began, the front of the building aglow in a hair-raising explosion that sent a shockwave through the cool night air.

Moments later, she saw the two armed guards collapse to the ground from Clem and Wheeler's sniper work.

Medina stood, running to the rear entrance and punching in the four-digit code on the numeric keypad. The door unlocked, and Miles swung it open while Medina swept inside first. With the central power out, the overhead emergency lights came on, casting the half-empty warehouse in a surreal orange glow. She skirted alongside rows of wooden crates towards the west end of the building.

Three armed men burst from the office on the opposite side of the room, heading for the stairwell in the corner, which led to an open walkway above the rooms.

Once they left, she shifted her attention back to another room where she could hear Levi Tanner and Sheriff Rudensky having a heated argument.

"That has to be where Zoe and Heather are at," she whispered to the cowboys beside her.

The crates beside her head splintered apart as four gunmen on the overhead walkways began firing. Medina ducked behind some Tanner steak crates as the cowboys scrambled to do the same.

She leaned out, squeezing off a barrage of rounds as the targets became available. Cavell's guys weren't being methodical, just spraying in the direction of where they thought everyone had gone until the magazines on their automatic rifles were depleted.

She took cover again, waiting until the next barrage passed, then crept out, sending a half-dozen bullets into a stocky shooter's chest. The man careened over the railing, splattering on the concrete floor below.

Miles and his guys were using a pocket-gopher approach with one cowboy springing up and shooting as a decoy while the other three guys identified the target and punched him full of holes.

Medina slid between two crates, watching the movement of a lone gunman on the far left, who kept darting out behind a metal beam and taking potshots before disappearing behind the cover. She crouched and walked down the next row of crates until she could get a better angle to shoot. Medina waited and watched. The third time that he crept out, she had him. Her Glock 17 barked out four rounds, zippering his chest. He fell back against the post and slid to the ground.

————

"So it's true… you've resorted to kidnapping now?" snapped Rudensky as he stood in the office with Levi Tanner. The sheriff kneeled in front of Zoe, gently stroking her head with his right hand as he slowly extended his left towards Heather, depositing a handcuff key in her palm.

"What the hell you mean, 'it's true'? You been talking to someone about what's going on here?"

Rudensky stood. "It's pretty clear what's going on. You've become a fucking monster since you joined up with that gangster Cavell." He moved to the other side of the desk so Tanner's line of sight was away from Heather. "This isn't you, Levi."

Tanner shook his head, grinning. "All you know about me is that I'm a steady paycheck, so you can keep whoring around Phoenix on your nights off."

Rudensky shot a nervous glance at Heather. "He's making shit up. Don't believe him."

Tanner slid his hand into a pants pocket, removing a white flash drive. "This is why you really showed up here, isn't it, so skip the white-knight routine. Even Heather knows you're a rent-a-cop, like most everyone else in this town."

Rudensky had a plaintive look in his eyes as he glanced at Heather again.

The air was shattered by the sound of gunfire coming from the rear exit door.

Rudensky used the distraction to remove his tactical baton and lunge at Tanner. He slammed the weapon down on the man's forearm, watching the flash drive tumble to the ground.

The sheriff slammed his boot downward, smashing the device. "Now you've got nothing on me, you piece of…"

The shot that rang through Rudensky's ears was louder than the ones outside. His stomach felt like a bowl of jelly as stabbing pain raced through his midsection. He stepped back, glancing down at the crimson fluid soaking through his tan shirt. He slumped against the wall, sliding to the ground.

———

"You idiot, you didn't think that was my only copy? I only got that out when I saw you pulling up on the security cameras." Tanner stepped closer, squatting down and tapping the barrel of his .380 Ruger pistol against Rudensky's head. "It doesn't really matter. We were going to replace you anyway."

Tanner never saw the laptop coming as Heather swung down, smashing it against the back of his skull. Despite the force, Tanner rolled off to the side, shooting up to his feet and sending a vicious backhand across her right cheek.

Heather careened into the filing cabinet. "You bitch," shouted Tanner, rubbing the back of his head. He coiled his arm for another strike, his shoulder blowing apart as Rudensky fired off a single round from his Glock.

Tanner hollered in pain, hinging his upper body forward on the desk.

Heather rushed at him, grabbing a pen and stabbing it down on his weapon hand. He recoiled his arm, dropping the gun.

Heather retrieved the .380 and kept it fixed on the man while she freed her terrified daughter from her restraints.

A second later, the door slammed open, and a look of relief flashed across Heather's face, seeing Miles and Medina rush in.

Medina squatted down beside the pale sheriff, feeling for a pulse. She looked up at the others, shook her head, then lowered his eyelids and removed the service pistol from his limp right hand.

Payne darted down the hallway, passing a conference room on the left and a small cafeteria on the right. He paused at the next hallway, recalling Wheeler's description of the first floor.

He stepped out, only to have the corner explode with splinters of drywall as a cacophony of automatic weapons fire erupted.

Payne leaped back, retrieving a stick of dynamite from the saddlebag and lighting the fuse. He kneeled, tossing it into the hallway. The explosion must have taken out most of the walls as an eruption of wood, ceiling panels and glass spewed from the opening of the corridor.

Payne sprang up, charging into the passage. Three men were splayed on the ground, their pulpy torsos a part of the flooring now. He scanned the empty rooms on either side, then headed to the last door at the end.

He stepped to the side, turning the handle. Chunks of the door blew apart from someone on the other side dumping buckshot rounds from a shotgun. The roaring sound of gunfire continued until the shredded door was little more than a patchwork.

Payne heard the shooter's weapon run dry, and he made his move. He swung inside, sweeping his weapon from left to right. Only there was no time to react. Cavell sprang out, swinging a lead pipe down on the UZI, sending it to the floor, then rushed at Payne's side, slamming him into the wall.

Payne sent a headbutt towards Cavell's nose, but it glanced off the sweaty right cheek. The mobster shot out a vicious jab into Payne's ribs, then reached for a fixed blade on his hip.

Payne grabbed a porcelain vase off the conference room counter and slammed it into Cavell's head, the knife dropping from Cavell's grip.

Payne followed up with a roundhouse kick to the man's left shin. The knee buckled slightly, and Cavell grunted like a feral animal, rushing at Payne again.

Both men exchanged blows, with Cavell dodging a palm strike to his throat while Payne barely missed an eye gouge. Payne shifted his weight to the inside and closed the distance, grabbing the gangster's vest and pulling him closer before executing a judo hip throw.

Cavell went down hard on the bare floor, the smacking sound echoing throughout the room. Still, the man seemed unfazed, rolling to his side and dodging an incoming stomp kick from Payne.

Cavell quickly snatched up the lead pipe, waving it in a figure-eight pattern.

Payne withdrew his folding knife and kept his distance as the two circled one another. Then the mobster shot forward, striking at Payne's blade hand. Payne sidestepped, shooting a straight jab into the man's right side. The leather vest prevented full penetration, but the tip caused Cavell to spring a small leak.

Cavell backed up, glancing at the wound. "The worst cuts are the ones that go just past the floating ribs. You'll have to do better."

"I'm just irritated that I only get to kill you once."

Cavell shifted the sixteen-inch pipe to his other hand and unzipped his vest. Beyond the Serbian mob tattoos on his chest were numerous scars, some over six inches in length. "I've got a few lives left."

Payne shot in with a snap-cut that hit the man on his

empty hand. It went in deep, but the serrated edge got hung up on the palm bone, slowing Payne's withdrawal.

Cavell gritted his teeth, sweeping the lead pipe in an arc down towards Payne's left leg. The pain was excruciating, nearly causing him to vomit. His quadriceps was temporarily wrecked, and he collapsed to his other knee, immediately trying to roll to his right to avoid another incoming strike, which impacted the tile floor, splintering it into pieces.

Payne came up on his feet but partially collapsed against the counter. Cavell's next strike was directed towards Payne's head, but he veered to the left, catching a faint grazing hit along the shoulder.

"I was hoping we'd get to play a little more before I bust your head apart," seethed Cavell.

Payne fumbled in his back pocket, removing the brass knuckles he'd taken off one of Cavell's thugs in the diner parking lot. When the mobster swung again, Payne ducked and sent an uppercut into Cavell's jaw. Bones and teeth splintered apart, sending a rivulet of blood and white particles from Cavell's mouth.

The enraged man swung again, still only seeming slightly fazed by the damage.

Is this guy on PCP or something?

Payne came at him with another punch, but his injured leg failed him, dropping him to one knee. Cavell exploited the opening, kicking Payne back down to the ground.

Now Cavell leaped on him, straddling his torso. He raised the pipe to strike, but Payne sat up and grabbed the shirt collar, yanking him down to restrict his striking ability. Now he could prevent himself from being pummeled while dishing out violence.

I need to end this rabid animal.

He grabbed Cavell's left ear and twisted down hard, tearing it off. The gangster shrieked, trying to pull free, but

Payne seized the man's greasy hair, forcing his head to the right so his neck was exposed. Payne sent a straight punch into the trachea, followed by another. The brass knuckles doing their job to shatter the cartilage.

Cavell was growing limp, and Payne bucked his hips up, then drove the man to his side, coming up on top. Cavell was gasping for air, trying to reach for the pipe on the floor. Payne leaned over, grabbing it instead and sending one end down into Cavell's right eye. He shoved it through until it came out the back of the skull.

Cavell's hands thrashed for a second, his body not getting the signal that his life was over.

Payne hobbled to a standing position, retrieving the UZI and his folding blade. He scanned the hallway for signs of movement. When he was sure there were no other threats, he glanced at Cavell, seeing the final twitches in the man's near-lifeless limbs.

Payne moved around the body, heading to the stairwell in the corner. He felt like he'd just been crushed in a stampede, each step an agonizing move.

Arriving on the last level, he gazed at the immense auto-mated door with a security keypad that was smashed to bits, evidently damaged by Cavell. He leaned against the wall, glancing up at the stairs, and slammed a fist against the door as his leg throbbed in agony.

"You've got to be fucking kidding."

He heard noise on the other side. A second later, the air seal on the vault-like door hissed as it began opening.

Payne stepped back, barely able to hold up the UZI.

Nothing could have been more pleasing than the face he saw on the other side.

"Damn, we gotta find some other places to spend our time besides canyons and warehouses."

Medina moved towards him, hugging him and gazing at

his banged-up face. "And you seriously need to think about reducing the scars on your body."

"I'd agree, but then there'd be two wise people between us, and I can't have that."

She turned sideways so he could lean on her, and they made their awkward way through the door. The sight of Miles escorting Heather and Zoe from the warehouse eased his pain for a moment.

They staggered towards the rear loading docks. After everyone reconvened in the back parking lot, they stood gazing at the silent building and the bodies scattered around the grounds and loading docks.

"Rudensky's dead. Took a round from Levi Tanner, but he was able to free Heather and Zoe," said Medina.

"And Levi?" inquired Wheeler.

"I hog-tied his ass to a forklift inside," said Miles. "And may have busted a few ribs by accident."

Payne looked at Miles, Clem and the other cowboys. "You fellas should head home. This place will probably be swarming with FBI and DEA in the coming hours."

"And ATF, the marshals and DOJ," said Medina in a flat tone.

Miles rested a hand on Heather's shoulder. "You and Zoe oughta come back to the ranch with us for a few days. Bee and I will take care of you both."

She nodded, pulling Zoe closer. "Thanks, that's much appreciated, Miles."

Payne glanced at the girl's teary eyes. "And Mochi's safe in John's cabin."

Her face lit up, and he saw the presence of the sweet child inside start to emerge again.

"You gonna be alright?" said Heather as she walked by Payne, clasping a hand around his arm.

"Nothing a few bottles of ibuprofen won't handle." He

nodded at the ridge overlooking the back of the parking lot, which suddenly seemed like a mountain slope as his leg ached with each step. "You guys go up ahead. I'm gonna be draggin' behind."

"We arrived together; we leave together," said Wheeler, who put his arm around the opposite shoulder from Medina as they helped Payne move up the slope.

"Always the Ranger, aren't you?" asked Payne as he hobbled along between them.

"Nah, this is the medic in me. I can't stand to see a grown man cry."

Payne frowned. "The only tears I'm gonna shed is when I have to pull out of this town."

"Guess that means he's gonna miss us," said Medina.

He chuckled, squeezing their arms. "I meant the food at Monique's."

CHAPTER 41

THE NEXT MORNING NEIL STROZZI GUNNED HIS VEHICLE BEYOND the speed limit on the two-lane highway, only slowing once to take the turn that led to Templeton Federal Prison.

"I never thought the sight of a slammer would be so pleasing," said Strozzi as he drove the black SUV past the security checkpoint at the east end after pausing to show his credentials.

His second-in-command, Mitch Brenner, glanced at his tablet. "The judge's paperwork went through, so that's three warrants we have now to search Davey Tanner's office, vehicle and home."

"Did Delgado get relocated already by the marshals after we told them about the threat on his life?"

Brenner nodded. "Still not sure how I feel about saving Delgado from being assassinated along the interstate. Somehow that just seems wrong."

"It's neither a good thing nor a bad thing," said Strozzi, who was weaving through the employee parking lot. "I've come to think of stuff like that in this manner: would you rather have a contented tiger at the top of the pyramid or a shitload of ravenous hyenas as the bottom who will maul everything in sight? For now, guys like Delgado have a cohesive systemic effect along the border, keeping the other cartels in check. He gets eliminated and it's power-grab mayhem for years to come until the next Delgado comes along."

"With all those fancy words, it sounds like you're working on your next PowerPoint lecture for the Academy."

Strozzi lifted a wry eyebrow, pulling in beside a blue and white bus with reinforced windows. The two DEA agents exited their rig and made their way to the front doors.

"You search Tanner's vehicle while I head inside to his office," said Strozzi, who opened his suit coat, hoping the breeze would cool him off.

"Might not be a need," said Brenner, pointing to the warden, who had just exited the main building and was walking towards his pickup truck while feverishly stabbing at his iPhone.

Both men quickly changed direction, making a beeline for Tanner.

Nearing his truck, Davey glanced over his shoulder towards the two agents, who were moving like linebackers. Davey froze like he'd been struck by a paralysis dart, dropping his cell phone. He backed up, trot-walking to the front doors, then changing directions and running along the side of the fence.

"Where the hell's he going?" inquired Strozzi as he and Brenner ran a parallel route.

Numerous convicts stopped their activities and moved to the sixteen-foot-high fence, shouting expletives at Tanner.

The warden made an abrupt turn and bolted for the open desert, which was surrounded by another fence a quarter mile away.

Strozzi and Brenner picked up their pace, darting around parked cars until they reached the end of the lot. Strozzi was burning high-octane adrenaline at this point, being spurred on as much by the surprise at Tanner's actions as from the fact that he was pursuing a supposed officer of the law.

A few seconds later, Strozzi was on Tanner's heels, the warden turning and casting a rollercoaster-wild gaze back at him. Strozzi increased his pace and could have grabbed his collar but waited one more second, shoving him in the back instead so he tumbled into a clump of prickly pear.

The DEA boss came to a halt, panting, as he rested his hands on his knees.

Tanner was writhing in the cactus restraints, his face and neck covered in spines as he groaned.

"David Tanner, you're under arrest, you motherfucker," said Strozzi. "The drug operation at your family's company in Pineland went boots-up last night. We know about your involvement with your brother and Aiden Cavell in starting up your own fentanyl distribution network. And that truck convoy heading to California with the designer drug you guys had Torres create is now sitting in a DEA warehouse."

Tanner tried to pull his shirtsleeve free of the cactus, but it only entangled him further. "You've got nothing on me. Whatever Aiden and Levi were up to was their doing, not mine," claimed Davey as he finally rolled off the bristly patch.

"And what about the sniper rifle in your possession and the storage box along the interstate north of Tucson to take out Delgado? Oh, yeah, and the truck convoy of fentanyl that left your family's fucking warehouse in Pineland last night."

Tanner stopped squirming, hanging his head back.

"Yeah, your brother ratted you out. It's over. And your pal Cavell had his head bashed in, so he's not gonna be watching your back anymore."

Brenner stepped on Tanner's right arm, then shoved him

on his stomach, cuffing his hands. He glanced at Strozzi. "You want me to read him his actual rights now?"

Strozzi waved at his agent, kicking sand in Tanner's face as he walked past. "Let's waltz him by the prison yard one more time on his way to the vehicle."

CHAPTER 42

A<small>T</small> 9:30 <small>A.M.</small>, P<small>AYNE</small> <small>PULLED INTO THE</small> I<small>NFINITY</small> EMS <small>PARKING</small> lot on Heller's Indian motorcycle. The sound of the engine was enough to draw attention from the open ambulance bay, and a second later, Wheeler emerged.

Payne stepped off the bike, lightly rubbing his aching leg for a moment as he glanced at the police tape cordoning Earl Hedley's mechanic shop across the street. He wondered how many other people in Pineland who were connected with the Tanners or Cavell were going to be in cuffs by week's end, that or on a wanted poster.

"Wow, nice rig. I recall John zipping around town on that beauty," said the medic. "Just don't let Miles see those leather saddlebags, or he might make you an offer."

"How are he and his guys doing?"

"They're back to the grind, but Miles is going to talk to the ranchers who used to sell beef to Tanner and see if they might all be interested in teaming up and running their own steak distribution company. Only this time, it'd be managed by an actual rancher."

"Sounds like a good way to keep the economy rolling in

Pineland." Payne hobbled to the curb, looking into the ambulance bay. "You already back in the thick of work, eh?"

"I missed enough time lately. Not gonna sit at home on
the couch when there's others in need of help."

He admired the man's sense of duty and knew that the
vestiges of the Old West would live on with people like
Wheeler and Miles.

Payne noticed the medic gazing at the bulbous saddlebag
on the right. "Just returned from Payson after picking up
John's ashes. He always said if he died, to spread his remains
in a place with a great view."

"You got somewhere in mind?"

Payne pursed his lips. "I have an idea of such a place, but
nothing off the top of my head seems quite right. I think I'll
let it come to me."

"So, what are you up to now? Going to stick around
Pineland?"

Payne glanced in the direction of Main Street. "I've gotta
run back to the cabin to grab a few things; then I'm meeting
Medina for breakfast in town. After that, who knows?" Payne
paused for a moment, as if in reflection. "You know, Garrett,
after what this community has been through, it could use
someone to steer things in the right direction. With your background and standing here, I think you'd make a helluva
sheriff."

Wheeler allowed himself a faint grin. "Funny, but Miles
and I were just talking about that very thing recently."

"You give my best to that old cowboy." He extended his
hand, and the two men gave each other hearty shakes.

"I hope we cross paths again," said Wheeler.

"Never can tell."

———

Back at the cabin, Payne tidied up the kitchen and removed the few laundry items from the dryer and put them away. Afterwards, he swept the floors and porch. The act of cleaning felt very Zen-like and helped his mind to settle down after the tumultuous events of the past few days.

All he really wanted to do was spend another night or three with Medina at her motel. But that joyous interlude was about to end. She had people to answer to, reports to handle, and endless debriefings to attend with the numerous alphabet agencies who were going to be sifting through Tanner's illegal operation for months to come.

And he needed to be long gone before Pineland was inundated by the feds.

When he had finished cleaning, Payne sat down on a rocking chair on the porch, inhaling the sweet fragrance of wildflowers and spruce while watching Mochi and Zoe playing fetch in the distance.

For a brief moment, the setting enveloped him. The thought of having roots in his adult life was appealing, but the pores of this place were saturated with someone else's dreams and hopes. Payne forced himself up and headed inside to the bedroom. He popped open the faux wooden hatch in the corner and opened the gun safe. Payne placed the HK pistol and mags inside and removed the .38 Smith & Wesson snubbie. It would be more compact and not cause too many legal issues in less gun-friendly states compared to a semi-auto.

Payne was about to close the door when he noticed something he'd missed at the back of the top shelf. He slid aside some boxes of ammo and removed an envelope. Flipping it over, he felt a chill run down his spine at the sight of his name. It was written in pencil by Heller.

The envelope seemed as heavy as a bowling ball, and he leaned back against the wall, stroking the edges as if it would spring to life. He removed his folding knife and sheared open the envelope, pulling out the one-page letter, which was also handwritten.

My friend, if you're reading this, then I've moved on to other shores. Always know that I didn't choose an easy life, no one in our line of work does, but it was one full of marrow and hopefully made a difference in some small way.

The best part of it all was knowing you, Kyle. You were the finest student I ever had and a hell of a case officer. But beyond that, you were like a son to me. I will miss you most of all in whatever land I'm off to next.

If I could leave you with one piece of advice, it's this:

Remember to live fully and not just exist, as is all too common in our profession after a while. Keep close those values and interests that make you feel most alive. You already know what they are... just don't let the nature of our work erode them. Cling to them ferociously, for those things will become beacons pointing the way in the years to come.

Regarding this property and cabin, use it how you see fit, but don't feel tethered to it.

And please look in on Heather and Zoe from time to time. I've grown very fond of them.

I wish you many fine trails ahead, amigo.

John

Payne slumped back, remaining still for a long while, the breeze in the aspens outside fading away as dozens of memories of Heller flooded over him.

He didn't know how much time had passed when he finally stood up. He returned the letter to the envelope and folded it, sliding it into his shirt pocket.

You old dog. You fought the good fight, trying to do the right thing as always.

He closed the gun safe and the wooden hatch.

Returning to the front porch, Payne glanced around the property and at the Indian motorcycle.

And his next move came without hesitation.

———

An hour later, Connie placed a plate of blueberry pancakes and scrambled eggs on the table in front of Payne, followed by an order of French toast before Medina, who sat across from him at Monique's Diner.

"You two enjoy," said Connie, who leaned a hand on Payne's shoulder. "And you'd best stay out of trouble for a while, though that ain't a complaint, only a suggestion."

"Yes, ma'am. I believe I will do that," he said.

She walked back to the grill, pausing to make small talk with some of the older patrons sitting on barstools by the counter.

"Looks like another woman whom you've worked your charms on," said Medina, cutting her French toast.

He winked at her. "Just glad that charm worked on you."

"Saw an Indian motorcycle outside. That the one of Heller's you told me about?"

He nodded, shoveling down a forkful of eggs. "Figured I'd take it for a spin out towards the coast for a while. I left the keys to John's cabin with Heather and told her to watch over the place for me. Not sure what I'm going to do with my life after this, but it sure as hell doesn't involve anything back at Langley. I emailed my resignation earlier. I thought I'd enjoy the sights along Route 66 instead. After that, I might keep pushing up the coast to Oregon, Washington, maybe even Alaska."

Medina slid her hand over his. "I wish I'd known John. He sounded like a quality guy. He'll be with you on every mile of that trip." She gazed out the window at the sun hanging over the treetops. "Strozzi and his team will be up here later this afternoon. He's going to wanna talk with you about how things went down."

"Tell 'em I headed east out of town, planning to take the backroads into New Mexico."

"I'll pretend I didn't hear that."

He squeezed her hand, staring into her brown eyes. "John has another bike in his garage that I could get ready if you want to join me."

"Sounds like quite a proposition." She tried to contain a wolfish grin.

"But?"

"But my family and my life are here. Plus, Strozzi is going to let me head up a new taskforce in Tucson."

He was only half serious about the invite but had to pitch it. He didn't envy the grilling she was about to get from her boss, but from the little he knew of Strozzi, the man would probably focus on the end results at the Tanner warehouse and not so much on the means.

At least he hoped that was the case.

"Duty calls, then."

Medina finished her last bite of breakfast and slid the plate away. "Plus, I think you and I are both so bull-headed that we'd get into a major argument at the first crossroad, trying to decide which way to go."

"And I'd convince you that my way was right, and then we'd continue on."

She laughed, holding up a fist. "Except, we'd need to stop soon after that to buy some ice for your bruised jaw."

He let go of her hand, leaning back. "Well, maybe next time. I'm sure I'll be passing through this *epicenter* of South-western culture in the near future."

"Then you can take me out on a proper date."

"You mean to the truck stop at the other end of town? I bet you know their menu by heart."

She lightly kicked him under the table. "Shut up." She dabbed the corners of her lips with the napkin. "I know a fantastic Mexican place in Scottsdale that will make an unfor-gettable impression on you."

Payne smiled, knowing Medina had already made a lasting impression on him, and he was going to have a hard time with this particular goodbye. He gazed at her lovely face, feeling the tension in his shoulders from weeks of stress melt away. "It's a deal. Dinner in Scottsdale."

He paid the bill, leaving a fifty on the table and a hand-written note on the napkin for Connie.

You're the town treasure. I'm going to miss you.

Payne followed Medina outside, limping to the side of the building where his motorcycle was parked.

Medina closed the distance, sliding her hands around his hips and hugging him. "You take care, wherever the road leads you."

He nodded, raising her chin and kissing her. When he finished, they shared another hug before she reluctantly pulled away.

"Be seeing you, Agent Medina."

She smiled, sliding on her sunglasses and giving a two-fingered wave as she walked to her SUV. "And I'd better not hear about you lighting up another small town somewhere out West."

"You won't," he replied, climbing on his bike.

At least not anytime soon.

ABOUT THE AUTHOR

Did you enjoy *Knife Edge*? Please consider leaving a review on Amazon to help other readers discover the book.

————

JT Sawyer is the pen name for author Tony Nester who writes survival and vigilante-justice thrillers. Before becoming a full-time writer, JT spent 30 years teaching survival courses in the American Southwest for the military special operations community, at the university level, and for a variety of federal agencies. He also served as a consultant for the film industry and provided training in mantracking and fieldcraft for actors Josh Brolin and Emile Hirsch. Nowadays, JT prefers having a roof over his head and placing his fictional characters in dire straits. He lives with his family and several rescue dogs in Colorado.

————

Want to connect with JT? Visit him at his website:

www.jtsawyer.com

ALSO BY JT SAWYER

Made in the USA
Las Vegas, NV
24 March 2025

20032765R00163